THE VAMPIRES' CURSE

DECIMUS BOOK 1

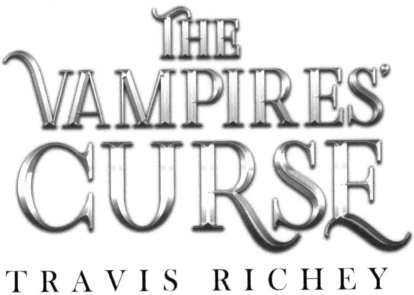

THE VAMPIRES' CURSE

TRAVIS RICHEY

4 Horsemen
Publications, Inc.

4 Horsemen
Publications, Inc.

4 Horsemen Publications, Inc.
1497 Main St. Suite 169
Dunedin, FL 34698
4horsemenpublications.com
info@4horsemenpublications.com

Cover by Emily's World of Design
Typesetting by Autumn Skye
Edited by Devora Gray

Library of Congress Control Number: 2023938089

Paperback ISBN-13: 979-8-8232-0195-7
Hardcover ISBN-13: 979-8-8232-0197-1
Audiobook ISBN-13: 979-8-8232-0194-0
Ebook ISBN-13: 979-8-8232-0196-4

Dedicated to Pamela Jill Alwin Fullerton,
My mom

For literally everything

TABLE OF CONTENTS

PROLOGUE

Los Angeles
October 31, 1982

Los Angeles was drowning.

Overcast skies had burst into a deluge of rain for which the city was unprepared. Children, and the adults minding them, were caught outside in the middle of trick-or-treating and were instantly soaked to the skin. The grown-ups scurried to get their costumed offspring to drier places, while the kids frantically tried to preserve their sugary hauls.

In a nascent West Hollywood, a neighborhood two years from incorporation as an actual city and five years before the first official Halloween carnival, old hippies and young punk rockers reacted in mixed fashion to the torrential rain. The latter retreated into the clubs and bars of the Sunset Strip, while the free spirits danced in the downpour, their body paints streaming down their bare skin and into the streets and gutters in a Technicolor runoff.

This rain had a chill to it. Even those who celebrated, attempting to grab joy out of the shower that was so unusual in the semidesert climate, felt something beneath the skin with the impact of every drop of water. It was a cold that threatened to burrow down to the bone. Nature herself seemed angry, as if She was trying to inflict a punishment on the city. That feeling heightened as the wind intensified, howling in fury and turning the deluge sideways.

A mile southeast of West Hollywood, in the shadow of the dilapidated Pan Pacific Auditorium, a figure roared in agony. As furious as the storm was, it couldn't hope to compare with his rage as he held in his arms another man, this one drooping and lifeless. Bathed in the darkness of the unused park, only the distant streetlights of Beverly Boulevard glinted off their soaked skin and clothing. The lifeless man's body was beaten and stained with blood which ran in rivulets down his limp arms. The source of the blood flow, two ragged puncture wounds in his neck, had already slowed to a trickle as the supply depleted. The screams of the man holding him became ear-piercing, and his upturned face revealed crimson-stained fangs, still dripping with his companion's lifeblood.

The figure howled against nature's wrath as if he were being torn asunder. He wailed in impotent anger at the heavens and, through the white-hot anguish of his torment, he made an oath; the most common promise in the history of man, and the one all sentient beings are powerless to keep.

I will never love again.

CHAPTER 1

West Hollywood, CA
May 22, 2023

Summer never stayed away long from Southern California. The noonday sun of late spring radiated warmth on Los Angeles like a soothing caress. The oppressive heat of late August had not yet arrived, and conversations about the current weather, which were only slightly less frequent than conversations about traffic, invariably contained the word *perfect*.

A delivery truck marked only with biohazard and medical waste warnings turned off Sunset Boulevard and headed into the Hollywood Hills, straining at the steep grade of the ascent. Half a dozen turns on the maze-like roads brought it to a stately yet subtle home. The stone and brick house was elegant in its simplicity, evoking a classic design and timeless architecture. The grey of the stone called to mind a European castle, but the style was somewhat less grand. It stood in stark contrast to the conspicuous ostentatiousness of some of the surrounding homes, which sported bright paint jobs, copious landscaping, or walls made of shimmering glass. This house, though well-maintained, could have been built three centuries ago somewhere in England or Germany. It was the home of someone who was very wealthy but didn't want to advertise the fact.

The delivery truck pulled off the narrow road into the long driveway, where it parked. The Latino man who emerged from the driver's side was handsome but nondescript, much like the house he had come to. His dark hair was neatly trimmed, and his so-navy-blue-it-was-almost-black jumpsuit contained no identifying logos or name patch. Behind dark sunglasses, his eyes scanned the area. It couldn't really be called a neighborhood, but there were a few houses within line of sight and the occasional dog walker on the road. Checking for witnesses was more of a habit than a necessity. He removed a portable cooler from the back of the van and—always keeping one hand free, just in case—moved towards the front door.

The man listened at the door for a moment before looking over the locking mechanism. There was no doorknob, no keyhole, no buttons. There was only a simple touchpad. The technology was in stark contrast to the rest of the home. He tentatively touched its surface and a virtual keypad appeared, silently asking for a code to be entered. He touched the series of numbers his contact had given him, and with an affirmative blink of green, the sound of a thick deadbolt could be heard retracting within the heavy oak, unlocking the door, which automatically swung open a few inches, allowing access.

With a final glance at the outside world, which was still clear, he slipped inside and closed the door behind him with a heavy thud and the low whir of the deadbolt re-engaging.

The difference in light from the brightness outside to the dim interior was extreme. Even after taking off his sunglasses, the man's brindle eyes took fifteen long seconds to acclimate to the gloom. The interior of the house was meticulously appointed. The stone floors seemed to suck any excess heat from the room, and the still, cool air tingled against his skin. The walls were adorned with intricate tapestries lit by track lighting recessed into the ceiling, so that the illumination seemed to originate from nowhere. What furniture there was looked rarely used and placed as much for aesthetic value as practical use. There were a few pieces of art on the walls and a handful of sculptures on short columns. It all looked very, very expensive.

The man crept further into the home, careful to make as little noise as possible. He heard almost no sound. There was virtually no traffic on the high road that the house was on, and the city was far enough away to be little more than muffled white noise. The thick stone walls dampened any but the loudest disturbances. Yet he didn't hear the figure creep up behind him until a low voice growled menacingly behind his right ear.

"You should know better than to sneak around someone's house in the dark."

The man felt a breath on the nape of his neck, but it wasn't normal, like when a lover hugs you from behind. It was warmer; a hot breeze tickling the fine hairs above his shirt collar. He tried to force his senses to attune to the figure that had managed to sneak up on him and spoke carefully, holding himself as still as one of the statues he'd glimpsed. "The door was open."

"The door was locked," the figure growled. "With a very expensive high-tech security system."

"I mean the door was open after I unlocked it ... and opened it." The man could almost feel the being behind him. He had a sense of its size and weight, but still thought the best course of action was to remain still. He felt a bit like a deer who knows it's been seen by a hunter but can't overcome the instinct to freeze.

"You don't seem very scared to have been discovered."

The voice was now almost a whisper and came from so close to the man's right ear that he couldn't help a shiver running from the top of his head all the way to his toes. He'd had absolutely no sense of movement at all. "Should I be?"

"I would think so. This *is* the home of a vampire, after all..." The low voice now growled in the interloper's *left* ear, again with no sense whatsoever of movement behind his head, and then another sound... something that could be fangs sliding into place.

"*Rahhhhr.*"

The visitor contemplated his next words carefully. "I don't think ... vampires actually go '*rahhhhr*', do they?"

The breath left his neck. There was no relief, however. The voice now seemed to come from everywhere, even from inside his own skull.

"How many vampires do you know?" it said.

Neat trick, the man thought. "Just one that I'm aware of. And he never went '*rahhhhr*'."

There was a silent pause. It could have been the prefatory moment before a predator strikes its prey, but instead, the voice took on a slightly timid quality. "And '*rahhhhr*' isn't scary?"

The man shifted, turning to glance at the owner of the house, who by all appearances looked like a handsome, if nondescript, thirty-something man, wearing a t-shirt and jeans. "Okay, well, now it's just getting kinda weird. Can I put this down?" The man indicated the cooler he was carrying. "It's heavy. Not all humans are super strong like you."

The vampire sighed, his menacing pose relaxing. "In the kitchen."

The man moved to the kitchen, which was also spotless, and put the cooler on the counter. "You're not sulking, are you?"

"Vampires don't sulk, Rafaél." The suddenly non-sinister vampire followed to the kitchen and leaned against the doorframe. Not helping, but not *not* helping.

"Now I know you're sulking, *Joseph*. You only call me Rafaél when you're upset. What is it? Are you lonely? Why aren't you asleep?" He checked his wristwatch, an analogue number that had once belonged to his birth father. "It's after noon."

"*Rafi.* No, I'm not lonely, and just wasn't tired." Joseph shifted his weight so that his back was against the doorjamb. He liked feeling the solidness of the house, and the subtle vibrations in the stone. "I was just playing around a bit. You were creeping in so quietly I thought I'd have a bit of fun."

Rafaél opened the cooler, and dry ice smoke spilled over the side, rolling its way along the floor until it evaporated into invisibility. He reached into the smoke and moved the cooler's contents into the refrigerator: bags of crimson blood, each with a label that identified the blood type, plasma percentage, and the source—Tetractys Blood Supply.

"I was creeping because I didn't want to disturb you in the middle of the day." Then, softer, "I'm not exactly the age to play games with you anymore."

Joseph's head had been against the doorway and his dark blue eyes had been tracing the grain of the wood. It was some old oak or maple, stained dark like an espresso coffee bean and polished to a shine. He sniffed as his nose picked up the scent of blood and turned his head towards his friend. He put out a hand, snapping his fingers in a toss-me-one way. "Pssh, you're barely sixty. I'm almost five hundred and still going strong."

"Could have fooled me," Rafaél admonished and paused to look at the vampire he had known for over half a century. He lobbed Joseph the bag he had been about to put in the fridge. "I mean, really, you live like a hermit, trapped in this house all the time. Who else besides me have you talked to in the last week?"

"I'll have you know I had a spirited discussion with Cardinal Filoni about the nature of love and sex." Joseph lifted the bag to his nose and inhaled, savoring the scent that was escaping even through the plastic vessel. "On Zoom."

Rafaél lifted his hands as if to say, *See what I mean? What kind of life is that?*

The blue-eyed vampire changed the subject. "Oh, hey, what do you think of the new lock, by the way?"

Rafaél turned to finish loading the blood bags into the fridge. He cautiously lifted a bag to his own nose, steeling himself for the metallic odor, but barely smelled the sterile plastic, let alone its contents. He spared a thought to marvel at Joseph's olfactory sense. "Oh yes, it looks very expensive and high tech," he teased, "Did you feel that you were in need of heightened security?"

"It's the twenty-first century. Security is everything these days. Plus, the guy in the infomercial was cute."

"There it is. You really need to get out. Tonight. Go out."

"It's Tuesday. Nothing happens on Tuesday."

"It's summer. There's plenty going on and you know it. Get your sulky butt out there and interact with some people. Dance, meet a guy, hook up. Or whatever kids who are the age you look do these days."

"Fine, jeez, stop. You know, I remember when I was the one telling you to go out and make friends."

"When I was nine. I'm taking a ginger ale."

"They're for you, go ahead. Are you going back to the office?"

"I have to, yeah. We just launched the summer blood drive. We've got fifteen trucks working six days a week through August. Means long days for the big boss."

"Mmm ... Tasty."

"Oh, knock it off. You can't be scary sounding when you're drinking donated blood instead of feeding on people."

"You are just no fun, *big boss*."

"Ha. I guess I deserved that." Rafaél downed the rest of the bottle of ginger ale and stifled a burp. "Okay, gotta run. Anything else you need before I go?"

"Nope. You go save the world. I'm good."

Rafaél made his way back to the front door, his soft-soled dress shoes thumping quietly on the stone floors. He paused at the door and turned back to the vampire who looked thirty years his junior. "Joseph. Seriously. Go out. Please?"

"I will."

Rafaél made a face that suggested that he didn't believe him. Joseph chuckled at the idea that he was now being told what to do by this older man who was a kid a seemingly short time ago. "I promise. Go!"

Rafaél laughed back as he opened the door, which automatically unlocked as he grasped the inside handle. "Good. I expect a complete report." He paused, considering the implications of his directive. "Well, maybe not complete. Don't need to hear all the naughty bits. Have fun, J, make good decisions!" The heavy oak door swung shut with a weighty thump, and the locking mechanism re-engaged. *Kaaaa-chunk.*

Joseph stood in the gloom for a moment and thought about how much had changed since he'd found a nine-year-old orphan wandering the streets back in the mid-'60s. He felt a familiar mix of emotions. A surge of pride at the man Rafaél had become, now the CEO of a multi-billion-dollar biotech company, mingled with a cloud of sorrow, with the recollection of his ward's mortality. With a sigh, Joseph shook his head and consciously dropped his shoulders, which had tensed. They did that. He smiled again, remembering Rafi's final order on the way out, then turned and walked to the bedroom and into the walk-in closet.

Tonight, he was going out.

CHAPTER 2

J oseph ordered a Lyft to take him from his house in the Hollywood Hills
to the clubs of West Hollywood. It had been ages since he'd been to
Boystown, the area of WeHo that was packed with gay bars and restaurants.
Having someone else do the driving allowed his mind to drift. He thought
about Rafi, of course. He hadn't stopped thinking about him since that afternoon. In the nearly five hundred years since he'd been turned, Joseph had let
very few people get close to him, either physically or emotionally.

Rafaél had only been nine years old when Joseph had rescued him from
a vampire attack. It was 1965, and the young Latino boy was an orphan who
had slipped through the cracks in the system and was living on the streets of
San Francisco. The vampire who was trying to feed on him had been turned
as a teenager and was easily scared off, and Joseph, not wanting the shivering
child in front of him to think that the world was all monsters, took him in.
After feeding and bathing the boy and seeing to his comfort, the child's story
had begun to emerge. His mother had died in childbirth and his father had
been drafted off to Vietnam and reported killed in action. Joseph's heart went
out to the orphan, and he used the wealth he had amassed over the centuries
to pull strings and adopt Rafaél.

The boy had proven to be remarkably adaptable. Within a year it was clear
that he was brilliant and creative. He made friends at school and quickly accel-
erated to become one of the top students in his class. The existence of vampires
was a closely guarded secret, and as humans progressed into the modern age,

belief in them had faded into the most remote fringes of conspiracy and myth. Yet Rafaél had been open to learning about Joseph's life and his true nature, both before and after being turned, and Rafi became his ward, confidant, assistant, and finally business partner.

Rafi was the closest thing Joseph had ever had to a child of his own, and indeed, it felt a little strange for him to now be taking on this fatherly role. *Go out. Have fun. Make good decisions.* Joseph laughed at the thought.

"What's funny?" the rideshare driver asked, trying to strike up a friendly conversation.

"Just something my son told me before he went back to the office," Joseph replied, turning his attention to the man piloting the Ford C-Max down the winding road. He was a typical taxi-driver type. Middle-aged, and Middle Eastern, with a middle-sized belly which probably wasn't helped by the extra-large Big Gulp he had sitting in the cup holder next to him. Joseph's heightened senses detected real tobacco and a mix of spices wafting off the man.

He was genial enough, though, and spoke English with only a faint accent, looking at Joseph in the rearview mirror with genuine surprise. "I'm impressed, you don't look old enough to have a kid who works in an office. What's your secret?"

Joseph smirked and quoted an old line from a comedian. "I decided to live forever. So far so good." This got a belly laugh out of the driver. "Also, I moisturize. A lot." The driver laughed again.

"Good one, bud. I don't know why I didn't think to just stop aging. First thing tomorrow, that's the plan."

Joseph instinctually leaned forward in his seat and put on a broad smile. "Why put off until tomorrow what you can start today?"

"That is a good point. Okay, no growing old, starting now!" The driver laughed again. Joseph allowed himself a wry chuckle. The car passed Sunset Boulevard, and after a couple of minutes of banal conversation about the weather, the Lyft pulled up in front of Micky's, a gay bar on Santa Monica Boulevard that had a good mix of dancing, drinks, and go-go boys.

Joseph stepped out of the car, thanked the driver, and turned to survey the sidewalk. Numerous gays made their way to numerous bars to consume copious amounts of alcohol and who knows what else. Nothing caught Joseph's eye, but the music wafting out of Micky's open front patio was a pretty good remix of a Kylie Minogue classic, and he could see some underwear-clad boys dancing on the stage inside, so he decided this was the best place to start the evening.

It was only 10:00 PM, so there wasn't much of a line to get into the club. He flashed his ID, which read *Joseph Franz Walter III*. He had been just *Joseph*

Franz Walter when driver's licenses became a thing in the early twentieth century, but eventually he had to kill off that identity and become his own son, and now his own grandson. He wasn't sure if he wanted to carry on the Walter family name for another generation. It wasn't a huge deal to change it, legally speaking, and Walter wasn't even his birth name. Back in the 1500s, when he was human, living in Munich, and a citizen of the Great Holy Roman Empire, his family name was Knoblauch, a fact he had pondered ruefully many times over the centuries. Knoblauch was German for *garlic*.

At the Micky's entrance, Joseph lined up behind a jockish college boy to pay his five-dollar cover. He grinned as the jock got in for free for showing his dick to the doorman. Since he was behind the jock, Joseph couldn't sneak a peek himself, but he made a mental note of the boy's face and outfit in case they ran into each other on the dance floor or cruised one another in the bathroom. He felt a slight tinge of hurt when the doorman didn't make him the same offer. At his actual age, he would have thought that a petty thing like vanity would be a thing of the past, but sometimes he wished he'd been turned when he was ten years younger.

Once inside, Joseph surveyed the place. The layout was fairly mundane, though a fire a few years back had allowed the owners to completely remodel the club with a sleeker, modern flair. The main bar was a chrome rectangle in the middle of the larger room. From the entrance, going left led to a large open patio directly off the sidewalk, and there was another smaller bar for easy drink ordering from outside. To the right was the dance floor (and bathrooms), and on the far side of the bar, a stage was set up for the scantily clad go-go boys, most of them wearing Andrew Christian underwear and shaking their barely covered asses and semi-hard cocks at the patrons in their attempts to earn tips.

Joseph began a circuit of the club. It was the perfect level of crowded; full enough to seem busy, but not packed to the point where you had to push your way through. There *was* something to be said for denser crowds; it allowed for more casual physical contact, the brushing of butts with hands, which usually led to eye contact, which led to whatever it led to. Now, however, Joseph was able to amble through the varied collection of guys and began a lap around the bar. He waited to buy a drink until he'd made at least one round and decided what he actually wanted to do tonight. Pick up a guy? Dance all night? Both? Neither...?

Now that he was here, he was definitely feeling his libido rising. Joseph had been turned at the age of thirty and was thus forever in that perfect balance of sexual desire and control over that desire.

As he moved around the bar, Joseph felt a shift in his body. His posture unconsciously transitioned into that of a hunter on the prowl. This he remembered from when he was purely human, in his late teens, attending village events where he was expected to seek out young Bavarian women and make them his own. More frequently, though, he would be sneaking away to rendezvous with some Roman soldier who was only a couple of years his senior.

Now, though, Joseph was much more than human. As he floated through the throngs of men, his vampiric senses reached out to give him far more details on the surrounding males than could be afforded by sight alone. He could hear not just their conversations, but their breathing, even their heartbeats. He could smell the mélange of colognes, of course, but could also smell pheromones, blood types, the very hormones coursing through young veins, not to mention which boys were carrying various diseases and infections. He could tell who was here from Santa Monica by the smell of sea salt air on their clothes and hair and who was visiting from the Midwest by the faintest trace of cow manure.

So strong were these senses that Joseph could almost know the very thoughts of humans he focused on. He wasn't a mind reader, no. Telepathy was not a gift of the turning. But humans were, frankly, awful at hiding their thoughts, so directly did the unconscious mind control the body. These abilities evolved in vampires for hunting, but over the centuries, especially in more recent centuries, they came in useful for seduction. Vampires were not sexless creatures. On the contrary, their blood ran warmer than the average human. This fueled their thirst, but also fired their passions.

On the far side of the bar, Joseph's attention shifted to the stage on his right, where the go-go boys gyrated. As he passed, he drew the gaze of each of the dancers, and made eye contact with them in turn. They looked at him as a potential tip, of course, but he was used to men and women being drawn to him and staring. Especially in sexually charged environments like this. The dancers' smells were so alluring he could practically taste the sweat that glistened on their lithe bodies. The first was a buff black guy of around twenty-five. He looked like he lived at the gym; his muscles bulged, and his underwear did little to hide his large semi-hard phallus. Joseph could also smell a cocktail of substances in him. Cocaine and Ecstasy, to fuel his long night of work. Without too much moral judgement, Joseph kept walking.

The next was a slightly beefy guy who reminded Joseph of the boys in his home village. Dark blond hair and slate grey eyes regarded him as he walked past the gyrating dancer. A chest full of trimmed hair led to a treasure trail flowing directly into the leather jock strap he had chosen to don this evening.

Joseph detected no illicit drugs in him, but beer was definitely his chemical of choice. A little too much like those boys from home. Joseph moved along. He quickly passed by the skinny twink that was swaying more than dancing, whose eyes had dark circles under them which were counter to his age in the low twenties. Crystal meth was his elected drug, which was a turnoff to Joseph, on par with hair pulled into a man bun.

The fourth and last dancer was interesting, though, and Joseph could see why he had been placed on the end of the stage. It was closest to the front, where passersby could see him from the sidewalk. He was, as far as Joseph could tell, perfect. Somewhere around twenty, probably still in college. Fit and lean, but not overly muscle-bound. The type of body shaped by actual work, or through intense sport, rather than in a gym. If Joseph had to guess, it was a running sport like soccer, or possibly swimming.

The dancer's blue eyes swept the crowd from under a damp mop of dirty blond hair as he gyrated sensually, and his face wore a perpetual smirk, like he knew a secret none of the patrons or other dancers knew. His gaze slid past Joseph at first but then he did a double take to observe his admirer.

Joseph was no slouch himself. His auburn hair was coifed stylishly over a chiseled clean-shaven face. Intense, dark blue-steel eyes that seemed much older than his thirty-year-old body met with the dancer's lighter eyes. Joseph stepped up to him, and the go-go boy slowly lowered himself to a squat position and then to his knees and sat on his heels so he could lean over to talk to the older man.

"Hey, stud. Having a good night?" the boy said, his sultry lips close to Joseph's ear to be heard over the music.

Joseph tilted his head up so his own mouth was close to the boy's ear. "Better now, handsome. How's the dancing?"

"Oh, you know, always on the lookout for a nice sugar daddy." The dancer ran his finger along Joseph's shoulder, feeling the expensive modal fabric of the T-shirt that hugged his toned torso. The boy had an eye for high fashion, Joseph would give him that. "Five bucks and you can touch my dick. Twenty and you can finger me..."

Oh, Joseph thought, disappointed. *I'm the daddy. Well, I guess I don't know what I expected.* Still, Joseph admired the boldness of the probably struggling model. He raised one hand to caress the dancer's face, locking eye contact. With the other hand, he reached into his front pocket and pulled out a wad of bills. Joseph sensed the other dancers turn their attention his way, but he was using his will to lock the dancer's mind to him. It was the kind of thing he used to do back when he would feed on humans. Joseph didn't intend to feed on this boy, of course, and was no longer even interested in him as a sexual conquest, but he still wanted to leave him with something he would remember forever.

Without looking, he leafed off two twenty-dollar bills, putting the rest back in his pocket. He held the bills between his face and the boy's, which were only inches apart, but the go-go boy's eyes never left his own. He was trapped. Their minds were linked via Joseph's gaze, and the dancer was entranced. His mouth parted slightly as Joseph touched the bills to the young man's chin and slowly traced them down his neck, his chest, his abs, to the waistband of his designer jock strap. Joseph used one finger to lift the elastic away from the dancer's perfect tight skin, and another finger to push the bills into their new home. He released the waistband with a snap, and the dancer, his attention still rapt, widened his eyes a bit and gasped. A fresh sheen of sweat had broken out across his body and a single rivulet ran down from his temple past his cheek.

Joseph projected a warmth through his gaze and the dancer's skin flushed in response. The music fell away and the two became the only thing in each other's worlds. Joseph moved his hand from the boy's waistband and down between his legs, across the pouch containing his manhood, which was rapidly swelling, then past the point where the pouch connected to the two straps of fabric that split off to surround his toned ass but left everything in between completely open to the air. Joseph ran his hand up one cheek, relishing the smooth skin over the taut muscle underneath, until his fingers reached the waistband on the dancer's backside. Then he pulled his hand slowly back, his middle finger naturally falling into the crease between the two mounds.

The boy moaned involuntarily, low and guttural. When Joseph's finger crossed the pucker of the jock's hole, he parted his own lips and blew softly into the dancer's already open mouth, never breaking eye contact. He applied just the slightest pressure to the rosebud of the dancer's ass, and the boy spasmed in orgasm. His eyes tried to roll back in his head in ecstasy, but they were still locked to Joseph's, and his pleasure came out as sweat and groans of bliss.

Joseph drew his hand back, across the pouch of the jock, which was now being pushed away from the boy's body by the straining erection it held, and being soaked through by his ejaculation. He ran his middle finger in a reverse course of the bills he had given. Up the abs, over the still-quivering chest muscles, up the neck, over the chin, and pushed his middle finger into the boy's mouth, which reflexively clamped down, eagerly sucking on it like a pacifier, and muffling his moans as his orgasm continued to send waves of pleasure through him. The young man could taste his own sweat, musk, and cum on the finger and his mind nearly short-circuited from the sensations overwhelming him.

Joseph pulled the finger out from the soft lips with a quiet *pop* and another "*ohhhh*" from the boy. He tilted his head up to bring his mouth back to the dancer's ear and said matter-of-factly, "You're welcome. I'm not much of a daddy, though."

The dancer, his gaze finally released from Joseph's arresting stare, slumped back on his heels, his head falling back and eyes rolling up, still in the thralls of the most powerful orgasm of his young life.

Joseph stepped away from the dancer and turned from the stage to get a drink at the small bar on the patio. He made his way through a gawking crowd that had formed around him to watch the show, some of them pawing their own erections. They flowed into the empty space in front of the dancer, pulling out bills to offer as tips, and salivating over the still-erect boy whose cum was leaking through the fabric of his jock strap.

For Joseph, it was a relatively empty experience. Something about the boy had turned him off once he actually started talking. He couldn't put a finger on it, ironically, but something about the willingness to be reliant on someone else made him disinterested. Joseph could certainly afford to take care of some hot young thing, but he tended to like independent, intelligent guys. If that could come in the physical package that the dancer embodied, all the better.

Joseph ordered two fingers of Killepitsch, neat, tipped the cute bartender the cost of the drink just for being pretty, and then completed his circuit of the bar. The crowd had filled out a bit since he'd arrived, and he scoped out the boys in attendance. It was a usual West Hollywood mix. In Joseph's estimation, Los Angeles had the hottest boys, but the *average* hotness was lower than other places he'd been. That dichotomy amused him when he thought about it. The boys *on average* were cuter in Minneapolis when he spent some time there. But perhaps the strong northern European presence just reminded him of his home in Munich.

One thing Joseph loved about Los Angeles was the diversity. He had spent much of his five hundred plus years traveling the world, but here, every part of the planet was represented. Even in this room, around the bar, he spotted a young black man whose skin was such a deep brown it looked like dark chocolate, and a Pakistani guy with a highly elevated sense of style that made him stand out in stark contrast to his more plebeian friends. Joseph knew non-whites had it harder in the gay community, as in the world at large, and didn't really understand why. When he first ventured away from home (ran away, really, after his transformation), he had been amazed at all the faces that didn't look like his own. And the bodies... Joseph delighted in the differences he encountered, embracing the chance to experience new things and learn about other cultures.

In recent decades, as the LGBT communities had begun to find their voice, he was dismayed to see that racism still imbued itself into that world. Joseph thought that since they were outcasts from society at large, it was natural to embrace others who were oppressed as well. Instead, too often he saw fear and distrust of the *different*. He supposed being a vampire was the most different thing of all and would never be something he could live with openly; even if he hadn't fed on a human in over two centuries.

Joseph returned his attention to the bar and its patrons. So far, no one had caught his eye. There were lots of groups but not a lot of single boys. Not that that really mattered. If he wanted someone who was out with friends, it was only a *tad* more difficult to convince them to break off and join him for the night. He headed to the dance floor in the back.

The music was a good blend of gay pop remixes, heavy on the bass and the Britney, and Joseph felt it permeate into his body. He sipped his drink, a blood-red liquor, and tasted the complex mix of fruit, spice, and alcohol as he watched the bodies sway and groove on the dance floor. It was too early for shirts to start coming off, but the dancers all moved in rhythm to the thumping beat, and Joseph felt himself swaying along with them, his shoulders moving to the tempo and then his hips, back and forth. He hadn't danced in some time, and the pure pleasure of it came flooding back. He set the remainder of his drink on a ledge along the wall and glided onto the dance floor.

Movement overtook his body, and he allowed the music to hypnotize him. He closed his eyes for several seconds, just concentrating on feeling the beat inside him, and when he opened them he unfocused his vision slightly to let the effect of the laser lights, strobes, and mirror ball create a kaleidoscope of light all around him. Before too long, his dancing style took on a more deliberate form, reaching his arms up and across his body, grabbing an invisible rope and pulling it back, spinning a one-eighty on the bass dip, and freezing everything just before the key change sent him into the floor on a full squat that took a few beats to rise back up, his ass thrust out behind him on the way. Joseph danced for an hour, without a trace of fatigue or even sweat. He had energy to burn and the joy he was feeling at the movement, while sensing other bodies doing the same thing around him, made him forget everything outside of this dance floor.

Then he opened his eyes and saw him. A boy, a *man*, dancing just to his left. Something about him arrested Joseph's attention. He was exquisitely handsome in a boy-next-door kind of way. Dark brown, almost black, hair styled classically over a face that appeared to be late twenties, with a darker complexion that seemed Latino, but not obviously so, Joseph guessed Cuban ancestry. The boy's shirt was off, and his body was drool-worthy. He would have fit in perfectly with the hottest go-go boys. His pecs and abs were defined but not so cut you wished he'd eat a sandwich or something. And his skin was totally smooth, with a sheen of sweat from his movements.

The guy felt Joseph's gaze. Their eyes met. The boy almost immediately broke the eye contact with a sheepish smile that made Joseph's groin flush with heat. He had entirely forgotten his desire to make a conquest tonight, but now he not only remembered, but suspected he had his choice picked out. He kept looking casually at the boy as they danced, and after a few seconds, the boy's light brown eyes darted back to meet with Joseph's blue ones. The man smiled again, showing off two rows of perfect teeth, and Joseph moved in. At six foot one, he was only an inch or so taller than the other guy, so he didn't have to bend over to talk in his ear.

"Hi. I'm Joseph." The music was loud and thumping and the crowd had grown denser, which meant he practically had to shout in the guy's ear.

"David," he shouted back. "And you're wearing way too many clothes, Joseph." The boy took a step back, bumping into another dancer, and gave Joseph a once-over as if to confirm this. He brought his gaze up and cocked a single eyebrow.

Joseph laughed good-naturedly. It was true, at some point in the last fifteen minutes most of the dancers on the floor had lost their shirts, and he hadn't even noticed. He crossed his arms over his stomach to grab his own tee at the bottom and removed his shirt in one smooth motion. Joseph's body was not skinny, but not muscular, either. His liquid diet meant he was thin and toned. His smooth skin seemed vacuum-sealed to his musculature with almost no fat, so as he danced in front of David, every movement of his abs and hips could be seen flexing with the beat. His low-cut designer jeans revealed the alluring V-shape that pointed directly to his groin. He had a small treasure trail that began at his belly button and led tantalizingly down into his pants. He cocked his own eyebrows at David, who raised his chin and mouthed "better" in response.

They closed the gap between them and grabbed each other's hips, grinning and looking lustfully into each other's eyes. Their groins pressed together as their bare torsos touched, and they instinctively offset their feet so they could get as close as possible, each placing their left foot between the other's feet. Being similar heights, their heads were positioned perfectly to speak in each other's left ear.

"You're really sexy," Joseph said over the music.

"You're hot as fuck," David said at the same time.

The synchronicity caused them both to laugh, Joseph throwing his head back, while David buried his face in his new dance partner's neck to stifle his outburst. They were both already semi-hard, but David took the opportunity to lick Joseph's neck up to his ear, and lightly nibbled his earlobe as they ground into each other with the beat, and *semi* became *mostly*. Joseph's hands moved from David's hips to his ass, squeezing the jeans-covered muscle, while David's fingertips slid to Joseph's lower back and up his spine. All the while they moved and grooved to the music.

Joseph pulled back a little to look at his dance partner. He hadn't even turned on his vampiric charm, but the young man was already entranced, and Joseph had to admit he was smitten in return. There was something about him that seemed to offer a little more than most boys Joseph encountered in West Hollywood. A hint of intelligence behind the eyes. Joseph found that he really wanted to *talk* to him. Get to know him a little before getting completely naked. Just a little, though. He really wanted to get naked as soon as possible. They could cuddle and talk after if they wanted to.

He pulled his head back enough to make eye contact. "You want to get out of here?"

David smirked the cutest smirk that Joseph had seen in two decades and gave Joseph a brief up and down before replying, "Desperately."

The pair exited Micky's onto the Santa Monica Boulevard sidewalk into a throng of gays going from one club to another or waiting to get into the one Joseph and David had just left. Joseph pulled out his phone to get a Lyft, but David pushed his hand away and pulled him in for a kiss, his six-foot-tall frame matching Joseph's nicely. The pair kissed softly in front of all the other gays, but the gaggle quickly ceased to exist for them, and the relative quiet of being outside of the club somehow made the kiss more intense. Their arms wrapped around each other's bodies, and their mouths pushed together passionately, tongues playing a delicate game of tag.

After a minute or two, David broke the kiss to catch his breath. "Wow," he panted.

"Yeah," Joseph replied lustily, and with just a hint of surprise, added, "Right?"

David reached his hand up to touch Joseph's face, running a finger along his left eyebrow and back across his temple and through his sweat-damp hair. "You're really good at that," he said, looking into Joseph's blue eyes, before glancing down at his own crotch and admitting, "I don't think I've ever been this hard in public."

"Do you want to stay in public, or...?" Joseph held up his phone.

"Definitely not. My place or yours?" David asked, pulling closer to Joseph and speaking seductively into his ear, "I'm only a few blocks down, on Kings. It's walkable."

Joseph didn't want to take the boy back to his place. It wasn't that he never did. In fact, sometimes he used the large house in the Hollywood Hills to his sexual advantage. It added an allure to the experience for most of the models and wannabe-actor types he found in West Hollywood and bedded, and the display of wealth tended to get them really hot in the pants.

But this one … he didn't want this one to know he was rich. *It's stupid*, Joseph thought to himself. *It's not like I'm going to get into a relationship or anything*. Still, though … it felt different for this gorgeous man to be so into him without knowing of his means, and without him applying any of his vampiric charm. It felt good.

"Your place. I'm a bit of a drive." He put his phone away. He'd have been happy to call a Lyft for them, but walking a few blocks was better than standing around waiting for a ride to take them five blocks.

"Come on, then, before I rip your clothes off right here in the street." David grabbed Joseph's hand and led him away from the *thump thump thump* of Micky's and the neighboring clubs and up the colorfully lit exuberance of Santa Monica Boulevard.

CHAPTER 3

"Roxana, come now, you've drained him dry."

The woman lifted her head from the neck of the Uber driver she was feasting on and threw a predatory glance at her companion. "He's still alive. Just one more minute, my love..."

"Of course, my goddess. As you please." Alexander turned from the murder in progress and regarded the view as he used the cleaning wipes the driver had on hand to mop the blood from his chin. They had told the Uber driver to take them to the middle of Kenneth Hahn Park, which was both secluded and featured a high hill from which they could look north over Culver City and West LA all the way to the Hollywood Hills.

They had ordered the Uber using a smartphone they took from their previous victim, a first-class passenger on the flight from Paris to LAX. They hadn't eaten anything on the ten-hour flight and were famished. Alexander's appetite had been sated halfway through the Uber driver, whose Middle Eastern blood tasted of curry and spice, but Roxana always did have a deeper thirst. It was one of the things he admired about her.

Behind him, he heard the final gurgling death of the driver, followed by Roxana exiting the rear driver's side of the Prius and pulling the corpse out of the front door, dragging the body to a stand of trees, and tossing him effortlessly down the hillside. Another advantage of this location: plenty of scavenging animals, coyotes, and even a mountain lion or two to gnaw at the body and hide the true nature of his death. Roxana was hundreds of years older than Alexander, descended from early Syrian blood, and had taught him volumes about survival in the human world. Together they had negotiated the centuries, feasting decadently and avoiding unwanted detection.

"Clean me," Roxana purred as she approached her mate from behind, wrapping her arms around him and turning him away from his view so they stood face to face.

He gazed at her, his pale blue eyes meeting hers, which were a bright hazel with flecks of gold and red. They almost glowed in the semidarkness of the city night, and entranced him, as they had for centuries.

"My love, you barely have a drop on you." Alexander knew better than to utilize the wipes he had used for himself. His mistress demanded a more personal approach. He found a trickle of blood that wound its way from the corner of her mouth and down her chin. With one hand, he stroked the side of her deceptively delicate face, and with the other, he gently lifted her head to reveal the crimson trail on her neck and licked it clean.

Roxana's hand traced his arm from elbow to wrist, her ecstasy flowing across her face. Her hand covered his and she intertwined their fingers, squeezing them into a fist, their two hands enmeshed as one. His fingers against her head grabbed her hair and pulled lightly but insistently, increasing the pressure of his tongue on her throat and chin. His mouth opened wider, and his fangs traced twin trails along her flesh. She moaned softly in response. When the human's blood was cleaned from her flesh, he continued to kiss and lick her cinnamon skin, moving down her neck.

Finally, Alexander pulled on her hair to tilt her head back and sank his fangs into her neck. Not feeding, but devouring her in his passion. She in turn twisted her head to align her mouth with their entwined hands and bit into his wrist. They were bound to each other through blood and desire, and they sank slowly to the ground, sipping each other's essence as they made fierce love on the grass. Their groans and cries attracted a couple of the larger animal predators in the park, who came to investigate the sounds of potentially vulnerable humans (and the smell of fresh Uber meats), but as Alexander and Roxana climaxed simultaneously, even the mountain lion was frightened away.

After, as Alexander rose to re-dress, Roxana remained on the ground, one arm under the back of her head, not bothering to cover her naked body with the dress that had been hiked up to her breasts. Even the warm evening air felt relatively cool on her skin.

"I hate this city. There are no stars."

"Would you rather live in the country, my queen?" Alexander asked facetiously, knowing the answer.

"Don't be stupid, my *batal*," she chided gently, using her pet name for him, a Syrian word that roughly translated as *hero*.

Alexander turned his eyes up to the dark grey night sky that enveloped the light-polluted metropolis. Even with his superior vision he was only able to see a few dozen stars. "The whole world is pushing the night away. Just two hundred years ago, we could see the galaxy in the sky, every night from almost anywhere. I miss it, too." He moved to gaze at his mate. "Still, there is no better place for us to flourish than here." The Americans had created the perfect society for people to disappear without question. Homeless humans flocked to the City of Angels because they could live on the street in relative comfort. "We must go where the cattle are."

"It is wise. And still..." Roxana lifted herself onto her elbows and stretched her face into the air. "I hate the smell. The salt of the sea reminds me of home. But the smoke and oil chokes me."

"That will pass in time. In a few hundred years, humans will realize how stupid they were to burn things for energy, and the air will be clean again. Or they will destroy themselves and our worries will end with them." He smirked down at her, then offered her a hand to help her up. She reached a slender arm up and grasped his wrist, which had already healed from her bite, and pulled up to stand with him, her dress falling into place.

"I know why you have really led us here, my *batal*. I know your very soul," she said, her eyes narrowing. "You cannot hide your feelings from me."

"I would never think to try and do so, my queen." Alexander turned his head and looked north again. "*He* is here."

"Why do you obsess about your sire?"

"Obsess? About his weakness? About his willingness to reject his nature and befriend the humans, rather than feed on them?" He entwined a hand with Roxana's and gently pulled her to stand next to him, looking over the city. "No, my love. I do not obsess about these things. His betrayal of our kind is two hundred years old. But he has managed to build an empire that is thriving and amassed himself a fortune. We are going to take that from him and put it to better use."

Roxana lifted a hand and traced her middle finger along the scar that ran from above Alexander's right eyebrow down the length of his face to his jawline. "And what of him?"

Alexander's eyes glowed with hatred. "I doubt he'll part with his wealth voluntarily. And if he must die, so be it."

Roxana pivoted and placed a hand each on his back and chest, then slid them downward. "You are powerful, my love. I have always known it. Now you shall ascend to rule this world." Her hand reached his groin and ass and squeezed. "Show me your power again, my lord."

His cock grew quickly in his pants. He traced a hand up her spine, deftly undoing each clasp of her dress as he moved, until he reached the back of her neck. When he removed the small hook from its eye, the dress fell from her shoulders, its silky caress causing her to moan softly into his shoulder.

He took her again, and this time, their animal passion cleared the park of all wildlife.

CHAPTER 4

David's alarm started softly but gradually grew louder and more annoying until it pierced his slumber. He woke up to soft light shining into his room through the gauzy curtains and was forced to get out of bed and walk across the room to silence the alarm. He briefly considered going back to bed—he'd only gotten about two hours of sleep—but stumbled to the shower instead, after stopping in the kitchen to turn on the coffeemaker.

Once in the shower, with the warm water wetting his skin, he reflected on the previous night. His skin felt silky from the silicone lube he'd been too tired to wash off after Joseph had left. David ran his hands along his body, reliving the kissing, the licking, and the light nibbles he'd been subjected to. Even though he'd cum five times over the course of their tryst, his dick was becoming hard again just thinking about it. God, it had been good.

David's hands moved back to feel his own smooth ass, squeezing the taut muscle as Joseph had done. His fingers slid between his cheeks and finally to his hole, which was still slick from the lube and slightly sore in that perfect way that let him know he'd remember the sex for a while. He and Joseph had flipped, neither one the top or the bottom, but both experiencing every part of the other in what felt like all possible levels of intimacy. The first couple of times were animalistic and raw, while the latter was gentle and more deliberate, and each in a different position. David had never had an experience quite like it. He had been tempted to ask Joseph to sleep over when they'd both had enough, but Joseph politely excused himself before David had a chance, saying he had an early day. Joseph ordered a Lyft and slipped out an hour or so before sunrise. They had made out by the front door while they waited for the ride, David still naked, pressed against Joseph's expensive T-shirt and jeans. The kissing was gentle and passionate, in contrast to most of the intense frenching they'd done earlier. Joseph kissed like a pro. He opened his mouth at just the right times, just the right amount, and there was the perfect amount of tongue... God, he was a good kisser.

David laughed at his repeated mental invocations of His name and thought how much his mom would disapprove as she clutched her rosary. His parents didn't talk about his sexuality, and even if he'd been straight, would never have approved of quite so much sex outside of a committed monogamous relationship.

Relationship. David found he really wanted to go on a proper date with Joseph. Obviously, the sex was amazing. Maybe the best he'd ever experienced—he was still stroking himself thinking about it—and now he wanted to know more about this man. David was in no rush to become part of a couple, but he had always loved the idea of sharing his life with someone special; someone who had a good head on their shoulders, a good heart, and didn't go crazy after they moved in together like Brad from Orange County. Something about Joseph made David think he could have those qualities. His ability to be gentle and, let's face it, *versatile* in bed was a good sign. But also, he had a sense of humor and general good nature. Many of the gays in WeHo got bitchy when they were around each other, always passing catty judgement on every little thing. Joseph, on the other hand, had literally stopped last night to smell flowers on the way up to the apartment security gate, commenting on how he loved the way the star jasmine made the city smell.

At the end of their time together, when the Lyft app had notified Joseph that his ride was a minute away, he had asked David to put his number in his phone. He had texted <Joseph from Micky's> with a smirk, before giving one last kiss and slipping out the door into the hallway.

Back in the present, David reluctantly turned off the hot water of the shower and stepped out, grabbing a towel and drying himself while making his way to his computer where his phone was charging. He unlocked it with a touch and saw the message notification from an unknown number. He opened it, hoping there would be at least a couple of texts there, but only <Joseph from Micky's> appeared. David noted the blue chat bubbles of a fellow iPhone user, which was another red flag avoided. *If he has a decent job and likes dogs, he might be the one*, he thought with a laugh.

David pondered what to do, mulling over the classic dilemma of how quickly to text a guy you were interested in. He realized that waiting an arbitrary length of time to say anything was stupid and childish, which only meant the content of his reply needed to be considered. He decided not to be *too* forward, and just tapped out <I really had fun last night, thanks!>, adding a winky smile emoji at the end. He thought about saying he wanted to meet again but couldn't make his sleep-deprived brain work out how to say it without seeming too slutty or too desperate. But if Joseph replied, they could go from there.

Around noon, Joseph had not yet replied. David was on the studio lot in the writing offices of a show gearing up for its fifth season. His Associate Producer credit was a technical promotion from assistant to the show runner, but basically it was the same job. His real passion was directing, but he'd stumbled into an assistant job out of college with the creators of the TV show he was now working on, and he'd enjoyed decent pay while slowly climbing the production ladder. David directed the odd short film to satisfy his passion.

A couple weeks into the new season, the staff and crew were in a groove and knew their jobs well, but currently there wasn't much to do. The show's writers were writing the first few episodes of the season and mapping out the rest. Which was good today, because David was starting to crash from his sleep deprivation. Instead of lunch. he decided to go out to his car and have a nap. He had a parking spot in the ramp nearest to the soundstages now, so it was cool enough to do that, and also fairly dark from the shade. On the way to the car, he held his phone, checking it every minute or so, hoping a text from Joseph would come through, but it remained stubbornly notification-free.

The rest of the day crawled by. A trip to the restroom turned into a masturbation session once David saw his own dick at the urinal, unencumbered by his jeans, and memory from the previous evening's sex came flooding back. He came fast and hard, moments before a production assistant walked in. David regained his composure quickly enough to exchange pleasantries with the younger guy, stuffing his still mostly hard penis into his pants.

Sitting at his desk later, staring at a spreadsheet with the production budget on it but not really seeing it, he was startled by a hand on his shoulder and let out a small shout.

"Damn, sorry dude! I said your name like five times, but you were zoned out!"

Dana had stepped back with her hands up to signal a non-threat. The two of them had come up from the bottom as PAs together, and she was basically

David's best friend. Her dark hair was in a pixie cut that looked boyish on her five-foot frame, and her ever-present smirk was darkened a bit by her worried face.

David took a couple of deep breaths to slow his heartbeat. "Sorry, I was totally spacing out. I'm a little sleep deprived."

"For good reasons or bad reasons? Everything okay?" she asked, momentarily dropping her usually snarky attitude and showing some genuine concern.

David blushed. "For good reasons. Like, really good reasons."

"Ooooohhh, David got laaaaaaiid," Dana teased in a singsong voice. "Was he hot?"

"Really hot, yeah," David chuckled back. The pair had no secrets from each other. They were so inseparable the rest of the crew sometimes referred to them as DayDay. They were constantly making each other laugh, which had earned them unofficial bans from the set during filming after they'd been overheard on the audio track during a scene at the beginning of the previous season.

"Aww, that's great! It's been too long, boyo." She sat on the edge of his desk, settling in for the details. "So how big is he?"

David laughed, "That's the first thing you want to know?"

"Obvi. So?" Dana mimed filing her nails and started chewing a nonexistent wad of gum.

David leaned in and lowered his voice. "A bit above average. But like, really nice..."

Dana matched his tone and leaned in conspiratorially. "Omigod, you slut. Are you going to have his babies?"

"No, but not for lack of trying," David shot back.

"Omigod, that is so damn hot, D." Dana fanned herself with an invisible fan. "My Lawd! D got some D!" She leaned back in. "So, tell me everything!"

"I'm not going to tell you everything. We met at Micky's and after some dancing we went back to my place and had some fun." David glanced around to make sure none of the interns were nearby. "Several times..."

Dana put the back of her non-fan hand up to her forehead as if about to faint. "I've said it a thousand times, gays are so lucky. Are you seeing him again?"

David sighed. "I don't know. I don't think so. I texted him this morning when I got up, but he still hasn't replied."

"But he gave you his number."

"Yeah. Well, he asked for mine and texted me before he left."

"Oh my gods, then don't be so dramatic. You saw him write a text to you and send it and it then appeared on your phone?"

"Yeah..."

"Then he's obviously interested, ya dink. If he wasn't, he wouldn't have asked for your number, and *definitely* wouldn't have texted you *while* he was there. And if you'd asked for his number, he would have given you a fake one."

"I guess you're right," David conceded.

"Trust me. I am, alas, an expert in such things." Dana noticed the doubt on his face. "Dude, there are a hundred reasons why you might not have gotten a reply—" she glanced at her watch, "eight whole hours later? Man, you're such a girl!"

"And you're practically a boy, that's why we get along so well," David shot back.

"Yeah, so maybe he has a job? Like you and I do? Did you ask what he does? Did you talk at all or just move right to the...?" She tried to stick one index finger into the other fisted hand, but the fist was too tight, and Dana started biting her lower lip with the effort to push it in. David let out a barking laugh at the visual.

"Stop! Gross," he laughed before addressing her actual question. "Yes, we talked, a little. No, I didn't ask about his job, but he was wearing designer jeans, so I think he has one, at least."

Dana threw her hands up. "Great! And maybe he works late! My point is, knowing only what I know about the text thing, he definitely wants you again. And dude, why wouldn't he? You're a catch and a half."

"Oh, stahhhp..."

"I will not stop! Seriously, you blush when you talk about this guy. You're like *so* into him."

She was right, David could feel the heat flushing his skin.

Dana continued, pointing a finger at him to drive her point home, "Don't even begin to worry about not hearing from him until at least twenty-four hours later. Mmkay?"

"Mmkay."

"Mmmmmm kay." She straightened. "So what did you need again?"

"Me? This is my desk, you grabbed me."

"Oh! Right." Dana stood up from his desk. "I just wanted to tell you that you. Are. A buttface."

David laughed. "Your face is a buttface."

Dana faked an offended gasp. "I'm going to HR!"

They both laughed. A couple of the other staff looked their direction. David asked, "Seriously though, did you need something?"

"No, I'm just bored and was trying to get your attention, but you were in your own little world. Drinks after work?"

David turned back to the budget spreadsheet. "For sure, as long as I can stay awake."

"I'ma get you a coffee. DayDay's gonna get their drink on tonight!" Dana turned and headed for the snack room where the office had recently gotten a fancy coffeemaker that ground fresh Starbucks beans and made espresso drinks.

"I would love that and love you for it!" David started reviewing the data and managed to push Joseph out of the front of his mind.

CHAPTER 5

Joseph awoke in his basement bedroom as soon as the sun set. The room was pitch-black with no light leaking in from the outside, but still he woke with the setting sun. He sometimes wondered how that could be possible, from an evolutionary point of view, especially since the time he woke up changed from day to day as the time of sunset changed.

But not this evening. The first thought to cross his mind was David. If he had dreams anymore, he never remembered them. Joseph suspected that something about the transformation from human to vampire had erased his ability to dream, but the fact that his last thought before falling into his daylight slumber was the boy he'd met the previous evening made it feel like he'd dreamt of him continuously.

He pushed back the covers of his bed and swung his bare feet to the cold stone floor. With his higher body temperature, he felt the coolness of the stone and the brisk dry air on his naked body as he stood and made his way to the bathroom.

He could smell David on himself. The saliva from his kisses and licks, his sweat which had commingled with Joseph's own, and of course his sex fluids, which Joseph hadn't bothered to wash off when he returned to the house. It had been late, yes, with the sun rising shortly after he got back to the castle-like house in the Hills. But he also found it intoxicating to feel and smell the results of their repeated lovemaking on his body.

When he walked into his master bathroom, automatic lighting accents gradually illuminated the floor and sink with a soft, warm glow while giving the eyes time to adjust to the change in brightness. Joseph entered the huge walk-in shower and touched the button to activate the half-dozen shower heads. He stepped back while the water warmed to a comfortable temperature and stretched his arms above his head while he waited.

After thirty seconds or so, the shower was steaming. Joseph dropped his arms, his hands running over his lithe body on their way down and stepped into the shower. The multiple heads felt like walking into a gentle, warm rainstorm. Joseph had felt such rain when he had explored the jungles of South Asia, and just as he had a hundred years ago, he longed to have another man's body pressed against his now. Only this time, as the water washed the aftermath of their sex from his skin, he was thinking of a specific man.

Joseph's morning routine was uncomplicated. He had no need for lotions or skin creams. He shaved every other day and got a haircut once a month. He didn't need soap or deodorant. The only luxury he permitted himself was a small dollop of leave-in conditioner for his hair, a habit which started back in the 1980s when ... well, when he learned to enjoy so very much the feel of someone running their fingers through his hair.

He dressed casually for the evening in jeans and a T-shirt and ascended to the main floor of the house, proceeding to the kitchen to retrieve one of the fresh bags of blood from the refrigerator. He popped it in the microwave for a minute, which brought it to a temperature that was pleasantly close to that of fresh, live blood. The plastic of the bag was thick and felt somewhat similar to skin as his fangs pierced through, allowing him to suck at its contents while he sat in his office and perused the day's numbers from the company and review the news.

Joseph hated the news. The world felt like it was going to shit, with rich people getting richer and more powerful while poor people, after a brief period which felt like progress, began to get poorer and more destitute again. Joseph didn't hate it because this was new; he hated it because it was exactly the same as the rest of history he'd experienced. He had hoped as humanity evolved and grew, they would become less greedy and less prone to violence. And he had to admit there were some places in the world that felt closer to that ideal, but here in the United States—in the promised land—the oligarchy was alive and well and getting stronger. Joseph tried to live by example. Though he and Rafaél were more than comfortable, his own wealth was directed almost exclusively toward making the world a better place.

The ringing of his cell phone roused him from the shit show of political coverage. His waking routine was so habitual he had completely forgotten to check his phone. It had only been a few years since the handheld devices began to hold power over human attention, after all.

It was Rafaél. "Hey, J, just checking in on my way out of the office. Everything good?"

"As a matter of fact, Rafi, it is. I was just looking at the quarterly numbers. Sales look good." Joseph got up from his desk and walked back to the kitchen with the empty blood bag, putting the phone on speaker mode.

"Wow, you *are* in a better mood. You never talk business anymore. And it's back to *Rafi*? Did you bring someone home last night?"

"No," Joseph replied, "but it was a very good evening."

"I'd love to hear about it. Want to have dinner?"

"I actually just had breakfast."

"So we talk while I eat, same as every other meal." Rafaél laughed.

Joseph considered for a moment. He looked at his phone, swiped out of the lock screen and saw a missed text notification. It was from David. "Can I let you know in fifteen minutes? I have to check on something."

"Sure thing. I'm just leaving, and I'll be in the car for an hour on the way to the Valley. Let me know and I can stop by on the way."

"Will do. Bye." Joseph tapped the button to end the call. He switched over to the texts and looked at David's reply. It had been sent a bit after sunrise, a couple of hours after he'd left David's apartment. Fourteen hours ago.

Joseph felt no need to be coy. He really liked this guy and wanted to see him again, and that was the end of it. He tapped out a reply, asking if David wanted to meet up again tonight.

The animated dots indicating that the other party was typing popped up immediately. Then disappeared. Then popped up again. Then disappeared. Joseph chuckled. David was struggling on how to formulate his reply. Either he wanted to get together but didn't want to seem too eager, or he didn't want to meet and was trying to figure out how to be nice about it.

David's reply was a third option Joseph hadn't considered. <I want to so bad, but I'm out with a friend, and heading home soon. SOOO tired after last night>

Joseph did some quick math in his head and realized the poor guy must've only gotten two or three hours of sleep at the most. A tiny pang of guilt hit him. <I completely understand. Luckily I managed to get a nap in. Ima bit of a night owl. Tomorrow maybe?>

The reply was immediate. <Yes plz> Then the toothy smiling face and horny devil emojis.

Joseph called Rafi back to confirm dinner plans.

Half an hour later, Rafaél pulled up outside the house in his gigantic Ford Expedition. Joseph had teased him about getting the oversized vehicle while living in Los Angeles but thought he understood the psychology of it. Even in his mid-sixties, after living in relative luxury and safety with all his needs attended to and wanting for nothing, Rafi longed for security and safety. The large SUV would surely destroy the average LA car in an accident, while sustaining minimal damage itself. Joseph would have gone for a Tesla, himself.

The ride to the restaurant consisted mostly of small talk about the business. Joseph had spread his wealth wisely over the centuries and invested heavily in technology (Tesla included), but the bulk of Rafaél's focus was on the bio-pharmaceutical division. Very exciting developments were in the pipeline with the cancer research and genetic engineering arms. He got a bit geeky when he talked about these things to Joseph, so it was fortunate the ride was short.

The younger (but older looking) man drove them to Studio City on the San Fernando Valley side of the Hollywood Hills to a quaint Indian restaurant. There was no waiting on a Wednesday evening, and they were led to a table in the back corner where they could talk without being overheard. A cute young server, who appeared to be of South Asian descent but not actually Indian, immediately brought them water and menus.

"Hi, welcome to Gangadin. I'm Kaung. I'll be your server today. What drinks can I get you while you look over the menu?"

Joseph noticed the proactive phrasing and the fact that Kaung made direct eye contact with each of them. The young man also had a very slight but constantly present Mona Lisa smile. Normally Joseph ordered something cheap to sip on while Rafaél ate his human food, but he suddenly felt the urge to support the kid.

"We'll split a bottle of your most expensive red, please." He glanced at Rafi, who cocked an eyebrow in his direction. "And I'm just going to have the wine, I ate already." He smirked back at his adopted son, who these days looked more like his father to anyone who saw the two of them together.

Rafi picked up the menu. "I think I know what I want, just hang out one second..."

Joseph knew that *Rafi* knew he thought the server was cute and was keeping him waiting for his benefit. He took the opportunity to give the server a once-over while his ward confirmed his selection.

Kaung was young but legal. His caramel skin looked clean and smooth. He was more fit than skinny, with some good muscle tone. The server's gaze shifted back to Joseph while he waited for Rafi to give his order, and his smile faltered as he locked eyes with the younger looking man who was just going to have wine. Joseph turned on his vampiric charm just a bit, and it was more than enough. He could hear the blood rush to the young man's groin and smell the light sheen of sweat as Kaung's skin flushed.

Joseph held the server's gaze captive for an extra beat, then let his scrutiny fall to the boy's crotch. The bulge there was impressive, and he raised an eyebrow as he returned his eyes to the dark brown eyes of the sexy waiter. But he was just playing with him and he knew it. He had no intention of bedding this guy, at least not tonight, so he showed the kid some mercy.

"Why don't you go grab the wine," he told the server, nodding his head at Rafaél. "He's not as fast as he thinks he is."

"I..." The waiter swallowed hard. His accent came out a bit heavier. "I, okay, I'll be right back with that." His light smile turned lascivious as he turned from the table and headed to the back of the restaurant.

Rafi didn't look up from the menu. "You're incorrigible."

"Hey, kiddo, you're the one who told me to get laid last night."

"Yeah, last night, on your own. Not tonight *while* we have dinner. Ironically, a meal we're having so you can tell me about your 'very good evening.'" He placed the menu down neatly and took a sip of water.

"Right, right! Oh, and it was good." Joseph looked down, losing himself in the memory. "You know what you want?"

"I knew what I wanted when we got here. I just knew you'd like the waiter when you saw him." Rafaél nodded in the direction of their server.

Joseph chuckled. "He's cute, for sure. Kind of reminds me of you when you were that age. Though you didn't smile as much."

"I was an introspective kid. Doesn't help when your new dad literally finds you living in a box in Chinatown."

Joseph made a new connection in his head, a fairly rare thing in his advanced years. "Is that why we never go out for Chinese food?"

Rafi shrugged. "I just don't feel like it. You know what I had to do before you found me."

Joseph did know. Rafaél's whole story had taken years to unravel, but in that moment in 1965, seeing the pile of boxes the child had been using as a shelter, it was clear he'd been dumpster diving for food. Eating old wontons and slimy meat. Joseph shook his head. How stupid was he not to realize the connection before? Of course, Rafi probably wouldn't want to eat sweet and sour pork or Kung Pao chicken for the rest of his life.

"What about Mexican food?" Joseph asked, suddenly curious about Rafaél's culinary experiences.

"What about it?"

"Do you like it? It's the food of your people, isn't it?" Joseph traced a finger absently around the edge of the water glass but didn't bother to drink.

"Actually, I never mentioned it, but a few years ago I got my DNA sequenced."

Joseph sat up, suddenly intrigued by this new revelation. "You did?"

"Yeah, well, we have several providers we work with and the cost had come down so much… Well, I was just curious." Rafi took another sip of his water and continued, "Turns out my mom was Puerto Rican and my dad, who we thought was Mexican—"

"That's what it said on his military record."

"Right. Well, he was from Peru. Mom was a mix of native and European, like most Mexicans and Puerto Ricans, but Dad's lineage was old Peru. Like, I've got some Incan heritage in me."

Joseph found himself speechless for a moment. Mostly, he marveled he was learning something so big about someone he thought he knew so completely.

They were interrupted by Kaung returning with the wine. His erection had subsided. "Sorry for the delay, I had to get a step stool to reach the top of the wine rack." He uncorked the wine at the table, and his coy smile returned as he looked at Joseph again. "Our chef said he was jealous you get to taste this bottle. According to him, it's very good on the tongue." He chuckled but looked directly at Joseph when he did so, which made Joseph wonder whether the chef had actually made the innuendo-filled remark.

"I'll definitely make sure you know how my tongue feels," he quipped back. He sensed Rafaél's bemusement and could practically hear his eyes roll. "About the wine, I mean."

"I look forward to a detailed review." Kaung's erection was returning.

Rafaél cut in, putting on a cheerful tone of voice, "Well, I'm ready to order."

The young waiter turned to the older-looking man, suddenly aware of his job. "Yes, sir, what would you like?"

Later, as Rafaél finished his lamb samosas and began tucking into his chicken tikka masala, Joseph sipped on the Catena Zapata Adrianna Vineyard Malbec. Though not terribly expensive as wines went, he hadn't really expected a small Indian restaurant to have anything pricier than a hundred dollars. It was good. *His tongue was happy*, he thought cheekily.

Rafi scooped basmati rice onto a small plate and used the serving spoon in the masala to ladle chicken and sauce on top. "So, you got home before sunrise, but only barely," he said, a touch of reproach creeping into his comment.

"Oh, stop, I was home well before sunrise. That wasn't the point of the story," Joseph defended. "I haven't spent more than an hour with a guy in years. I thought you'd be happy for me."

"I am, I am." Rafi scooped the masala mix onto a piece of naan and took a big bite.

Joseph sipped. "But?"

Rafaél met Joseph's gaze while he chewed. When he had swallowed enough to speak, he chose his words slowly. "But ... I know you very, very well. You've been alone for a long, long time."

"For good reason, I feel."

"Well, yes," Rafaél conceded. "Wait, which reason do you mean? The—" he bared his teeth to mean vampire without having to say it aloud "—or the other thing?"

"Both. Plus, relationships haven't turned out great for me, traditionally."

"Right, that's kind of what I mean. The way you talk about this guy... David?"

"Yeah, David," Joseph nodded, suppressing a grin at the mention of his name.

"I can only remember you talking and looking like *this*—" he made a gesture that encompassed Joseph's whole demeanor "—one other time in my life."

"I know. But I just met him."

"Yeah, for sure. But..." Rafaél put the naan down and focused on his companion. "Dad, I just worry about you. I don't want to see you hurt the way you were after Rob."

"When was the last time you called me Dad?" Joseph asked, somewhat surprised.

Rafi shrugged. "This is a serious conversation. I'm being serious right now." He picked up his own wine glass, smelling the bouquet before taking a sip. "This is my serious face."

"Rafi, I love you. You are a better son than I ever could have imagined, you know that?"

"I know. And you're a pretty good dad. I wish *you* knew *that*. I used to wonder why you never adopted any other kids. All the good you could have done." The seriousness of the conversation subsided as they veered into old topics, and Rafaél picked up his naan again and piled more chicken masala on it.

"I've told you why."

"Well, you *say* it's not safe, but I don't think I could feel safer than I do. I was certainly safer than most kids who have to live on the street. Safer than I would have been if you hadn't brought me in."

"You don't know how much energy, and money, I spend to protect us, Rafaél."

Rafaél chewed, savoring the delicate mix of creaminess and spices. "Mm'kay." He didn't push.

They sat in silence while Rafaél ate. Joseph absentmindedly swirled the wine glass as he studied the decor of the restaurant without actually paying attention to it. The blackberry and tea notes from the wine wafted up into his nose and sparked little fireworks of color in his senses.

Rafaél broke the silence. "Do be careful, though. Personally, I think it's best if you don't get too involved with this David guy... before you fall too much for him."

Joseph set the wine glass on the table but grasped it with both hands, steadying himself. "I've been thinking about it. If I'm being honest, I'm very lonely. Most ... others of my kind find a partner. Someone to spend the many, many years of their lives with. But you can imagine there aren't a lot of gay—" he glanced around to make sure no one was in earshot "—*vampires* in the world. But does that mean I shouldn't try for happiness when I find it?"

Rafaél sighed, sadly. He looked into the unchanging blue eyes of the man who had rescued him, completely unable to see him as the monster that myth and legend made him out to be. "You know, when I was younger, I don't know, in my twenties or so, I sometimes wished I could have been that for you. I experimented with guys in college, did I ever tell you?"

Joseph reacted with a mix of humor and surprise, but he was touched at the revelation as well. "No, I had no idea."

"I knew pretty quickly I wasn't gay. I had a lot of gay friends back then, thanks to how open you were to me about it. I think most of them thought I was closeted and plenty were absolutely willing to try and help me find the way out." Rafi chuckled. "But I knew I was pretty far from the gay end of the Kinsey scale. Anyway, I thought if I could be more than just an adopted son, I could help you be happier. Took me a few years to realize that wasn't my role in your life. And then you met Rob."

"Yeah."

"I really liked him, you know. Other than having to tell him I was your cousin, at first. And I've never seen you so happy. But the last thirty years... Jesus, that's half my life... after he died, I know how unhappy you've been."

"It's hard, is all. About a hundred years after my transformation I fell in love with a soldier."

"Marcus."

"I told you about him?"

Rafaél nodded. "A bit." Joseph had told him many stories over the years; Of the wars he'd fought in, the corners of the world he'd explored. Rarely did he speak of his romantic relationships in more than ambiguous generalities.

"The great war was coming to an end—that is, the Thirty Years' War—and Marcus and I found each other in France. He was my everything and I was his. Even after the truth came out about what I was, he stayed by my side. A few years later, he asked me to turn him."

"But you wouldn't because of Decimus."

"That's what I told you." Joseph's eyes darkened as the distant memory solidified in his mind, and he averted his gaze from Rafaél's caring visage. "The truth is, I tried."

Rafi's eyes widened in shock. "What? But..."

"I know. I hadn't experienced the misery of Decimus for myself at that point. I suppose I thought my will and our love was stronger than some ancient curse." Joseph took a long, slow sip of his wine, feeling the alcohol warm his tongue and throat. "Of course, in those days anything we didn't understand was attributed to magic and curses and gods. Now we know it's just biology. But I wanted to give Marcus the gift of—" Joseph caught himself. This had become a moment of truth with his son, the person he never lied to. "No, that's not true. I wanted to give myself the gift of a long life with him, not aging, in his prime forever. As a human I thought I had experienced love, but it was a pale shadow of what I felt for Marcus. So I agreed to turn him."

There was a long pause while Rafaél waited for him to continue. Neither of the men drank their wine, and the tikka masala began to cool and congeal. Finally, Rafaél broke the silence.

"He died?"

"I killed him."

"It wasn't your fault." The response came reflexively. Rafaél knew his adopted father so well, the urge to defend him was automatic.

"It kind of exactly was. The fang marks don't lie."

"You said he asked you to turn him."

"He begged me. But I knew the rules. My sire had told me the dangers before he sent me on my own into the world. I just ... didn't believe them, and Marcus died for my arrogance and greed." Joseph inhaled sharply and let out a tremendous sigh.

He could feel the empathy from across the table. Rafaél clearly wanted to say something, or perhaps wanted to say so many things. Offer platitudes about everything being okay and assure Joseph of what a good man he was, but anything that came to mind seemed hollow, so after a moment he stopped trying and just sat quietly with the only father he ever remembered having.

"And of course you know what happened to Rob," Joseph said.

"Do I?"

"Yes, I told you everything. I felt you deserved to know the truth." Joseph understood the question being asked, though. It had been a while since Rafaél had learned anything new about Joseph, so with these new revelations, he naturally must have wondered if there was anything else he didn't know. Joseph cocked his head, the sorrow of the memory momentarily pushed aside by the bemusement of another realization. "It is interesting, though, now that I think about it, the public perception of gay people was worse in 1980 in Los Angeles than it was in seventeenth-century France."

"Or the eighteenth, from what you've told me."

"Oh, Rafi, I loved Europe during the Enlightenment. Marcus and I were able to walk in public together, even showing affection, with impunity. With Connor it was the same, but by then, my wealth shielded us even more than the tolerance of the time."

Rafaél knew about Connor Robinson well enough. He was the relationship Joseph had no regrets about, as far as he'd let on. The two met after the turn of the eighteenth century in Paris. The young Irish boy had made his way to mainland Europe in search of adventure and was making a meager living as an apprentice farrier and selling his body to rich clients on the side.

By then, Joseph had learned how to use his long life to financial advantage, growing a diversified business and owning several large manors around Europe. He first hired Connor as a stable hand before the boy successfully seduced him. Connor later admitted he was just trying to get ahead by bedding the master of the house, but Joseph turned out to be so kind and noble, in every sense of the word, that the young Irishman, who was in his early twenties by then, declared his love after only a year.

Joseph didn't push the boy away, per se, but did send him to the University of Cambridge to get a proper education, much as he would do with Rafaél over two hundred and fifty years later. However, even after exploring the world of University, including the virile young men there, Connor still came back to Joseph at every break, insisting his love was real. And so Joseph, who had also fallen in love with Connor, revealed his true nature to the young man. Connor had taken time to think about the revelation, that not only were vampires real, but he was in love with one. He approached the problem logically and ultimately determined he knew Joseph's true kind nature and was not afraid of him, just as he was not afraid of an African friend at school just because he heard stories about the tribesmen of the Southern wilds. Joseph moved him into his home completely and the two lived as husbands for over fifty years until Connor died an old man in his sleep.

Rafaél had never asked if Joseph had considered making Connor a vampire. He knew about Decimus and assumed that was the entire reason it wasn't considered. Even when Rob had died his tragic death in the middle of Pan Pacific Park on that torrential Halloween, Rafi hadn't connected it with stories he'd heard about Marcus.

Joseph sighed again. "At least until heads started to roll during the French Revolution. At that point, as I'd long since become a member of the *bourgeoisie*, and when it became apparent that my wealth could not protect me from the mobs and their guillotines, I figured I might give the New World a look-see."

Rafaél nodded. "Okay, I get your point. You know your heart and your life better than I do. And I do admit there's something about you tonight that is good to see. You seem ... lighter, somehow. I just don't want to see you heartbroken again."

"'Tis better to have loved and lost..."

"Tennyson. The same poem that warns of Nature, red in tooth and claw," Rafi reminded him.

"Tennyson was gay. I knew him, you know."

Rafaél grinned slyly. "No, you didn't. You were on another continent his whole life."

Joseph snorted lightly. "Okay, I didn't. Good for you, Rafi. But he wrote a ninety-page poem for his dead college friend. You can't tell me they weren't doing it."

"They might have been doing it," Rafi conceded, pleased that the conversation had taken a lighter turn. He paused. "You're going to call David?"

It was barely a question. "Nobody calls anymore, old man, jeez. Get with the times." Joseph winked. "But yeah, I'm going to get together with him again."

"Okay, well, just be careful. And if you call me old man again, I'm investing in some sharp sticks." Rafi playfully poked himself in the chest with his butter knife like a stake to the heart.

"Oh, you just try it, *Dad*." They both laughed as cute young Kaung took that opportunity to return to the table.

"How was everything? Can I interest you in any dessert?" It was apparent that the question was meant literally to Rafaél and as an innuendo to Joseph.

Rafi wiped his mouth with his napkin and replied to the young waiter, "Everything was perfect, thank you. Exactly what I was craving."

Joseph reached for his wallet and subtly drew the boy's attention. "On any other evening, I'd really show you what I was craving, and you'd wind up at my place," he said matter-of-factly as he fished out four one-hundred-dollar bills and handed them to Kaung. "I can't tonight, but I do want to make sure you know how beautiful you are."

Kaung took the bills, making a point to touch the older man's hand. Joseph didn't relinquish the currency immediately. He brought up his other hand to lightly caress the inside of the waiter's wrist.

Kaung gasped lightly, and his pants swelled noticeably. "Thank you..." he whispered. "Another time, maybe. I hope."

"Me, too. Please keep the change." Joseph released the money and smiled warmly as Kaung looked down and realized he just got a hundred percent tip on what was already a large bill.

"Wow. Thank you. Have a great night, guys."

Joseph could feel the heat of the young man's sexual desire. He suspected Kaung was going to have to take a break as soon as they left. The cute waiter might explode if he didn't get to the employee restroom and jerk off immediately.

"We will, thanks," Rafi said, rolling his eyes at the exchange. The pair got up and made their way to the door.

As they reached the SUV, Joseph made a decision to enjoy the night air. "Thank you for the delightful dinner, kiddo. I really do enjoy seeing you, but I'm going to walk home," Joseph said as he opened the Expedition's driver's door and stood ready to help Rafi into the high seat.

"I guess I prefer kiddo to old man, but I don't need help getting into my own car just yet," Rafi replied. Once in the seat, he buckled his seatbelt and regarded Joseph skeptically. "Are you sure? That's quite a hike."

"I mean, besides having the stamina of ten men, it's a beautiful night. Plus, it's out of your way. It's fine, really."

"Okay, I won't argue with getting home quicker." Rafaél's face turned serious. "Hey. You be careful, okay? LA might be kinder to gay people these days, but I'm not so sure about the other thing. Take it slow with this guy."

"You'd have made a good, if overprotective, father, Rafi."

"Oh, I've got my hands full taking care of you," he replied with a grin. "Good night, J."

Joseph closed the door with a heavy *whumph*. *They design them to make that noise*, he thought absently as the big Ford pulled away, taking up what seemed like three-quarters of the parking lot lane.

He turned and walked out to the sidewalk, setting a brisk pace along Laurel Canyon Boulevard, heading upward into the Hollywood Hills. As he went, he pulled out his phone, unlocked it using the two-factor authentication of his thumbprint and a passcode, and tapped into his chat with David. He had an idea. <Awesome. Let's meet 8:30 PM tomorrow at the Starbucks near AMC Sunset 5>

The response was immediate. <Perfect! Looking forward to it>

Joseph chuckled at the enthusiasm and had to admit he shared it. <Do you own a suit or jacket and tie?>

A moment passed as David typed an answer. Joseph's feet scuffed lightly on the sidewalk, but his soft footfalls were easily covered by the passing traffic on the busy road.

<What kind of self-respecting gay do you take me for? Of course I have a suit!> and then <but now I'm very intrigued why you should ask...>. A second later a curious face emoji with a monocle appeared. It was about three times as large as a regular emoji because it was in its own text line.

Joseph chuckled. He sent the face with a *shhh* finger, followed by <It's a surprise... Wear it. See you tomorrow!>

He forgot how fun this part was. He hadn't exactly dated in a while, but taking boys out for a good time before taking them to bed was not unheard of for him. And though he didn't want to show off to David, and certainly didn't want to tip his hand to reveal just how comfortable a lifestyle he enjoyed, he felt like treating this new guy to something special.

David replied with a GIF of a little girl doing an excited dance, and Joseph laughed out loud. He had always embraced new technologies. When he was a boy, the printing press had barely been invented, and he was fascinated by the ability to share a story permanently fixed in paper, even though his parents were strictly in favor of oral storytelling. Telegraphs, radio, television, the internet... Joseph had not only been in favor of these new methods of communication, he had helped develop some of them. When humans began texting on their cell phones, though, he hadn't seen the appeal. It was so clunky and required so much *work* when a quick phone call could accomplish more, faster. But then Apple (he owed a fair chunk of stock) created a phone with a full virtual keyboard that was easy to use, and suddenly Joseph *got* it.

Initially, he had despised the rise of emoji culture, but now frequently used them as supplements to a conversation. GIFs though... *They* were amazing. The ability to find a looping video clip that so perfectly represented one's mood in a particular moment was practically magic. Joseph liked it so much he had Rafaél purchase a GIF creation company over a year ago, and now they were an integrated part of the iOS, Android, and Facebook core user experiences. In the end, it didn't matter what Joseph liked or not. If he wanted to hook up with younger guys (and every guy was certainly a younger guy), he needed to communicate the way they did. Resenting progress didn't help. One might as well embrace it.

Joseph used another bit of technological magic. "Hey Siri, call Jeb Whitlock." Siri, using Joseph's preferred option, a male voice with a British accent, confirmed the call and the phone started ringing.

"Ahoyhoy."

"Hey, Chief, it's Joseph."

"Oh!" came the sarcastic reply. "Thank God the caller ID wasn't lying to me." Joseph heard the grin on the other end of the line.

"Ha ha," Joseph gave the corny joke its due. "Hey, I need a favor. Can you get me passes to the club tomorrow night?"

Jeb didn't hesitate a beat. "I can get anybody passes, I'm the president. And for you, anytime. How many do you need?"

"Just two, and reservations for dinner, please."

"Ooohooo," Jeb teased. "A hot date, huh?"

"Kinda, yeah. Are you performing tomorrow night?" Joseph inquired.

"I am indeed, buddy. I'll be on the main stage!"

Jeb was a perpetually cheerful guy. Joseph had met him when he saw him performing improv ten years ago. He was so impressed with the man's ability to create hilarity out of thin air, he waited to meet the comedian at the bar attached to the theater. He was convinced to start taking improv classes at a highly regarded comedy theater, and the pair became friends. Jeb had even invited Joseph to his wedding (a daytime affair, Joseph had had to come up with a very convincing reason to not attend). But it wasn't improv he wanted to treat David to on their first date. It was Jeb's other incredible skillset.

"Your show is so fun. I can't wait to see it again and share it. I'll see you tomorrow night, my friend. Thanks so much!"

"Of course, buddy. I'll have 'em put you on the list! Later, gator!" Jeb always called everyone buddy, and it was never insincere or annoying.

"Later, Chief."

Chief was a nickname he only used with Jeb, because when they'd met he reminded Joseph of a character on a TV show who people called Chief. Joseph chuckled at the kind of person he'd be if he called everyone Chief the way Jeb called everyone buddy.

With that task done, he shifted his awareness to his walk. He made it past Ventura Boulevard (*so many Boulevards in this city*, he thought) and came to a parking lot on the right side of the road. It was mostly empty except for a few teenagers who were making out, smoking weed, or some combination of the two. Just past the lot marked the entrance to Fryman Canyon Hiking Trail. It was supposed to be closed after sunset, but Joseph supposed the restriction was more of a guideline than a rule. And anyway, he didn't want to walk the whole way up the side of the road, especially since the sidewalk was about to end as Laurel Canyon continued up the Hills. From here, dark masses of shrubs and scraggly trees butted up against the road.

Joseph turned and headed up the trail.

CHAPTER 6

The night was cool and as clear as things got in Los Angeles, yet only a handful of stars could be seen thanks to the light pollution of the sprawling metropolis. The moon was new, and with no clouds to reflect the city's glow, the surroundings became much darker once Joseph moved onto the moderate hiking path. The trail itself was an easy incline, especially for Joseph and his heightened strength and endurance. Spring rains had eroded small channels through the dirt, and he had to pay attention to where he stepped, even more so in the dark.

It was several minutes before Joseph realized he was being followed. He scolded himself for lowering his guard. LA wasn't a dangerous city, especially away from the city center. The downtown Hollywood area had been tamed twenty years ago and successfully gentrified, and the Hollywood Hills, through which he now walked, had a minuscule incidence of violent crime.

He reached out with his senses, trying to identify the person or persons behind him. It was surprisingly difficult. Whoever it was had light footfalls and didn't make much sound. They were downwind, but the breeze was light, so Joseph should have been able to smell *something* from them, but all he could detect was the dusty trail, the sweat of the evening walkers who had been on it during the last hours of daylight, and the various animals in the area. He sensed the many dogs who hiked with their owners, some deer that inhabited the Hills, and the coyote that hunted the deer (and sometimes the smaller dogs).

Joseph didn't have enough information to determine whether the person following him was actually following, or just coincidentally behind him on the same trail, which was closed, on a dark night. The darkness was a clue. Most human beings required flashlights to walk safely on this dim a night on a path as poorly kept as this one. The pieces fell into place. Joseph stopped and turned towards his pursuer, his eyes picking up the ambient light and flashing with warning.

"I am not prey," he called out. "You will find no meal in me."

A figure stepped out of the shadows from the brush along the side of the trail. "I didn't think I would."

He moved closer and Joseph suddenly recognized him. The only vampire he had ever created. "Hello, Alexander. It's been a very long time."

"Joseph. It has indeed. How long did it take you to detect me?"

Joseph ignored the dig about his sensory abilities. "What are you doing in Los Angeles?"

Alexander spread his arms to show his peaceful intentions. "Can't I come to see my long-lost progenitor for a visit?"

Joseph looked at him with narrowed eyes. "Is *she* still with you?"

Alexander closed the distance between them, casual and silent. "If you are referring to my dearest love and *wife*... She is hunting. She decided to see what your Venice boardwalk had to offer, though after feasting in the real Venice, I doubt this one will compare." He looked around them. From here, the trail had climbed enough up the hill that it afforded a decent view of the San Fernando Valley which stretched out like a blanket of lights before them. "I don't suppose you're also hunting? Here, where there don't appear to be any humans to prey on?" He made a show of looking around them, searching for any humans they might feast upon.

Joseph stood his ground. "I am not."

The amiable look on Alexander's face dropped in unmasked disappointment. "I had hoped you might have changed in the hundred years since we last saw each other. You have always been too involved with humans."

"They dominate the planet. Even more now than when you traveled by my side. It makes sense to fit into their world or risk discovery and death."

"That's not why you don't eat them, and you know it." Alexander turned to look at the lights sprawling beneath them. "They are sheep. You are the wolf. I've never understood why you don't act like it."

"I would have taught you, but you left to be with that lunatic you love so much." Joseph moved to stand next to his progeny. "I wanted to teach you, as I was taught."

The younger vampire snorted derisively. "Uh-huh. And your progenitor, your ... *teacher* of vampire life, where is he now?"

"He was slain shortly before I made you."

"Good that I did not learn from his student, then. I would rather a similar fate not befall me."

Joseph pointed at the scar on Alexander's face. "By the look of it, it nearly did..."

Instead of turning to hide the deformity, he presented it to Joseph. "A battle scar. When we returned to Europe, we were tracked by a group that fancied themselves vampire hunters. They were delicious, and they died slowly. This was their only hit. A silver blade, it never fully healed."

"I would have taught you to avoid silver if you hadn't left."

Anger roiled suddenly in Alexander's eyes, flashing red. "*You* sent me away! Your pity for the humans caused our rift."

"Your loathing of them did that."

Alexander closed the distance between them, baring his teeth at the man who created him. "I do not loathe humans. I don't think highly enough of them for that. You, on the other hand, you ignore your nature. You are a predator, yet you completely fail to behave like one."

Joseph remained calm but on guard for any sudden moves the younger bloodsucker might make. "I recognized a changing world and adapted with it. You would be wise to do the same or the next silver blade you encounter might do more than leave a scar."

Alexander sneered. "You bend truth like one of their politicians would. You hated feeding on humans since before I was born. Tales of your weakness are told among our kind."

Joseph grew tired of the tit for tat. "Why are you really here, Alexander?"

The other vampire began backing away, arms spread apart. "Why, I'm merely a tourist in your great city, Father."

Joseph stiffened at the moniker. "I don't believe you."

"What you believe holds little concern for me." Alexander sighed theatrically. "I must leave your company, though; the smell of humans on you sickens me. Good night, *Father*."

With that he stepped off the trail, jumping into the growth below. Such a show should have raised a ruckus of rustling brush and breaking branches, but he was virtually silent. Joseph was able to follow his path down the hill, between houses and through the light woods, until he lost sight almost half a mile away.

Joseph turned up the hill and resumed his walk, now preoccupied with the problem that was Alexander. He never intended to create a vampire. Contrary to popular superstition, it wasn't an easy thing to do. Joseph had seen many depictions of vampires in popular media over the centuries. Stories around the hearth, then books, and these days, movies and television. But none of them ever had it quite right. There were too many wrong details, like the ridiculous ability to turn into a bat or glitter in sunlight or not make reflections in mirrors. Some omitted true facts, like the limitation in the process by which vampires were created.

Alexander had been a sloppy accident. In the years after the death of Connor, Joseph had been distraught and careless. One hunt, he had beset a highwayman who had plagued a stretch of road between Paris and Brussels. It had given Joseph a sense of justice and righteousness to feed on men who preyed on other humans. On this occasion, however, after draining the thief, some of his blood from a lucky blow landed on the thief's lips, and against all odds, the thief gained his immortality.

Joseph would never have considered giving such a gift to a person with that much cruelty in them. Increased power, strength, and long life only served to exacerbate a person's evil tendencies. That mistake turned Joseph away from feeding on humans ever again. He shifted his diet to cattle and other easy prey. Joseph initially felt a responsibility to keep the thief with him, and tried to train the young vampire how to live nonviolently. He attempted to adapt the lessons his own creator had bestowed, but Alexander's bloodlust was overwhelming, and the pair were constantly working to quash problems caused by his indiscriminate killing. Too many young women were lured by his hypnotic energy and bitten at the height of orgasm. When the French Revolution happened, Joseph and his protégé were already under close scrutiny, so out of an abundance of caution, they fled to the New World and settled in New Orleans. It was French, and thus familiar. But it was also wild and exacerbated Alexander's wanton dismissal of Joseph's insistent teaching.

Then Roxana came. Alexander's bloodlust was easily eclipsed by hers, and they quickly fell in love. It was a passion fueled by mutual distain for humans and, by extension, Joseph and his benevolence for them. They hunted together more and more until she was ever-present in their lives. The female vampire was older than Joseph and Alexander combined and physically powerful. She was a perfect huntress, but she depended on Joseph's hospitality, having never taken advantage of her longevity to develop wealth or resources.

Before long, Joseph found himself unable to tolerate their wanton cruelty towards humans or their disrespect of his house. He would occasionally bring men home, but always feared for their safety. Instead, it was in hotels and brothels he would appease his sexual needs, and when they grew to know him by name at an establishment, he would never go there again. After perhaps a dozen years of this, he saw an opportunity as the American expansion into the West began, and Joseph left New Orleans behind. The last time he had seen Alexander was in 1820. He had closed his affairs and burned the house to bring closure to that identity (giving fair warning to the bloodthirsty lovebirds, of course), and moved west. When gold was discovered in California, he was there, with enough wealth to build mines and hire men to dig for him. He bought land, developed farmland in the fertile area, and built his financial empire, though always through a veil of secrecy. His companies had fingers in almost every type of business, from food to technology to healthcare to banking. And of course, scientific research. Various businesses under the corporate umbrella held thousands of patents worth billions of dollars. Tetractys was not a household name, but it was one of the most powerful companies on the planet.

Joseph stopped walking. Alexander's parting words came back to him. *"I must leave your company..."* The phrasing seemed oddly formal for the former bandit.

It's something to do with Tetractys. Perhaps he knows what I've built and means to take it from me. Joseph started walking again. He was relatively certain Alexander couldn't know all the parts of his financial empire; a huge percentage of the wealth generated by his companies was directed into research towards green energy production, space exploration, human medicine, and, clandestinely, the genetic study of vampirism. On paper, Joseph was worth billions, but only had ready access to a tiny portion. If Alexander was after a massive payday, he was likely to be disappointed. And if Alexander was disappointed, he could be a violent problem. And if, and if, and if...

Joseph shook his head. It was not a problem that needed to be solved now. Alexander would entertain himself in this new city, and if he needed money, Joseph could easily provide some to tide him over until a more permanent solution could be found.

CHAPTER 7

The next night, Joseph's phone alarm went off promptly at 7:30 PM, a good bit before sunset. He went through his wake-up routine, showered, and tried to pick out a nice semi-casual outfit for the date with David. Joseph appreciated Rafaél for keeping his wardrobe current via a quarterly stylist, but he wished he had some help right this moment. He wanted to impress David but hadn't been on a real date in thirty years. Cruising West Hollywood or Soho in a casual shirt and jeans, or attending board meetings in a high-end suit—these were looks he was comfortable with. But this in-between place confounded him. A quick Google search for "*men's first-date outfit*" gave him some ideas, and Joseph ended up picking out a warm grey sharkskin suit and paired it with a blue-striped fitted dress shirt. He added a blue-grey tie and a sharp pair of brown dress shoes with matching belt to complete the ensemble.

Joseph took a step back from the mirror. "Rahhhhr," he said, smiling. He looked pretty good for north of five hundred years old. He glanced at his watch—a classic Uhrenmanufaktur Heuer he'd gotten to celebrate the end of the first World War—and realized he was running late. Joseph called for a Lyft while he popped into the kitchen and heated up a container of blood. He didn't suppose there was going to be much on the menu at the club that would sit well with his stomach, and it wouldn't do to be hungry for what was sure to be a fun-filled evening with the hot young man.

The empty blood bag was just being dropped into the incinerator when Joseph's phone pinged him that his ride had arrived. He quickly rinsed his mouth at the kitchen sink and suddenly found himself feeling nervous about the date. *What? Nervous?* He had fought in hand-to-hand combat in the hellscape of war. He had traveled the world and met kings and emperors and dictators. He controlled the livelihoods of thousands. How was he nervous about a date with a man he just met?

The answer came to him in pieces as he rode in the back seat of the mercifully unchatty Lyft. From his dinner conversation with Rafaél where he admitted his loneliness and reminisced extensively about his past loves, to his long night with David. It had mostly been sex, sure, but everything leading up to it, and the in-between breaks, had been great. Little clues pointed to him being a genuinely good guy. The way David spoke about family when they were covering the basic get to know you stuff. His passion for life and compassion for people. And the fact that he spoke in complete sentences, which set him apart from the usual WeHo boy toys.

And that waiter at the restaurant with Rafi! On any normal day, he would have been back at Joseph's castle bent over an extra-plush pillow *that night* (or, given the bulge under his apron, had Joseph bent over one). But no, Joseph had walked home alone. Well, mostly alone.

The fact of the matter was that he felt differently about David than he had about any guy in decades. It was a scary and exhilarating feeling. Joseph spent most of the Lyft ride trying to bring himself back to Earth. In all his life, Joseph had been in love only three times. Four, if you count the teenage love for that Roman soldier when he was still human. It just didn't happen in one night. His romance with Connor had taken years to develop. There was no reason to get overly excited just yet. *Although*, another part of his brain countered, *we are going on an actual date. What gays do that anymore in the age of Grindr and Scruff?*

He tried to distract himself with other thoughts. What was the stock market doing? What about the rocket work that was being done in the space division? But business led his train of thought to Alexander and what Joseph suspected his progeny of being up to. That was too far in the wrong direction, so he thought again of David, and the last moments he saw him. As Joseph had been getting dressed to leave the apartment following their night together, David had remained naked; his smooth, toned torso glowing with the sheen of sweat, lube, and cum. The younger man had been completely at ease with his nudity, leaning on the kitchen counter and cocking his hip to the side, one foot crossed over the other. He looked so sexy with his weight on one leg like that, the abs on one side of his stomach flexing to maintain his balance as he watched Joseph pull on his shoes, the hallway light highlighting one side of his body, and the curve of his butt...

"Wow," Joseph said aloud at the visual memory. He noted with interest that his skin was tingling in a very not-unpleasant way.

"Everything okay?" the Lyft driver said. He was a Persian or Armenian fellow, probably been driving a taxi since he got to America, but now relegated to trying to make a living as a gig worker.

"Yeah, yeah, just thinking about someone," Joseph replied, making eye contact in the rearview mirror.

"You are in love, yes?" Joseph started to disagree with the assertion but the driver cut him off. "Yes, yes, I can see this." He continued defending the point as if Joseph had been insulted by the accusation. "It is good to be in love! Love is the purpose of life. There is nothing without love."

"I agree completely, my friend. It's just a little early to call it love."

"Pah! You can love little, or love completely, or anywhere in between. What they say? Love is love is love." He made a wave with his hand to demonstrate that *kids today don't know and just trust me with this.*

Joseph smiled but didn't say anything. He supposed tonight would prove or disprove the driver's theory. Either way, the world would keep spinning and life would go on. David and Joseph could be a part of each other's lives or they could not.

The Lyft turned onto Sunset Boulevard and then pulled off into the parking garage. Joseph got out, thanking the man for the ride. On the way to the Starbucks, he tapped the max tip option on the rideshare app and noted the time before he put his phone away. Despite the time spent trying to figure out his wardrobe, he was still a few minutes early. He decided to surprise his date with a drink and was thinking about what David might like when he opened the cafe door and spotted him sitting at a table already, facing the door so he could watch for Joseph's arrival. And he already had two to-go cups in front of him.

Joseph found himself charmed out of words. He took a few steps towards the table, hoping his brain would get in gear.

"Hey," he said. *Good one*, he thought.

"Hi, handsome. You look fantastic! Love the outfit." David rose from the table and met Joseph with a hug, like they'd known each other for years. When they parted, David grabbed Joseph's face gently and kissed him deeply. Joseph's hands wrapped around David reflexively. After a couple of seconds, they parted naturally. It was a perfect hello kiss between lovers. Not too much for public, but clearly not chaste either.

"Wow," Joseph said for the second time that evening. "Hello to you, too." He took in David's wardrobe selection, which consisted of a subtle hound-stooth jacket with a bolder burgundy windowpane pattern that played off his dark pink button-down Oxford shirt. He wore charcoal slacks that matched the slim tie and pocket square. White sneakers featuring rainbow accents completed the outfit. "You look great, too."

"I didn't know if you were a kisser, but since we already did way more than that, I figured throw out the first-date rules," David rambled.

Joseph couldn't help but smirk at the adorable nature of it all. "I like the way you think," he said.

"Oh!" David remembered, stepping to the table for the cups. "I got here a little early so I got you something. I figured green tea would be a safe choice; I hope you like it."

"Actually, that's my favorite thing here, thank you!" It was true, in that it was pretty much the only thing Joseph could stomach at Starbucks. Most teas were fine for him to drink, and it was what he always got during "coffee meetings."

"Awesome. I figured it wasn't enough caffeine to worry about, and I didn't want to risk any dairy allergies on a first date."

David ended the explanation with a cute little shrug that made Joseph swoon the tiniest bit. "You didn't have to get me anything, but that is incredibly sweet. And I do, in fact, have an aversion to dairy, so really good call."

A slight look of concern crossed David's face. He indicated his own drink. "I got an almond milk chai, is that going to cause any problems?" He paused while he tried to think of what possible problems it could cause and laughed. "Really, *really* bad nut allergies, maybe?"

Joseph laughed, too. "No nut allergies. You're good." There was a comfortable moment while they both just kind of enjoyed standing in front of each other, then Joseph broke the silence. "It's really good to see you again."

"Yeah, me too. I'm just going to risk it and say I have thought a *lot* about you the last couple of days."

"Really?" Joseph replied, feigning mild shock. "Because honestly I almost forgot we had a date tonight." He was teasing, but as soon as he said it, he regretted it. They didn't know each other's senses of humor yet and he wouldn't want David to think he was being a jerk.

As if reading his mind, David retorted, "Oh, I know you're lying, my friend, because this— " he waved his index finger at Joseph's ensemble, "Is a man who dressed to impress."

Joseph meant to say, *You got me!* and laugh roguishly, but instead he just stood there, a smirk blooming into a grin. He pushed into the moment, leaning in a bit. "Is it working?"

David leaned in the rest of the way to close the gap between their faces. "Oh, yeah." He pressed his lips to Joseph's. He only held the kiss for a second or two, then pulled away a few inches, looking Joseph in the eyes. Joseph tried to lean in for another kiss, but David backed off just an inch so Joseph missed his target. They both grinned at the game.

"So this date you have planned, is it super cool or should we ditch it and go back to my place? I mean, as much as I love you in a suit, I really dig you out of one, too."

Joseph acted as if he were considering the idea. "Well, that depends. How do you feel about magic?"

David sniggered. "Ha! Good one." He waited for the back and forth to continue, but Joseph instead had a slight but very genuine look of worry cross his face. "Wait, you're serious? You're taking me to a magic show?"

Joseph faltered. "Kind of. I mean, it's more than that. Dinner—"

"Oh, no, that's cool, I'm sure it'll be great." David tried to hide his disappointment, but the truth snuck out of his mouth. "I mean, I've never really been a fan of magic, but I trust you." He tried to recover the moment. "Hey, if I'm with you, I'm sure I'll have a great time. That's what's important."

Joseph eyed him skeptically, assessing the man, and his plan. He suspected his idea for the evening was still a good one, but though he had wanted it to be a surprise, he decided it was better to be safe than sorry. "Have you ever been to the Magic Castle?"

David's eyebrows scrunched together at the name. "No... It's a private club, isn't it? You have to be a member to get in?"

Joseph was relieved. A magic show was one thing. A night at the Magic Castle was something else entirely. "I know people," he said simply. "I think you'll have a good time."

David straightened to his full six feet and stated sincerely, "I trust you."

The second Lyft of the evening drove north on La Brea Avenue towards the Hills until it turned right into Franklin, driving behind the Hollywood &

Highland center and tourist trap. On the left, set up high on the hill, was a great gothic Victorian mansion. The stained-glass windows were brightly lit, as was the rest of the building, and a large sign next to the driveway proclaimed it "The Magic Castle: Academy of Magical Arts." The car turned into the drive which banked steeply up and curved around to the front door, where a valet opened the back doors for David and Joseph. The gentlemen said thanks to the Lyft driver, who was directed to keep driving forward to get out of the lot.

In front of the building, there was a small red carpet set to the side with a step and repeat backdrop behind it so people could take pictures to commemorate their visit. There was an awning jutting out from the door (which people could wait under for their cars in case of inclement weather, which did happen in Los Angeles a few days a year), a valet station, for those that brought their own cars (a Tesla Roadster was pulling in behind them just now), and there was a large swinging double door leading into a foyer where a greeter station was set.

"Do you want to take a picture?" Joseph asked tentatively, gesturing to the red carpet, where a group was doing that very thing. He still wasn't sure where David's mindset was on this.

"Our first picture together? Ooh, at least we dressed up for it," he said, putting his best foot forward. Joseph could tell he wasn't yet sold on the magic aspect of the evening but liked the fact that he was making it about them being together.

One of the other guests took their picture, arms around each other like they'd been boyfriends for months, and David returned the favor, taking the strangers' picture with proffered phones. The pair then made their way into the foyer, where the club hostess confirmed reservations and made sure dress code was being followed. The man in front of them, a cocky actor-type dressed sharply in an expensive-looking designer shirt, was being told that he needed to have a jacket and tie to go in. He was trying to argue his way in (a solution that almost never worked, in Joseph's experience), and the hostess, with the help of an intimidating-looking bouncer, informed him that the only options available were to leave and return with the required wardrobe, or use one of the items available from the club's supply. But, being a magician's club, those were considerably less flattering. The actor pushed past Joseph and David and stormed out in a huff.

Joseph leaned over as they moved up to the reception counter and whispered, "They're very strict about the dress code."

David was looking over his shoulder at the irate guy. "He acted like he was really important, but I've never seen him before in my life. He'd be handsome, but bitchy looks really bad on him."

Joseph elbowed him playfully and gave his name to the host. She gave them tickets to present to the dining room, welcomed them to the Castle, and gestured to a wall of bookshelves opposite the desk, saying, "Just say the magic words."

Joseph turned to David. "Go ahead. You know what the phrase is for doors, right?"

David looked curiously at the door and then back to Joseph. "Please? Please is the magic word, isn't it? But that doesn't make any sense."

Joseph grinned. He loved watching other people solve puzzles he already knew the answers to. "No, the phrase Ali Baba used to get into the cave of wonders." He was delighted when an expression of recognition dawned on David's face.

"Oh ... Seriously? Open sesame?" he said to both Joseph and the woman at the counter.

"Not to me, to the owl." Joseph pointed at a bronze statue of an owl that was sitting on one of the shelves.

David turned to the owl. "Open sesame!" At the utterance of the phrase, the owl's eyes glowed red and one section of the bookshelf slid into the wall, revealing the interior of the mansion beyond. David was unable to control a small squeal of glee, and Joseph knew the rest of the evening was going to turn out just fine.

David's delight only increased the more he saw. Immediately inside the Castle was a bar room, and they each ordered drinks to carry with them as they explored. David got a rum and pineapple juice while Joseph got another Killepitsch, the drink he had the night they met. Behind the bar, Joseph led them into a smaller sitting room that featured a grand piano, the seat of which was roped off. The piano was playing itself.

"That's Irma the Ghost," Joseph explained as if it were the most natural thing in the world. "She's been playing here since she was alive. She takes requests and can play pretty much anything, but only for tips." He pointed at a large gilded birdcage that was hanging next to the piano. It had singles and five-dollar bills stuffed between its thin bars. David looked at Joseph doubtfully, but he only shrugged in response. To prove his story, Joseph pulled a skinny wallet from his jacket pocket and dug out a fiver.

He approached the piano. "Hi, Irma," he said amiably. The version of "Magic to Do" from *Pippin* stopped, and the piano trilled two short chords that somehow sounded exactly like *Hello*.

"How are you tonight?"

Another sprightly series of notes played, and David realized that the keys were indeed moving, apparently of their own accord.

Joseph slipped the five into the birdcage, and the piano trilled in thanks. "I'm glad to hear it. Could you play 'Canon in D'? I'm here on a date."

The piano chirped a congratulations and immediately began playing Pachelbel's 'Canon in D' beautifully and romantically. Joseph turned back to his date, whose mouth hung open in bewilderment before dissolving into a grin as he made eye contact.

"That's cool," David admitted. He very much wanted to ask *how do they do it*, but something inside him really enjoyed the enchantment of not knowing how the illusion was pulled off.

"Thought you'd like it. The story goes that Irma played the piano here at the club like fifty years ago. She loved playing so much that she died while performing one night and just kept on playing," Joseph said with absolute sincerity. "Go ahead and request something."

David excitedly dug out a dollar bill, looking at Joseph for confirmation, who nodded that it was just fine. He turned back to the piano but paused. "Actually, I want to hear the rest of this."

Joseph sat in a plush loveseat facing the piano and patted for David to join him. They put their drinks on the table in front of them, and David sat, Joseph wrapping one arm over his shoulder. They enjoyed the music together.

People wandered in and out, but the club wasn't too busy this early, and they had the room pretty much to themselves. At one point, Joseph felt David's gaze on him and turned his head to meet it. They both smiled and kissed lightly. No need for an intense makeout, not when they could enjoy the romance of being serenaded by a ghost.

The song ended and David stood up, pushing on Joseph's knee to get out of the soft cushions of the sofa. "Irma, that was beautiful!" Irma tickled the ivories in thanks, and again when David stuck the bill into the cage bars. "Could you play 'LoveGame' by Lady Gaga?" He looked over his shoulder at Joseph, who smirked knowingly. "I want to see if I can stump—"

The piano started a pulsing beat. The hard electronic chords that opened the original version of the song came out strong and loud from the strings of the grand. Irma somehow managed to play the bass line and the melody and the talking rhythm that began the song. It was so good David could almost hear the words talking about taking a ride on a disco stick. His mouth dropped. The normally techno dance song sounded amazing on piano. People started wandering in from the bar to hear Irma the Ghost positively *slay* the Lady Gaga tune.

David started getting into it, dancing a bit despite the trickle of patrons wandering into the sitting room. He dance-walked back to Joseph and sang the lyrics as they came up. When he got to the part where he got his ass squeezed by sexy Cupid, he included the appropriate hand gestures.

Joseph laughed and stood up to meet him on what was becoming an impromptu dance floor. They got close and moved their bodies together. Some of the other patrons wandered in and started dancing and singing, too. When it got to the chorus, the voices of half a dozen people joined with the pulsing piano rhythm.

Instead of repeating the chorus and all the dance breaks, Irma found a spot to end the song on a high note with a flourish and a hard double-beat chord. The room united in applause.

"Irma, that was incredible!" David effused, and Irma trilled a bashful series of notes. He turned to Joseph. "How?"

"I have no idea." He jerked his head to the room's exit. "Let's look around. I want to show you some stuff before dinner."

The next hour was spent wandering the labyrinthine maze of the mansion. Down a flight of stairs led to a series of basement corridors and performance spaces. Every room had a magician doing a show: close-up magic, card tricks, mixed shows with comedy. There must have been a dozen magicians performing in all corners of the club. Some were in rooms that had scheduled shows, and others sat at tables set in various corners where patrons could come and go as they pleased. In the lowest basement, there was a small theater where a magic practitioner was performing with a stuffed monkey who hypnotized the audience. David had never seen anything quite like it. Every performance amazed and delighted him.

The Castle itself had tricks and secrets, including a phone booth that looked empty, but when you went inside and closed the door, a skeleton appeared in the mirror behind you. There were bits of history crammed into every nook and cranny—videos about WC Fields and his early comedy, programs and posters from Houdini (and even one of the large milk cans he escaped from).

Before they knew it, it was time to report to the dining room for dinner. Joseph informed David that they dare not be late, because the reservations were strictly timed to lead from dinner to the show in the large theater.

They were seated in the dining room at an intimate table with a candle and cloth napkins folded in the shape of roses. "Order anything you want, it's on me," Joseph said, adding, "But please excuse me, I'm on a liquid diet at the moment. Not the way alcoholics say it, it's for a medical thing." He realized he had not needed to explain away his inability to eat solid food in quite some time. He hadn't spent much time coming up with his excuse for tonight, and now that he said it out loud, it sounded stupid and unbelievable. He immediately wished he had just skipped dinner reservations and brought David for the shows, but then plenty of the actors and models he'd taken to bed had claimed to be on liquid diets in preparation for shoots—

David interrupted his mental flagellation. "I hope it's nothing serious?"

Joseph was impressed that David's first reaction was concern for his well-being. It was somehow an unusual reaction among men in Los Angeles. "Yeah, totally, no worries at all." He changed the subject. "I recommend the filet mignon, by the way, it's amazing."

Dinner *was* amazing. David ate his steak, salad, mashed potatoes, and grilled Brussels sprouts while Joseph ordered wine for them both and sipped that. He had asked David to request no onions or garlic, as he was allergic to that group of vegetables, and David was happy to order his dinner without them. Of course, onions weren't really a problem, but broadening the scope of the fib somehow made it more believable and, more importantly, less suspicious.

During the meal, the conversation flowed as naturally as if the two men had known each other much longer than two days. The topics were very get-to-know-you things. David talked about being the only child of two staunch Southern Republicans, while Joseph spoke truthfully of his childhood on the farm with four siblings, though he strategically omitted certain details, such as the century, the country, and that one brother and one sister had died before the age of fifteen due to a contagious disease, leaving only him and the remaining older sister. They talked early sexual encounters: David's in a bathroom stall at the mall with an older man at the age of sixteen; Joseph's a year younger with a soldier at his sister's wedding.

They spoke of their life's passions. David told Joseph about the show he worked on called *Hardly An Angel*, and about how he wanted to be a director. He enjoyed narrative filmmaking but had a love for documentaries and wanted more than anything to inspire people. When asked, Joseph spoke vaguely about also wanting to help people, while doing a little of everything for work. It was technically true, if lacking in specific details.

They both opted to skip dessert. Joseph paid the check, and they exited the opposite way from which they'd entered the dining room. They went down the stairs into a completely new part of the mansion, which David was amazed could exist. How was the building he'd seen from the outside big enough for all this?

There was another bar at the bottom of the stairs but neither of them felt like another drink. It was about fifteen minutes until they were allowed to get in line for the show, so they explored this previously unseen section of the club. Another close-up magician was doing card magic at an octagonal poker table at the other end of the bar. They passed him and his ecstatic audience of seven people (plus a few more standing and nursing their drinks) and came to a velvet rope line that led to a smaller theater.

A club employee (or perhaps a young magician's apprentice) saw them and gestured to the entrance. "The show starts in two minutes. There's a few seats left!"

"How long is the show?" Joseph inquired.

"About ten minutes."

"Perfect!" Joseph turned to David. "You want to...?"

David grinned amiably. "Oh, I am following your lead on all of this."

Joseph returned the grin, and they entered the small theater. It wasn't that small, in actuality. About seventy or eighty seats, set stadium style in ten rows, gave everyone a perfect view of the diminutive performance area. Just as they got to their seats, the apprentice/employee came out to give the club speech about not taking pictures or video, and basically don't be a jerk. The sign next to the stage read "The Incraigible Cred!" The young maybe-magician finished the spiel, and the lights dimmed.

A drumroll started as a voice over the speakers said dramatically, "Ladies and Gentlemen, children of ... childhood age ... prepare yourself for the show of a lifetime. Direct from the Orient, where he was sightseeing after growing up in Cincinnati and going to college *all* the way in Columbus but dropping out because he wanted to be a magician..." The drumroll built in intensity and dramatic music swelled. "Please put your hands together and then apart in a sort of clapping motion as we bring to the stage..."

The curtains parted to reveal a thin man holding a microphone. The audience laughed, realizing that the awkward magician was providing his own awful introduction.

"The Incredible Crai—" He stopped short when he saw the sign. "The Incraigible..." He trailed off in disbelief. He waved his hands at an imaginary sound guy. "Stop the music! Stop! Jeff, stop, turn it off." Craig pulled a music player out of his upstage pocket and pressed pause. The music stopped.

It was supposed to be obvious, and his timing was perfect. The audience loved it.

The rest of the show was a mix of storytelling, comedy, and trick magic. Like putting a bottle of ketchup into a bag and then crumpling the bag like nothing was there. The tricks weren't impressive, at least to Joseph, who had been around the block a few times, but the performance itself and the story accompanying the trick was solid and funny, and David was enjoying himself.

When the Incredible Craig finished, he got a nice loud ovation, and the audience obediently filed out of the theater. Joseph gently took David's hand for the first time and directed him towards the large theater space called "The Palace." There was a moderate line, and the door had just opened to let people file in. They joined the end of the line and were able to ogle more magical memorabilia along the wall as they moved, until they were inside and seated, with approximately a hundred and fifty other people. A waitress was walking the room to make sure everyone was drinked up. She stopped at the pair, who now each had their hand on the other's thigh. "You boys are adorable. Need a drink for the show?"

Joseph was fine, but he turned to check in with David, who was sporting the most contented little smirk and looking at him. "Mm-mm," he said, shaking his head slightly.

"No, thank you, we're good," Joseph told the waitress, and then directed his attention to the stage. Just looking around. But then he sensed David's gaze was still on him and turned his head. The young man was still grinning slightly and trying to fight it getting bigger. "What?" Joseph laughed.

"You held my haaaaand," David accused, teasing in a singsong voice.

"Oh my God, I did? I'm sorry, it won't happen again," Joseph jibed in return. "I wouldn't want anyone to think we were—" he looked around conspiratorially and leaned closer, whispering "—*gaaaaaaay.*"

David matched his volume, whispered, *"Heaven forbid,"* and closed the gap between their lips for a quick kiss. Then he looked around, pretending to make sure no one had seen.

"Mmm, I think we're safe from suspicion," Joseph purred and grabbed David's nearest hand, entwining their fingers.

In perfect timing, the lights dimmed and the show began, as every show should, with a song.

"At the Magic Castle…" David sang as they rode back to his apartment. It was a refrain from the opening number of Jeb's show, sung by his beautiful assistant, and included instructions for the audience, as in:

Make sure you turn off all your phones,
At the Magic Castle…

Then it was used as a punchline throughout the first act.

Jeb had been on fire. One time, literally. His show was hysterical and amazing, with illusions that even Joseph in all his worldliness couldn't figure out. The best part of the evening, though, was the moment when he looked over at David, the guy who "didn't really like magic," and the look on his face of pure childlike wonder had filled Joseph with a warmth he hadn't felt in ages.

After the show, they'd hung out with Jeb at the bar. All the patrons and performers mingled into the late hour, and David had met a couple of famous actors who were guests of member magicians. The club didn't close until 2:00 AM when they were forced to stop serving liquor, but Joseph had whispered something into David's ear around midnight that had perked up his date's ears, and they'd made their way swiftly to the entrance after saying quick goodbyes.

As they arrived at David's apartment, still laughing and recounting all the funny and incredible things they'd seen while they rode the elevator, Joseph pulled David close. "I'm really glad you had a good time," he cooed.

"I had a *great* time." He wrapped his arms around the ever-so-slightly taller man. "I didn't think it was going to be that fun, but it was perfect."

"Well, it's not over yet. I've got something special in mind for you," Joseph whispered seductively.

David shifted his gaze back and forth between each of Joseph's deep blue eyes. "Who *are* you…?" he mused out loud.

"I'm just a guy. But I'm a guy who keeps liking *you* more and more, mister." Joseph planted his lips on David, and they kissed deeply, the pent-up passion from the entire evening of romance and restraint spilling between them. It lasted the remaining ascent and was so intense they almost missed the doors when they opened on David's floor. David grabbed Joseph's hand and pulled him to his apartment, fumbling to retrieve his keys with the remaining hand and unlocking his door.

Their fervor intensified as the door closed behind them. They couldn't keep their hands and mouths off each other. They were both torn between touching and kissing and removing clothing. By the time they got to David's bedroom, they each had one sock, and a trail of semiformal dress strewn to the front door. They were both hard to the point of bursting and ravenous for each other's bodies. Blindly, they fell on the bed, David on his back and Joseph on top, their legs staggered and intertwining.

David's hands roamed everywhere they could reach on the body of this amazing man he'd somehow found on the dance floor. Joseph didn't bother to use a hand to hold himself up, instead wrapping them around David and pulling them together as they ground their dicks between them, their sweat and precum creating a slick lubricant for their straining. David grabbed Joseph's head in his hands and held him above, looking in his eyes with lust and wonder. This was different, and they both felt it.

As his hips continued to gyrate autonomously, Joseph unlinked his hands from behind his lover and with one hand on the bed, used the other to stroke David's face. David looked like he wanted desperately to say something but couldn't bring himself to do it. Instead, he shifted so that both his legs were outside of Joseph's, and lifted his knees above Joseph's hips, wordlessly inviting Joseph to enter him.

Joseph looked into David's eyes, and then looked *into* him, allowing himself to tap into his vampire side. He shared hundreds of years of passion and lust and joy with the man under him as he swiveled his hips back, the head of his uncut member slipping between David's legs. They maintained eye contact as he slid slowly inside. It wasn't just fucking. It was deeper and a hundred times more intimate. They were both more connected with each other than they'd been with anyone in years.

This was *lovemaking*.

They lasted over an hour before they climaxed. By then, they'd switched positions at least half a dozen times, and David had taken a turn doing the penetrating. Unlike their first night, this time they were always face to face. Sometimes it got intense, the sound of skin slapping against skin echoing in the room and mingling with their moans of pleasure. If they weren't kissing, they were making eye contact, seeing each other deeply in the most intimate moment they'd shared yet. When they did climax, it was simultaneous, with David riding Joseph and unloading on his chest and stomach, while Joseph came inside him. The size of his load and the powerful release of the orgasm surprised David, and he laughed involuntarily. He couldn't help it; it was more intense than any sex he'd ever had. Joseph lay sweating below him, chest heaving and covered in cum. David could feel Joseph inside him, still hard and twitching with the aftershocks of his orgasm.

They looked into each other's eyes and David's giggles became contagious. Joseph's own stoicism cracked, and he laughed lightly, mostly because David was, but also a result of his own euphoria.

David's gaze fell to Joseph's chin, which had been hit by one of his first volleys. Then his neck, where the muscles and tendons still twitched from the exertion of their lovemaking. When he looked at the mess he'd made on his lover's chest, an uncontrollable and ridiculous urge took him. He took two of his fingers and ran them through the puddle of his own cum, then brought them over Joseph's forehead, which was already slick with sweat. Joseph looked mildly confused as David ran his two fingers in an arc above Joseph's eyes.

"Simba..." he said in a deep-voiced impression of Robert Guillaume's Rafiki.

There was half a moment of complete silence as Joseph put the *Lion King* reference together, and David waited to both see his reaction and process the fact that he'd done it at all. Then they both erupted into gales of laughter. It was the funniest, sexiest moment of either of their lives, and they both howled at the absurdity while they were still physically connected, one inside the other. It lasted about thirty seconds before Joseph softened enough to slip naturally out of David, who then laid on his side next to him, placing his head on his shoulder, still giggling.

Joseph was the first to speak. "That was incredible."

"I'm really glad you think so. I loved it, too," David replied softly as he ran his fingers along the other man's taut abs, spreading the fluids as the air began to dry them. He was thinking much more but didn't want to say too much.

Joseph sensed the reticence and acknowledged his own, for different reasons. He had never connected this quickly with another person. The conflict he'd felt leading up to the date was washing away. Of the several times he'd been in love over the centuries, the one thing they all had in common was that they were all different in the way the relationships matured. There was enough anecdotal evidence for love at first sight. Joseph's reason for restraint was more complicated, but he was, for the first time in decades, powerless to resist his feelings.

"We fit together really, really well."

"Yes!" David replied excitedly, clearly relieved to hear some confirmation that Joseph felt the same way. "I was thinking the exact same thing. I've never felt this way with someone before." He stopped abruptly, afraid of having said too much, too enthusiastically.

Joseph was staring at the ceiling, trying to make mental relationship calculations, but his pleasure at just being with this man interfered with his thoughts. He traced his fingers lightly around David's back, his free hand rested on his hip. One clear question came forward, though, and he asked it, "Hey. Have you ever been in love? Like, not just love someone, but *in love*?"

It was the first time either of them had said the "L" word out loud in reference to a relationship, and David's heart sped up. Though he didn't answer right away, Joseph could hear the increased heart rate, and feel it through their pressed bodies.

After thinking a moment, David said, "Yeah, one time. I was just about to graduate college and I met this guy online. We eventually moved in together, had a dog and everything. It lasted three years before something changed in him and everything went wrong. I had my heart broken. But I know the difference you're talking about. How about you? Have you been *in love* in love?"

Joseph thought of Marcus, and Connor, and Rob... "Yes. A couple of times. Each relationship was different. And I know what heartbreak feels like, too." He wanted to ask *the question*, the hardest question, but he was also afraid of his own answer. He had sworn a vow to himself while holding Rob's lifeless body almost thirty years ago that he'd never love again. But hadn't he also made similar promises to himself after Marcus and after Connor? Was it a fair promise to make?

"Do you..." David began but stopped.

"Hmm?" Joseph thought he knew how he'd answer if David asked the question. He just didn't want to presume to ask it himself.

"Want to sleep over?" David changed the question mid-sentence.

Joseph glanced at the clock on the bedside table. It was just after 2:00 AM. "I would love to, but I have to be up early for a morning meeting. I'd have to leave by 6:00 AM, is that okay?"

"For sure. Let's just stay like this. I'm so comfy," David sighed. He wrapped his free arm around Joseph's chest and squeezed. Joseph wrapped his arms around David in return. "I really, really liked this."

"Me too. It was a perfect night," Joseph agreed. "And I should know, I've had a lot of good nights."

David loosened his grip and rolled back to put his head on its previous perch of Joseph's left shoulder. "I bet. I was going to say, I usually don't go for guys so very old as you." He resumed stroking Joseph's stomach innocently to counter the joke.

Joseph played into it while deciding to test the waters in the smallest of ways. "When five hundred years old you reach, look as good you will not, hmm?"

David slapped Joseph's abs in excitement. "And you're a nerd? I love that!" He turned his head and playfully bit Joseph on his chest above his left nipple. "I hate to be this guy buuuut ... Yoda was nine hundred years old."

"Oh, that's it, I'm going home!" Joseph feigned getting out of bed, but he allowed David to push him back down and climb over him. Their eyes met. It wasn't a searching or yearning stare but a comfortable one. A sure and steady delving into each other's souls. David leaned down, and they kissed, slowly and deeply, tongues flitting and flirting with each other. Joseph's arms caressed David's body until they were wrapped around him completely. The kiss ended and David lowered his body to snuggle into the man he couldn't yet admit aloud that he loved.

Entwined together, they slept.

Joseph's sleep was light but wonderful. The feeling of David lying against him was a soothing balm on his psyche. A contentedness filled him in a way he had nearly forgotten. The simple necessary thrill of sharing yourself with another human being. Not just sharing your body, but your mind and soul, too, if there was such a thing. He recognized the feeling for what it was, though he didn't know if he was at peace with it. His demons wrestled inside him as he sensed the imminent rising of the morning sun.

He stroked David's face softly to rouse him from his slumber. "Hey, handsome, I need to go. Do you want to shower with me first?"

David's hand moved along Joseph's torso then lengthened into a stretch, which accompanied a yawn, and he made the cutest little squeaking sound, making Joseph chuckle softly.

"Yes, please, I would like that very much."

Joseph slid out of the bed and helped David up. They were both a bit crusty from the previous night's climax, which made Joseph's skin looked like it was flaking off in certain spots on his abdomen. He led the way to the bathroom, holding David's hand behind him, who made more cute sleepy noises with every other step. By the time they got to the small standing shower, David was awake enough to turn it on, then wrap his arms around Joseph again.

"Good morning, beautiful man."

Joseph smiled and held him in return. "Good morning to you, sexy."

They kissed while the water warmed, and by the time it was ready, they were both hard and pressing their cocks against each other. David looked down as he grabbed hold of Joseph's tumescent shaft. They were both similar in size down there, each slightly above average, about seven inches, though David's was circumcised, and Joseph's was not. "I really like this," he said, admiring the penis as one would admire a work of art. "I like that it gets so hard."

"Yours does, too," Joseph pointed out. "And I like it quite a bit myself."

"But some guys don't, though," David continued, though Joseph knew this about men. Cocks were as varied as the boys that sported them, and he'd been with plenty of guys who just didn't get rock hard. "I also like that you're uncut. You don't see that a lot these days." He looked up into Joseph's eyes as he stroked him. "It's *exotic...*"

Joseph was also stroking David as he replied with the truth, "My parents were European," and silenced the subject with a kiss.

Steam billowed from the shower so David turned and walked inside. He grabbed a loofah that was hanging on the wall and squeezed bodywash gel into it, working it into a thick sudsy lather before handing it to Joseph, who followed him inside and shut the door.

"Wash me."

Joseph began gently rubbing the loofah on David's chest and used his other hand to work the slick suds over his skin. He felt the water and soap dissolve the sweat, lube, and cum from last night. He washed David's torso, massaging his abs and even running a finger into the boy's belly button, making him laugh. He then lowered himself and ran the sponge down each leg, cleaning them in turn. Lastly, he grasped David's member, which was hard as a railroad spike, and used the slick soap to jerk him off, causing him to moan. All the while, he was pelted with water from the showerhead.

Joseph stopped, stood, and physically turned David around. He started washing at the neck with the loofah and then David's back, stroking gently until David whispered, "*Harder,*" and Joseph started scrubbing with earnest. When he was done with the back, he grabbed David's hands and lifted them up, holding them both with one hand as he used the other, with the loofah, to wash each arm in turn, and then the armpits. They were so close that Joseph's cock was rubbing on David's ass, gliding against his cheeks and sliding between them.

Joseph continued to hold David's arms up with one hand as he squeezed the loofah, letting loose a small torrent of suds onto his back. Joseph dropped the soap-laden sponge to the shower floor and ran his free hand down the young man's back to his slick toned butt. His middle finger ran down the crevice of David's cheeks until it found its target and rubbed against the puckered sphincter. It relaxed with a soft moan from its owner, and the finger slid inside.

Joseph didn't intend to take long with the foreplay. Time was against him and, after all, this wasn't lovemaking. This was passionate morning fucking. After massaging David inside for a moment, just long enough to get him whimpering, he pulled his finger out and replaced it with his rigid dick, holding the head at the entrance to David's hole just long enough for him to prepare, then shoved the entire length of himself in with one easy motion. They both moaned in unison at the pleasure of it. Joseph with the hot pressure of David's hole, and David with the incredible feeling of hard fullness massaging his prostate. They wasted no time before each found the same rhythm, and the sound of wet skin slapping against skin reverberated on the tiles of the small space.

Joseph released David's arms and pulled his chin to the side to kiss him while he pounded him from behind. With the other hand, he grasped David's cock, still slick from soap and copious amounts of precum, and jerked him off. David kept one arm on the wall for support and reached behind with the other, grabbing Joseph's ass and pulling him in faster and harder. The sensation was so intense, it peaked sooner than either of them expected.

David scream-moaned as he shot all over the shower wall while Joseph came inside him for the second time that night. If they hadn't already been in one, they'd have had to take a shower.

As it was, they were able to rinse off as they descended from their orgasms, Joseph apologizing for needing to rush. David fetched an extra towel from the hall closet while patting most of the water from himself with the towel hanging by the shower.

When Joseph was dry and dressed, David walked him to the door as they had two nights before. And instead of the awkwardness of the end of a hookup, this goodbye felt more at ease and full of potential. Their kiss was passionate and affectionate, with the unspoken promise of many, many more to come.

Joseph rode down the elevator to the ground level, contemplating the extraordinary and wholly unexpected evening and the events of the last few days that led up to it. He realized as the doors opened, he'd forgotten to call a Lyft, and sat down outside on the short brick structure lining the sidewalk while he awaited his ride. He smelled the blooming jasmine in the air and marinated in an unaccustomed feeling of contentedness.

About twenty minutes later, Joseph walked into his house, which this morning somehow felt far more empty than usual. His phone buzzed the arrival of an incoming message.

<Tonight was amazing. I know I'm supposed to be all coy about it but eff that, I'm not in college anymore. I had a spectacular time>

Joseph typed back <I had an okay time too, thx>

<fuck you> with a laughing emoji.

<Kidding, of course. Best date I've had in a long, long time>

Joseph headed down to the bedroom and noted the animated dots that indicated a reply was imminent. When it came, he stopped, frozen in place on the stairway.

<I wanted to ask you something tonight, and I think you know what it is. But anyway, my answer is yes. I do. I hope you have a fantastic day!>

Joseph sat down on the steps, holding his phone in front of him like it was a precious treasure, and he was the first to see it in a hundred years. He read the text three more times. Then he realized that David might be on the other end waiting for a reply, and he was also suddenly certain what the answer was. His fingers flew on the virtual keyboard.

<I do too. And I can't wait to see you again> and then, to explain his day-time absence, <Heading in now, I'll be AFK most of the day. TTYL>

Joseph stood, feeling lighter than he had moments ago, and got ready for bed.

CHAPTER 8

David awoke the next morning as if he'd been sleeping on a cloud. After Joseph left, he'd gone back to bed for an hour or so, and woke feeling more refreshed than he had in months. He did some quick mental math and realized he hadn't gotten anywhere near eight hours of sleep, which would usually have left him groggy all day.

The last thing he'd done, after their textual professions of love (well, *implied* professions), was to suggest they go dancing tonight. It would be Friday, so Boystown in WeHo would be much livelier than on the Tuesday they met. Joseph replied just before he went into his meeting, and David didn't expect to hear from him until later, but he got the go-ahead to make plans. With things still slow at work, plotting out their evening was the main activity of his day.

On his way into the production office, he stopped in Hollywood at a corner lot lined by stores that featured a Starbucks and a donut shop and picked up coffees for himself and Dana and a dozen glazed to share with the office. It wasn't something he usually did (that was for the much higher-paid writers on staff or the show runners), but David was feeling especially good, and he felt like spreading the joy.

As he drove over the Cahuenga Pass to Barham, he noticed the huge cumulous clouds creeping over the San Fernando Valley. They were an unusual sight in LA, which was normally beset by unrelenting sunshine. The clouds were beautiful, though. Enormous, billowy balls of cotton, just floating in the air. They got him thinking about what it must have been like to be a human thousands of years before anyone had any inkling about the water cycle or what those titanic poofy things in the sky could be. Looking at them as the traffic crawled towards the studio lot, he could understand how people thought there were cities up there with gods living in them. David couldn't help but stare and admire the beauty. Which reminded him of Joseph smelling flowers along the sidewalk, and that just made him smile more.

When he arrived in the office, Dana eyed the box of donuts suspiciously. "What did you do...?" she asked slowly.

"Nothing bad; I just wanted to treat everyone," David replied, handing over her coffee.

"You know, we have Starbucks in the machine here," she chided.

"Yes, but this way someone else does all that work *for* you, and you don't have to go to all the effort of walking all the way to the kitchen," he pointed out, playing her little game.

She took a sip. "For sure," she agreed, "and it's also not so hot. Like, not even hot at all. Like barely warm this way. You're the bestest, thank you."

David reached for her cup. "If you don't want it, I'm sure I can find someone—"

She growled and pulled the treasured liquid closer to herself. "No! I wants it. My precious..."

They laughed as David deposited the donuts on the table in the center of the room and announced they were for everyone. There was a comical rush of people dropping what they were doing and moving to the table but trying not to *look* like they were dropping everything and rushing to get the sweet, sweet, delectable treats.

Dana took David by the arm and led him to his desk, which was further from the donuts than hers. "So, spill the tea, BooBoo! You had your date last night?"

"Yeah," he replied. "He took me to the Magic Castle." He tried to say it like it was a disappointing thing, but Dana didn't take the bait.

"Omigod, was it cool? I've heard it's cool, like there's magicians everywhere—

Ooooh I'm so jelly, tell me everything!"

She was bouncing from excitement so David dropped the pretense. "Okay." He leaned in. "It. Was. Amazing."

They sat conspiratorially at David's desk, and he recounted everything about the night. He told her about Open Sesame, and Irma the Ghost, and as much of the magic shows as he could remember. Dana was rapt with attention, asking for more details here and there, and otherwise making jealous sounds of disgust. He even told her the highlights of the incredible sex, because she was one of those girl friends who thought that boys putting penises in butts was super hot.

"David..." Dana began as if she knew the answer already, and it was the biggest news of the day. "Are you like, really, really into this guy?"

"I really, really am, D. I mean, as far as I can tell, he's perfect. He's sweet, intelligent, seems to be doing pretty well for himself, *and he's soooo fucking sexy.*" David leaned in and whispered the last bit, feeling a blush just talking about Joseph.

"Whoa, you are *really*, really into him..." Dana enthused, then turned all gooey. "Ohhh, I'm so happy for you! After what's-his-piss from Orange County, you deserve someone nice!" She grabbed David in a one-armed hug, decided it wasn't enough, and put her coffee down to bear-hug her friend.

"I really hope it stays good. We're going dancing tonight in WeHo, do you want to come?" he offered, half-hoping she'd say no. He felt bad about abandoning his bestie but wasn't ready to share Joseph with anyone quite yet.

Dana answered like she was reading his mind. "I would, but I think it's too soon to be introducing him to your friends. Especially me. I'm a lot."

"Are you suuuure?" he pushed, adding a little sarcasm this time.

Dana caught on. "You little bish, you didn't want me to say yes! You are devious!"

They bantered a while longer, and when David said he had to come up with the plans for the night, Dana helped with those, too. At one point, they had to take a break to read through one of the scripts that had been drafted by the writers, but afterward, they got right back to goofing off and planning a night out dancing.

It wasn't until one of the interns casually mentioned it looked like rain that either of them thought to check the weather. Why would they? This was Los Angeles, the land of dreams and sunshine. Even with the big puffy clouds this morning, it never occurred to David to check a weather app unless it was literally physically precipitating. Outside of the winter months, clouds were more of a tease than an actual portent of rain. Like Mother Nature delighted in dangling the *possibility* of moisture over the semiarid landscape but never actually giving it.

David was disappointed by the forecast they found for showers all evening. He tried to text Joseph to see if he wanted to change plans but got no immediate answer. He explained to Dana what Joseph had said about not being able to answer messages until later.

"What does he do? Is he a doctor or something?" she asked incredulously.

David thought, searching for a memory where Joseph might have disclosed his job. Nothing sprang to mind. "I don't know, but it seems important. He wears nice clothes and seemed really chummy with the guys at the Magic Castle."

Dana looked disappointed in David. "You never asked his job? He could be unemployed for all you know?"

"Or he could be a prince who is disguising his wealth until he knows if I love him for who he really is rather than for his money." David cocked his head, realizing something. "Actually, he does have a hint of an accent..."

"Oh, yeah, that's much more likely," she shot back. "A gorgeous guy in *Los Angeles* who isn't just an unemployed actor or model or something and who didn't just max out his credit cards to look more important than he truly is."

"Hey, I'm not an unemployed actor or model or something," David pointed out.

"I did say gorgeous, though, soooo..." She batted her eyes and gave her innocent *What did I say?* face, and he tried to look pissed, but they both broke and the moment was a pure joke again.

"But seriously," she told him, "This is night three, and you're super into him; it's time to find out what he does."

David continued with his pro-Joseph train of thought. "Maybe he's just cautious about letting new people into his life. All I know is, everything I've seen so far has been amazing. So even if he doesn't have a great job—"

"Or no job."

"—or no job, that's not a deal breaker. Did I tell you he literally stopped to smell the roses our first night walking back to my place?"

Dana looked at her friend and saw the adoration in his face. "Okay, that is pretty freaking sweet. Who does that?"

The end of the day finally came, and David walked to his car. He had his parking spot in a garage on the lot, but he still had to walk across the studio in the rain to get there. As far as rain went, it was more of a heavy misting, but the clouds were blocking out the sun just the same, and the late afternoon was gloomy and grey.

The drive home was slow and plodding. All the studios tended to get out around the same time, at 6:00 PM, so traffic heading to Hollywood along Barham was congested in the same way as it was in the morning, just in the opposite direction. The rain made everything worse. Even though it barely required the use of windshield wipers, Angelenos as a group completely lost their minds and forgot how to drive when water falls from the sky in even miniscule amounts.

When he was just cresting the top of Barham heading to the Cahuenga Pass, David's phone rang through the Bluetooth of his Accord. It was Joseph.

"Hey, hot stuff," David answered using the hands-free button on the steering wheel. He winced a bit, not sure if they were at the point yet where that kind of greeting was appropriate. Joseph's reply put him at ease.

"Hey yourself, sexy. How was work?"

"Boring. Still not a lot to do until the season starts to go into production in two weeks." The wipers squeaked as they made an intermittent swipe across the windshield, and David looked over to check his blind spot, changing lanes to avoid a bus he saw several vehicles ahead. "How was yours?"

"Pretty boring too, practically slept through it. I just got your text about tonight."

"Yeah, the rain. It's not too bad, do you still want to go dancing?" David hoped Joseph would say yes. Not only did he love dancing, but he kinda wanted to be with Joseph in public. His desire was a mix of mild exhibitionism and a bit of showing off to the world that he had a hot man on his arm after too many nights alone.

"I can certainly deal with the rain. I've lived in places with actual weather, so this doesn't bother me." Joseph laughed on the other end of the line.

David suddenly realized he was hungry. All he'd had besides a donut and coffee was some vegetables and hummus he kept in the staff fridge. "Do you want to grab food first?"

"Actually, I've got some stuff I need to wrap up here," Joseph answered. "Why don't you eat if you're hungry. I'll grab something on the go, and we can meet later, say, 9:00 PM?"

"Sounds perfect. Fiesta Cantina?" David picked a place that was central to all the bars, and easy to find.

"Fiesta *á nueve*. See you then, handsome." Joseph was smiling, David could hear it in his voice, and his heart melted a bit at being called handsome by someone he thought was so hot.

"Perfecto. See you then."

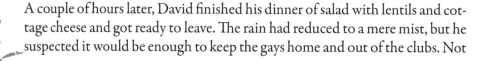

A couple of hours later, David finished his dinner of salad with lentils and cottage cheese and got ready to leave. The rain had reduced to a mere mist, but he suspected it would be enough to keep the gays home and out of the clubs. Not all of them, of course, but it wouldn't be quite so lively in downtown WeHo as a usual Friday night. Which suited David just fine. Usually, when a night out dancing alone was a numbers game of finding a piece of ass, the more asses the better. But tonight, he had a piece already. Guaranteed! So, a little more room on the dance floor was kind of perfect.

At 8:30 PM he was dressed and heading out the door. The weather created a conundrum in that David's normal attire for Boystown was tight and revealing. But the air had a chill, and it was wet. So the delicate question was whether to don a jacket or long-sleeved shirt, or, God forbid, carry an actual umbrella. He was sure he had one somewhere, if he looked hard enough. He could avoid that issue altogether by taking a Lyft to the bar, but it was so close that seemed wasteful, and he imagined such a short ride would annoy a Lyft driver.

Then he remembered that West Hollywood had started a free trolley service that ran up and down Santa Monica Boulevard on weekends. He wouldn't have to walk in the rain. It suddenly solved every problem, and he was out the door, looking sexy in a fitted short-sleeve shirt that showed off his physique.

David's apartment was only a block south of SMB, and the trolley stop was right by the intersection on the other side of the thoroughfare. He got to the bus stop and saw the westbound trolley was less than a block away. They only ran every twenty minutes or so and he felt very lucky indeed.

The streets were busy as they always were with vehicles of all kinds, but the trolley was virtually empty. David was mildly surprised to be getting onto an empty bus, but then understood it was still early for a Friday. Things didn't tend to pick up until ten-ish. The WeHo Trolley was made up to look like a trolley car from San Francisco. The seats were wooden benches on either side of a central aisle. Being West Hollywood, the front of the ride was home to bowls of condoms and cards featuring deals at the various establishments along the boulevard. One dollar drinks at FUBAR, no cover at the Factory, and so on.

The condoms gave David pause, as he realized he and Joseph had not only fucked bare every time they had had sex, they hadn't had the STI conversation he usually encouraged with every sexual partner. David got tested for the full panel of potential infections every three months as part of his Pre-Exposure Prophylaxis program, a daily pill he took designed to prevent HIV infection, and the PrEP itself reduced that biggest worry to a statistical zero. But still, there were things other than just HIV out there, so he usually used condoms with new guys, and *always* had the STI talk, verifying that potential partners were tested regularly and knew their status. He even usually insisted that partners be able to share results. A lot of guys balked at this and called him paranoid, but he got his test results sent to his phone automatically, so David figured it was so easy, it was a good habit to have and encourage in others.

Have the talk. David nodded in agreement with his own pledge and resolved to talk to Joseph about it.

The nearest trolley stops to Fiesta Cantina were two blocks away in either direction, so David got off on the first one, just past the car wash. He crossed Palm Avenue towards Fiesta and saw that there was a big commotion by the bar that used to be Eleven but was something else now that he couldn't remember the name of. There were lights and photographers and a step and repeat which meant celebrities or people who *thought* they were celebrities. It was craziness and David had no desire to try to push his way through throngs of wannabe influencers. Fortunately, he knew a shortcut through an alleyway behind the clubs he frequently used when nights got busy and the packs of college twinks were just too much.

He turned right on Palm and then left down the alley. The noise of WeHo died down significantly behind the buildings, as did the illumination of the streetlamps. What light there was glowed as the misting rain diffused it and created a sheen on every surface. The laughter and the honking cars and the demands of paparazzi to *"Hey, look over here! Over here! Over here!"* became dulled by several stories of brick and the moisture in the air.

David had his hands tucked into his jeans, his bare arms glistening below the sleeves of his burnt orange Henley shirt. His head was down to keep the chill drizzle out of his face, so he didn't see the couple standing directly in his path until he practically ran into them. He was stopped by a man's hand on his chest.

"Hey, watch where you're going, mate!" the man scolded with a detectable European accent.

David initially flinched at the direct physical contact that seemed to come out of nowhere. It wasn't like he was zoned out. He should have been able to see someone coming towards him with plenty of time to veer his path. "Oh, shit! Fuck, I'm sorry, dude. You okay?" He didn't know why he asked. It was reflex, he supposed. He had stopped before colliding with the pair, thanks to the man's outstretched hand. His companion, a woman with dark hair and caramel skin, giggled. David didn't wait for a response to his question; it was mostly meant as an "excuse me" as they each proceeded on their way, so he took a step to his right and resumed walking.

The man blocked his path.

"Am *I* okay? Listen to him, my love, he wants to know if *I* am okay. Such courtesy." He leaned in closer to David. "We have not experienced this since arriving in your city. I would say most people have been downright rude." He looked at the woman over his shoulder but maintained eye contact with David. "Wouldn't you say, Roxana?"

"So very rude, my *batal*," she replied, her voice silky and smooth.

Deep for a woman her size, David thought. He wondered casually if she was trans but a growing part of his brain was sounding an alarm. This was not usual.

"I'm ... really sorry people have been rude to you. Uh, sorry, I'm meeting friends," David stammered, trying to step around the man, who was wearing all black like he was coming from a funeral.

The woman *tsk-tsked* as the man blocked his path again. "He is *sorry* even for other people," he said to the woman, Roxana, and turned back to David. "But he does not know what he is really sorry for..."

David's mind flooded with panic. *Oh fuck, oh fuck, is this a gay bashing?* He had taken ten years of Soo Bakh Do martial arts training, but in this moment, off guard, his black belt meant nothing. He forgot every lesson, every combination of moves. This man radiated menace, and he was clearly out to impress his girlfriend, or maybe they were a psychotic pair like in *Natural Born Killers*. A homophobic Bonnie and Clyde. The only thing David could think to do was put distance between them, and he began to back away. He took two steps and was stopped by something. *Fuck, oh shit, there are more of them!* He turned to see what was in the way and saw it was the woman. *Roxana, her name is Roxana*, his brain somehow thought it important to remind him. David whipped his head back to the man who should have had a woman standing next to him. She was gone. Somehow, she had moved fast enough to block his exit. He was trapped.

"He is afraid, my darling," the woman purred, her accent unfamiliar.

David tensed his body, making himself ready to fight. The awful irony of being attacked in the middle of West Hollywood, a place created to be a safe haven for people who weren't welcome elsewhere in the world, suddenly surfaced. "You're in West Hollywood!" he told them, his voice raising in pitch and volume. "Go somewhere else if you have a problem with us!"

"You think we are prejudiced against men who lay with men?" the man said. "No, this is not a random act of violence."

The woman was suddenly right behind him, her hand at his throat and her voice next to his ear. "It is you we have questions for."

David's brain suddenly shifted out of neutral and slammed into gear. All his training focused his mind, and he knew exactly how to break a grip like the one on his neck. You started by grabbing the attacker's hand and using it as an anchor, holding it against yourself while dropping and spinning towards the thumb. Then thrust up with your legs to use the momentum to unbalance and flip the attacker. Once free, he'd take the open path back around the building and down to the main street where there were people and cameras and police and big burly bouncers at every club.

Those thoughts went through David's mind, but did not make it to his body. He could see the entire scenario play itself out in his imagination, but his vision was arrested by the gaze of the male attacker. David couldn't look away from his eyes. Were they *glowing*? That didn't seem right. His feet felt like concrete, his legs like lead. He could remember having moved his body before, but for the life of him, couldn't get the desire to move from his brain to his body parts.

I might die now.

The thought flitted like a lightning flash through his mind, interrupting all others before it was pushed away by more rational thinking. *Surely no. No one gets murdered behind the Yogurt Stop.*

The man broke eye contact and looked David up and down, his face twisting in a grimace of revulsion. "Look at him struggle, my love. How weak-willed they are. Disgusting." Though the man's eyes were no longer boring into his own, David still couldn't move. The longer he was trapped in his own body, the more he panicked. Adrenaline coursed through him, increasing his heart rate, but there was no possibility of fight or flight. He was a human statue.

The woman ran her fingernails across David's neck. The physical sensation was at once dull, like the echo of a touch, and like fire. He felt like his skin was being sliced by red-hot knives, but maybe it was not even his skin.

"I can hear his blood, Alexander, it surges through him. Ask him now so that I might have some."

She wants my blood? So this wasn't a simple gay bashing, it was a full-on hate crime. David tried to scream, but no sound same from his throat. His lungs began to burn. Was he breathing?

"I don't know who you are," the man (*Alexander!* David's mind shouted. *Remember that so you can identify the man who killed you.*) told him. "We were searching for another and found his scent on you." He breathed in deeply, smelling David's skin and clothes. "And in you. You have lain with Joseph? You may nod yes or no."

This is about Joseph? Who are these people? David silently asked. Another part of his mind thought the answer to Alexander's question, and he felt his head nod up and down as if controlled by remote.

"How embarrassing to have a father who lies with males," Alexander spat, though it wasn't clear if the barb was directed at David or the woman who held his throat.

Father? What? This can't be about my Joseph. They must have me confused with someone who slept with an older man named Joseph. My God this is insane somebody help me help me help me—

"He cannot help the way he is, love. Let me release him from his miserable existence," Roxana purred, giving David's neck a lick. "We must be quick. We are exposed, even in this back street..."

"You are right, my queen, of course. And if this whelp means something more to Joseph than a mere sexual conquest—" he leaned in close to David's ear "—all the better."

The man lowered his head, and David felt his attackers' breath on both sides of his throat. He was going to die, he was certain of it. He found he could close his eyes so he did, though he was sure it wouldn't spare him the pain of whatever came next.

What came next was a roar from behind that sounded like a large lion or a small dinosaur. The grip on him first loosened, then disappeared with the sound of an impact as his assailants were hit by something big and vicious. David found his body could move again but downward seemed to be the only reasonable direction. He collapsed to the ground. There was a flurry of movement as blows were exchanged and bodies were slammed into nearby dumpsters.

Great, David thought, his brain struggling to interpret the events of the last few minutes. *I've escaped one gruesome death only to be mauled by a rabid mountain lion. Did mountain lions live in the Hills? Did they ever come into the city?* His modern human mind crazily tried to recall if he'd ever read an article about mountain lions in Los Angeles while his prehistoric reptile brain screamed wordless prayers for a quick death.

There was a flutter of clothing and a whoosh of movement, and the screams were gone. The muted sounds of the city returned to David's ears. Of course, the lion had scared away the attackers, and it was now circling him, closing in for the kill. David found he was hugging his legs and decided it was best to keep doing that. He heard a scuffling that sounded like dress shoes on asphalt. It was probably a predator's paws and claws scraping on wet pavement, but the sound focused his mind and suddenly, he was not okay with being eaten by an animal in the middle of the city. If there was any way out of this, it meant fighting, not dying in a ball in a dirty, wet alley.

He had no idea how to fight off a mountain lion *(it could be a pack of coyotes, you've seen those in WeHo)*, and his mind could barely put two coherent thoughts together, so he just unfurled himself enough to scream as loud as he could. Once he got his head up he'd find the danger and direct his scream at it and then, well, he'd see what happened.

"David!"

The lion was screaming his name because he was going crazy from the stress of the attack, of course. David howled back louder in an inarticulate expression of fear and rage but mostly fear.

A gentle yet strong hand grasped his shoulder. "David, stop! It's me!" Another hand grasped David's other shoulder and shook him lightly. He opened his eyes and saw Joseph, his piercing blue eyes wide with concern.

David's scream died suddenly in his throat. Joseph was here. Holding him. He was safe. David didn't know how he knew he was safe, but somehow in his mind that was broken into a thousand puzzle pieces and trying to assemble a coherent view of the world, he knew Joseph. The kindness of the last few days flooded into him and soothed the jagged edges of his terror.

Joseph's eyes were full of compassion and worry. He had a cut on his forehead and blood was running down his temple. David looked at the rest of him, his mind yearning for context and saw that his lover's clothes were torn. Gashes were ripped across his maroon shirt. David's mind was still piecing things together and he thought, *Joseph fought off a lion?*

"Joseph?"

"Yeah, babe, it's me. You're okay. Everything's okay." He pulled David into a fierce hug filled with relief.

"Jmmsmmph..." Face buried in Joseph's chest, David began to cry, the adrenaline and stress and fear having nowhere to go but through his tears.

"Shhhh, shh-shh, it's okay. I've got you, you're safe." Joseph rocked him slowly, holding on to David as if he'd never let go.

A thought percolated through David's disjointed mind. "Babe..." he murmured. That's what Joseph had called him. It felt right. Then, another thought, "Hey... do you have a kid?"

Then David passed out.

CHAPTER 9

David woke with a start in unfamiliar surroundings. He was in a bed. Luxurious, but not his own. The room was dark, and it was hard to make out details, but the layout was equally unknown. The only light was a soft ethereal glow from the bathroom. David realized it was a night-light.

His nightmares had been disjointed as his mind tried valiantly to make sense of the attack. As he sat up and looked around, dual sensations of pain and a tugging came from his neck. He reached his right hand above his clavicle and felt a bandage taped to his skin. When he applied slight pressure to the area, a jolt of pain from something that felt like a cut made him stop.

"David?" A calm, gentle voice spoke out of the darkness. When he looked in the direction it came from, he could make out a figure in a chair. The figure rose in a fluid motion and approached the bed, settling lightly next to David. "How do you feel?"

"Joseph? Where am I?" David's voice came out scratchy. His throat was hoarse and sore from screaming.

Joseph reached to the bedside table. "Watch your eyes, I'm turning on a light."

David closed his eyes and heard a click. Through his eyelids, he saw the warm glow of a bedside lamp. He had meant to keep his eyes closed a moment longer to let them adjust but an instantaneous panic shot through him, and they flew open. Fortunately, the lamp was not bright, and the level of light was comfortable.

"Shhh, it's okay. You're at my house. You're safe. I…" Joseph stopped, unsure how much he wanted to say. He wanted to find out how much David remembered and what he knew, but more than anything, he wanted to comfort him. He grabbed a glass of room-temperature water from the table and held it for David. "Here, some water."

David sipped tentatively at first, unsure if it would hurt to drink, but it soothed his dry throat, and he downed half the glass before he stopped.

"How do you feel?" Joseph asked again, gently but insistently.

David had not yet looked Joseph in the eyes but did so now. He saw the love and concern Joseph felt for him and felt his own feelings begin to rise to the surface. But the trauma of the attack crashed over him like a wave, against the rocks and shoals that were the details trying to piece themselves together into a not-yet-coherent picture. He burst into tears.

Joseph held him, and David wrapped his arms around him in return, squeezing as if his life depended on it.

"It's okay… it's okay…" was all Joseph said as he gently rubbed David's back. David's hot tears fell between them and dampened Joseph's shirt, but he made no move to part. He would hold on to this man forever if that's what he needed.

David cried like a child, and it exhausted him just as it had when he was young. After ten minutes or so, his whole face felt swollen from the physical effort. His head throbbed, and his eyes burned. The sobs subsided, and he squeezed his eyes closed. He relaxed and lay back into the bed but didn't let go of his grip on Joseph, who followed David down and adjusted himself until they were both lying together in the bed, wrapped in each other's arms.

Feeling safe and protected, David drifted back to sleep.

He was roused hours later by the sound of a laden tray being set on the bedside table, and Joseph softly saying his name, "Daaaaviiiid…"

David's eyes were crusty with the salt of dried tears. The smell of chicken soup wafted into his nose from the tray.

His dreams had been quieter, less chaotic this time. Now that he was awake, certain details became clearer.

"There wasn't a mountain lion, was there?" It wasn't really a question.

"No." Joseph sat back on the bed. "Here, I brought you a hot towel."

David scooted up into a sitting position and took the washcloth from Joseph, who placed his hand on top of David's for a moment. David placed his other hand on top in a silent gesture of reassurance. *I'm okay. I love you. Give me a second.*

The towel was the perfect temperature to give his skin a slight sting when David pressed it to his face, and it contained the exact amount of moisture to effectively wipe away the remnants of his tears, sweat, and grime from the alleyway. When it had cooled, he lowered it from his face and looked at Joseph. Neither of them could decide what to say. A palpable silence hung between them.

"I have some chicken soup and ginger ale if you want," Joseph offered.

"What time is it?" David asked.

"Around 4:30 AM. You were out cold after ... what happened. You woke up the first time about 3:00 AM." Joseph was being careful, picking his words cautiously.

David felt at the bandage on his neck. "What is this?"

"You got cut. I cleaned and dressed it while you were asleep."

"*You* got cut," David countered, pointing to the spot on Joseph's forehead that had been bleeding earlier but now showed no sign of a wound at all.

Joseph reached up and touched the spot. "It wasn't as bad as it looked with all the blood. I..." He stopped. That was enough explanation. He was about to add that he healed quickly but caught himself.

David felt like he had a thousand questions jumbling around his head and couldn't grab onto the most important one. He grasped at the one piece of information he already had.

"There was no mountain lion," he said simply. Saying it out loud for the second time sounded ridiculous. In fact, he couldn't think of how the idea ever occurred to him in the first place, it was so preposterous. Okay, he pushed that one to the side.

The problem was he didn't have a complete picture. Whole chunks of the puzzle were missing. The pieces he did have felt nearly as improbable as a giant cat in the middle of Los Angeles. What he needed was more information. One potential source was sitting next to him. The vital question was, did he trust Joseph?

David looked at him. Even in the dim light, Joseph's blue eyes were easy to see. They were filled with ... what? Compassion, sympathy, for sure. Pity, maybe. Love? David's throat tightened involuntarily at the thought, and he felt the bandage tape pull at the skin. How did he really feel about Joseph?

That was the key. Did he trust this man he'd only met several days before? Did he ... love him?

At the thought, the lump in his throat dissolved and a warmth filled his chest. He had never fallen for someone so fast, but everything thus far had been perfect. It might not last, but for now, yes. He trusted him to fill in the pieces.

David reached for the open bottle of ginger ale and took a sip, feeling the carbonation tickle his nose and the spiciness of the ginger as it flowed down his throat.

"What happened?" he asked, his voice a bit stronger and more confident.

"You were attacked," Joseph replied, placing a hand on David's leg over the comforter. "I was on my way to meet you when I saw them and ... fought them off."

David's racing mind slowed. All the puzzle pieces that were flurrying around like glitter in a snow globe started to settle, and he set to picking them up and putting them in place. He had always been a problem solver. He couldn't help it, when someone told him something was wrong, he automatically tried to fix it. It had occasionally been a source of friction in previous relationships.

"Who were they?" he asked, picking up on an important detail in Joseph's statement.

"Um..." Joseph paused before deciding that feigning ignorance was the lesser of two evils. "I don't know."

"How did you find me? You just happened to go down the same alley a block and a half away from where we were meeting?" David's face set into a determined stare, reading Joseph for information.

"Yeah," was his reply.

"It wasn't just a gay bashing. I thought it was at first, but it wasn't. They were crazy." David could feel the events of the evening coalesce into coherent memory.

Joseph misunderstood David's irritability as panic and saw where it was headed. "You're safe, David."

"Why are you saying that?" David snapped. "You wouldn't keep saying that unless there was a reason to think I wasn't."

"I just think you should calm d—"

"Who are you?" David cut him off.

Joseph just looked at him. The vampire had just reconciled his feelings for this man but had yet to decide if he was going to let him further into his life. That decision would mean revealing his true self. The decision was being thrust upon him right now, this very moment. He couldn't think of what to say.

David saw the conflict in his eyes. He knew there were several ways this conversation could go. One way was for him to get out of the bed right now and leave, go to the police and report the attack. He didn't think Joseph would stop him. But he didn't want to do that. The other option was that he stayed. He took a deep breath.

"Joseph. I've never met anyone like you. The truth is, I haven't stopped thinking about you since the night we met, and I think…" David struggled to get this line of thought out in the midst of everything else he was reconciling. "I have never really thought that love at first sight was a real thing. Because I'd never experienced it." He placed a hand on top of Joseph's. "Until you."

A tear welled up in Joseph's eye and rolled down his cheek. David realized two things. One, Joseph felt the same way about him, deeply. Two, the expression in his eyes wasn't sympathy or pity; it was sorrow. In that moment, Joseph's eyes looked older than any David had looked into.

David continued, "I think I love you. I don't know how but I do. But there is so much I don't know about you. I don't know what you do for work, exactly. This—" he waved his arm to indicate the room "—is a nice place. But I don't know what your job is. I feel like you've told me a lot of half-things about yourself, but I can't quite put my finger on why."

Just then a detail from the evening lit up like a neon sign in his brain. "They were looking for you. The crazies." He waited for Joseph to respond with shock or ask how he knew, but he remained silent.

"You already knew that." Another piece fell into place. The picture was still indistinct. "Because you know them."

Joseph looked like he was about to be torn in two but still didn't speak.

"*Do you?*" David demanded.

Joseph barely whispered his answer. "Yes."

David was silent before he decided Joseph's earlier lie wasn't the important thing. "How?"

"They're from my past. A long time ago, from a different part of my life. I never expected to see them ever again."

More bits from his encounter with Alexander and Roxana clarified in David's memory. "They knew about us. That we'd slept together. Did you tell them?"

"No, David, no," Joseph said, grateful for the ability to answer honestly.

"Then how did they know?" David insisted, his voice rising.

Joseph spoke slowly. "David, I just want you to know that I love you. I do, I love you. I've never felt anything like what I feel with you and when I say that, it means…" He trailed off, not knowing how to finish the sentence. "I need you to know that you're safe. And that I love you." Tears flowed freely down his face. "I don't want you to hate me."

David's memory flashed back to ten years ago, when he was trying to come out to his family. He had said the exact same thing. But Joseph clearly wasn't trying to come out to him, so what was his secret? What was so awful?

The final piece slid into place and a horrifying and completely improbable realization occurred to David. He reached up to his neck to feel the bandage and started peeling away the tape. Joseph reached out to stop him.

"No, don't do that," he implored.

David didn't listen; he pulled the bandage off and touched the wound that had been cleaned and dressed. He felt two holes beginning to scab over. *What are these? What* are *they?*

David looked into Joseph's eyes. They were completely visible despite the lack of light in the bedroom, eyes that shimmered slightly and...

"Joseph... What are you?" David said softly, both wanting and not wanting to know the answer.

Joseph spoke slowly but avoided answering the question directly. "The people who attacked you... They were vampires, David."

"No... that's not possible," David said quietly but didn't believe himself. He said it because that's what you say when someone tells you that you were attacked by vampires.

Joseph closed his eyes and took a deep breath. This wasn't the first time he had revealed his secret to someone, but the last time had been Robert, thirty years ago. Before that, Rafaél, close to fifty years ago. And before that ... centuries. This may not have been different, but it felt too rushed. The decision was taken from him, and he felt unprepared for it. Joseph opened his eyes and exhaled slowly, making eye contact with David. "I... I was born in the year 1518."

David pressed his palms to his eyes. His brain hurt. Somehow this information, phrased that way, was more real than some mythical monster. "No..." Despite having pieced it together, there was a difference between a puzzle laid out in your mind and the stark reality of something so impossible presented to you in real life.

"Please try to stay calm. It's okay, I'm not going to hurt you." The truth was out and now all Joseph could do was wait to see what happened next.

David was calm. At least, he didn't feel particularly frightened. "That's what vampires do, though, right?" he pointed out. "They hurt people. I was almost killed tonight! I thought I was going to die." He lowered his hands and made eye contact again. "Joseph, I was *sure* of it."

Part of David's brain still fought the notion altogether. It was like mountain lions in LA. There were no vampires in the world, it was utterly ridiculous! But the calmer, problem-solving part of his brain answered, *Yes, but there are mountain lions in LA. You've seen them on the news. And you know there are animals that feed on blood. Vampire bats do it.* But it was a huge leap from vampire bats to vampire humans. The more likely truth was that he was attacked by coked-out whack jobs with fake vampire teeth...

"Show me," David demanded quietly.

"David..." Joseph tried to read the other man's emotional state. David's heart rate was steady, if a bit elevated. He didn't smell especially afraid. "Are you sure?"

David didn't ask again. He just jerked his head towards Joseph's mouth. His meaning was unmistakable. *Show them to me.*

Joseph noted that David's hands were no longer touching his. One was rolled into a loose fist within the other, over his stomach. Joseph opened his mouth slightly, then stopped. "I love you," he said. David said nothing. Did nothing. Waiting.

While maintaining eye contact, Joseph bared his incisors and allowed his fangs to slide slowly into place. When they were fully extended, he noticed that David was holding his breath. Joseph withdrew his fangs.

"David. Breathe."

David had no context to process this information. For the last few minutes, until that moment, it had been theoretical. And before tonight, it wasn't something he'd even conceived as a possibility. He sucked in a breath and suddenly the deep reptile part of his brain that dictated survival told him that he needed to be anywhere else but here.

"Are you going to kill me?" he asked. It was a question that needed asking, but the look on Joseph's face betrayed such hurt that David had his answer.

"I could never." He tried to reason through David's shock. "I *am* capable of love. And the last time I fed on a person was over two hundred and fifty years ago." Joseph wasn't sure if this last piece of information would help or hurt the situation, but it came out before he had a chance to censor himself.

"If I need to leave will you stop me?" David asked, confident enough that he was able to look Joseph in the eye again and not just at his teeth.

"No. I brought you here to protect you, but you can go whenever you want," Joseph said sadly, trying to be as soothing as possible.

"I need to leave. I can't be here with you right now." David pushed aside the comforter and sheets. Joseph stood up to give him room. He even stepped back a couple of paces, wanting to be as nonthreatening as possible.

"That's okay. I'll order you a car." Joseph reached to get his phone out of his pocket. But David shot the idea down.

"I got it. I..." He trailed off while he put on his clothes. Joseph had respectfully left David's underwear on and folded his pants and shirt in a neat pile on a chair on the other side of the table, shoes arranged primly underneath. "I have a lot of things flying around my head right now, and I don't want anything from you until I can sort it all out." David pulled his shirt over his head and tugged it straight. He gave Joseph a look that was not unkind, but also held little affection. "Okay?"

Joseph swallowed his sorrow and anger at the circumstances that led to this. "Mmhmm, yeah. Whatever you need."

David tapped into the rideshare app and ordered a car. It was late enough after bars closed and early enough to be ahead of morning commuters, so there were a few drivers within minutes. It was the first instance that David got an idea of where they were, looking at the map on his phone. "You live in the Hills?"

"Yeah." Joseph decided less was more in this situation. Best not to explain how he was loaded but hadn't wanted David to know until he knew their love was real. What did it matter anyway?

"Hmm," was all David said. Then, "The Lyft'll be here in a minute. Where's the door?"

"Follow me." It was still dark out, so Joseph led David up the stairs from the bedroom into the main part of the house. He was aware of David's reaction as he took in the huge space, the interior design, and the art on display. He caught David's mild fascination at the door that unlocked at a touch of the handle, the large deadbolt sliding open with a heavy but immediate *whirrclunk*, and saw him notice that there was no handle on the outside.

Outside, the rain had stopped, but everything still had a sheen of recent precipitation. The pair stood silently under the covered entryway, each of them wrestling with the urge to say something but not knowing what words could possibly be uttered in the moment.

David wanted to run. It took everything he had not to bolt from the house. But he also still felt Joseph's touch. The way he caressed David's skin (*he's a vampire!*) was better than any man ever had. The way they had that instant and effortless chemistry (*he drinks blood!*), and their shared sense of humor was undeniable. Everything David had experienced showed Joseph to be kind, generous (*he's five hundred years old!*), and gentle. But then, of course, he was also a vampire.

For his part, Joseph wanted to profess his feelings, again and again, until David couldn't help but believe him. He also wanted to beg David not to tell anyone his secret. For both of their sakes. The outcome of such a spilling of information could go a hundred different ways. David could be seen as insane. Or he could be believed. Either were awful to contemplate. Fleetingly, Joseph welcomed a public reveal of his true nature. Bring his tortured existence to an end. Then he remembered the feel of David's body next to his. The experience of feeling his heartbeat as if it were his own. And his kiss. A quote he once read flitted into his mind:

"It was the kiss by which all the others of his life would be judged and found wanting."

That was how good David's kisses were. Never in his five hundred years had he experienced kisses that excited him so easily.

The Lyft pulled into the driveway and the moment was over. Whatever was going to happen was going to happen. When David didn't immediately step off the stoop and head for the idling Prius, Joseph touched his shoulder gently. "David? Are you okay?" Then, before he could stop himself, " I meant it when I said I loved you."

David didn't answer. Or he didn't know the answer. Joseph saw him shake his head almost imperceptibly, and he stepped out of the entryway. After a couple of slow steps, he turned back, and Joseph's heart swelled at the hope that he might not leave. He would give the driver a twenty and they would go back inside and David could finish his soup and they could cuddle and kiss and—

"I won't tell anyone," David said simply. He was staring at the ground. "Other than that, I can't promise anything. Please don't call. I can't stop you if you wanted to, but…" He raised his eyes to meet Joseph's. They were filled with tears. "Please don't."

David turned and walked to the idling car and got in the back seat. The driver was a middle-aged black woman, who seemed preternaturally cheerful given the hour. She asked him to buckle up, and a moment later the hybrid pulled out of the driveway and down the curving road with an electric whine. Joseph's house disappeared behind the hill, but David wasn't even looking.

"You okay, sugar?" the driver asked. "Y'all lookin' like you got the world's worst news t'night."

"Yeah," David said, either affirming one question or confirming the guess.

"Mmhmm. I get it. I'm sorry if you're having a tough night. I got y'all's destination right here. You just relax, and I'll get you there safe and sound." The driver had been doing this long enough to know when not to be chatty. But she also knew some people needed an ear sometimes. "Y'all just let me know if you need to talk. I'm here for ya, sugar. I'm Madeline," she said with a long *i* like *fine*.

David realized he was holding his phone. He turned it over, looking for cracks, but it seemed unscathed, despite the events of the early evening. He activated it, not really knowing what he wanted to do, but his fingers automatically opened the iMessage app and tapped the most recent conversation. It was Dana. She had said:

<Have fun Romeo! Dnce a jig fr me!>

David typed back:

<Call me asap> Then, <Also, not coming into work Monday>

He turned the phone screen off and looked out the window. From up in the Hollywood Hills, the Los Angeles basin spread out in an ocean of lights as far as the eye could see. David had always loved that view. It had reminded him of the future and possibility and the remarkable things man could achieve.

Now it looked like endless hiding places for a thousand unknown terrors.

David closed his eyes and leaned his head back against the seat. *What the hell am I going to do now?*

CHAPTER 10

Alexander woke late in the evening, long after sunset. His body was battered and bruised and required rest to heal after his brief battle with Joseph the previous night. His joints were still aching and his face sore, and he silently cursed the man as he rose naked from the bed that had belonged to the Uber driver they'd fed on. He saw that Roxana was not in bed nor in the room and ventured out to see if she was elsewhere in the apartment. He didn't bother putting on clothes.

The single apartment was especially dark. They had covered the windows against sunlight and none of the lights were on inside. Nevertheless, Alexander's eyes were attuned to the darkness, and he saw Roxana standing at the bookshelf in the corner, leafing through the previous owner's meager library.

"Darling," he said.

Roxana looked up from the copy of *From Beirut to Jerusalem*. "Alexander. Are you well?"

He noticed the lack of her usual pet name for him. "I will be. You are upset with me, my queen?"

She closed the book deliberately and set it back on the bookshelf. She turned to him and pondered the question a moment before evenly replying. "No, my love. I am upset, but not at you. Your maker is the one who gives me ire. He attacked us without provocation. You, his own progeny."

Alexander moved towards her, speaking carefully, as if to a dangerous animal. He did not want her ire directed his way. "*He* would say he *had* provocation, since we were about to feed on his human."

Roxana spat on the floor of the apartment. "Humans are for food, not for fucking."

"I agree," he said, closing the distance between them. "Though Joseph is not the only vampire to use humans for sexual pleasure."

"You defend him? He could have killed you. If I had not been there—"

"Joseph would not kill me. He is too sentimental." Alexander stroked the side of Roxana's face. "And I find the fact that he dismisses his nature, refusing to feed on humans, more blasphemous than anything else. I lived with that insanity my whole life until you rescued me."

Roxana's expression softened at his touch, and she returned the gesture. "You are more vampire than he ever was." Her hand fell away from his face and she turned as anger crossed her features. "I despise the fact that he found prosperity despite having such weakness."

Alexander approached behind her, wrapping his arms around her waist. "You come from a different time, my queen. When your strength and savagery were all that was needed to rule, who could have known money would become more important than the strength of ten men, or the will to decimate those that cross you?" He reached up and gently turned her face to his. "Those are the things I have always loved in you and still do."

Roxana sighed. "My *batal*. You are my warrior poet." A look of concern passed over her eyes as she looked at him. "It has been two days since you fed and healing your wounds has taxed you. You need to eat."

"Then let us feast on this City of Angels until we are gorged on it." He grabbed her by the shoulders and turned her to him, pressing his lips to hers with a passionate kiss. He ignored the pain in his face, and she ignored his erection that was rising between them.

"Later, my lord," she cooed as they parted lips, running her fingernails gently along his shaft and making him gasp. "After dinner, I shall give you dessert."

Los Angeles truly was a banquet for vampire kind. They had taken the Uber driver's wallet to make it harder to identify the body, but it had the added benefit of providing them a few days of shelter while they got themselves situated in the city. The driver had a modest apartment in Glendale. They determined he didn't have a family before killing him; Roxana's connection to his Middle

Eastern ancestry charmed him into easy conversation. Now they also had a car to use. But they didn't have to go far, the unhomed were everywhere in this city. They came for the weather. If you're going to live outside, you might as well go to a place that rarely gets rain. The only tricky thing for Alexander and Roxana was getting them alone, away from the tent cities they congregated in under freeway overpasses and in public parks.

It wasn't *that* tricky.

The pair was closing in on an old black man pushing a rickety grocery cart through North Atwater Park, a strip of greenery between Glendale proper and the Los Angeles River across the freeway from the hills of Griffith park. The location was perfect for feeding. The River, a concrete trough courtesy of the Army Corps of Engineers that snaked through the city from Canoga Park to its mouth in Long Beach, served as a perfect dump for bodies, and the I-5 freeway provided enough noise to drown out screams.

The homeless man was muttering to himself as he pushed his cart, which was laden with all his worldly possessions, the supplies for a makeshift tent, and assorted junk. Alexander and Roxana were stalking him, waiting for when he passed between streetlights and when no witnesses were within sight. The moment came, and Alexander moved in for the kill when a voice came from the direction of the freeway.

"Alexander! We need to talk." Joseph stepped out of the shadows into the moonlight. The homeless man started at the sound and grabbed a bent golf club from his cart, waving it at the people he realized were following him.

"Git away, now! You git and leave me be!" He pushed his cart with one hand as he swung the club with the other.

Joseph stepped between the man and his would-be killers. "Go, old man, find a place to hunker down." He faced the other vampires. "A storm is coming."

Roxana swore at him in Arabic, *"Kess Ommak."*

"At least I *had* a mother," Joseph shot back, "and am not the bastard daughter of a slave whore."

Alexander erupted, "You dare speak that way to my wife!"

"Dare?" Joseph pinned Alexander with his gaze, which was filled with white-hot fury. "*I* dare? You attacked someone who is dear to me and you have the audacity to accuse *me* of insult?"

Roxana stepped next to her mate, her body taut and ready for combat. "You are a disgrace to our kind, Bavarian. If a fight is what you want, we shall mete out your destruction."

"Like you did last night?" Joseph taunted.

Alexander responded, his buttons deftly pushed by his former mentor. "You caught me by surprise so I was not able to stand by Roxana's side against you. Now it is two against one."

"I can tell from here that you're weak. I interrupted your meal last night and again tonight." Joseph gestured towards the homeless man, who was halfway across the park. "While I, on the other hand, am fully fed."

Roxana sneered. "On the blood of dogs and cats..."

Joseph tsked. "You are tragically behind the times, my dear. No, I feed on human blood." He omitted the part where it was *donated* human blood and stood tall, making himself as intimidating as possible. "I am stronger than you, Alexander. And Roxana... well, I feel pretty good about my chances."

Roxana pushed back. "You lie. For hundreds of years, since you turned my love, you have refused to feed on humans, yet now you change?"

"Do you wish to test my full strength against your weakness, then?" Joseph took a single step towards the couple.

"What do you want, if not a fight?" Alexander asked cautiously, unconsciously retreating half a step.

Joseph spoke slowly, enunciating each word clearly and deliberately. "It's not what I want. It's what *you* want. I know why you're here. I know why you attacked David. You were trying to get to me. Well, here I am."

Joseph took another step closer; this time it was Roxana who retreated next to Alexander. "I propose a bargain."

There was a moment while the words hung in the air between them. It wasn't what Alexander had expected, and Roxana was always more interested in a fight than talking.

"What sort of bargain?" she finally replied.

"You want what I have built. To join us here in the twenty-first century with money and influence. I want you out of my city. Leave and I will give you half."

The greed in Alexander spoke before he could think. "Two-thirds."

Joseph closed the distance between them in a fraction of a blink, the power of his gaze capturing Alexander the way Alexander had held David the night before. *"Do not presume you are in a position to negotiate, spawn!"* he bellowed. Roxana did not retreat but made no move to intervene.

"Why would you do this?" she inquired skeptically.

Joseph took a deep breath and released Alexander from his freezing stare. The younger vampire stumbled back a step. Joseph looked at the older female. "Because I value peace over conflict. If we fight, at least one of us dies." He gave Alexander a side-eye. "Probably two-thirds."

Joseph raised his hands in a gesture of peace and backed up a step to illustrate his desire for conflict-free resolution. "Besides, Alexander is my progeny, despite how our views may differ. We don't get along, the three of us, but I would never wish you harm. I know you have resisted this new world of business and finance, but I have done well enough to provide for you both. I can give you money or a portion of my company to run. You can learn to turn that into more money to do with as you please, or you can squander it. But you will do it in any part of the world except Los Angeles."

Alexander was clearly about to say something defiant and rash, but Roxana placed a hand on his shoulder, and he held his tongue. Instead, she spoke for them. "That is most generous of you, *Herr Knoblauch*. May we take some time to consider your offer?" It was barely a request.

"Don't take long. I know where you're living, and I could make that a very short-term arrangement," Joseph threatened.

"A week, then. No longer." Roxana bowed, her hands out in supplication. "Now if you'll excuse us, my husband and I must find a new meal."

Joseph nodded but did not move. It was clear who was to retreat from this confrontation. Alexander and Roxana backed away until they were far enough that they felt safe, and they strode into the brush and into the Los Angeles River Basin. It was dry this time of year, made for easy travel through the city, and any stray humans that might be down there were easy pickings.

CHAPTER 11

"Jesus Christ," Rafi said, taking a swig of his ginger ale. The pair were in Joseph's kitchen, drinking while they talked.

Joseph had caught him up on the highlights of the last few days, which had taken a good while. He started with Alexander's appearance right after dinner to the date with David and the attack the following evening. Finally, he'd described tracking the vampires to their temporary lair by following Alexander's trail of blood. Joseph leaned against the counter next to the refrigerator, and Rafaél sat on a stool next to the island.

"Mmhmm," Joseph replied. He paused to take a sip of his own beverage, one of the blood sacks, which had cooled slightly during the long recap of events.

Rafaél set his bottle down gently, the glass clinking softly on the granite countertop of the kitchen island. "You're really going to give them half the company?" he asked incredulously.

"Oh God no, of course not," Joseph replied, waiving his hand dismissively. "There's no way they know every part of the company or the extent of the corporation's reach. Hell, I barely know it all." He grinned, letting the plan realize itself for Rafi. "That's what I have you around for."

"Ah," Rafi said after a moment. "I see." He took another sip of the soda and contemplated the problem. "It's a bit of a gamble, don't you think?"

"A bit, maybe. But we have a week to work it out. What I need you to do is a bit of inventory. Figure out what we can part with that will still be profitable enough with minimal oversight. Something that will keep them pacified. It needs to be small enough not to harm us irreparably and big enough it could conceivably be half of what I own."

"Riiiiight." He finished the last of the sweet-and-spicy carbonated beverage in one swig, then eyed the empty bottle. "I'm going to need something stronger than this, I think."

"Sorry, all I have is soup. I thought David might want some when..." Joseph said, a touch of sadness creeping into his demeanor. "You're welcome to it."

Rafaél sighed. "I told you to take it slow, didn't I?"

Joseph held up a hand defensively. "I didn't take it anywhere! I was just along for the ride, and it went as fast as it wanted to go."

Rafaél decided it wasn't the time for I-told-you-sos, and took a more sympathetic tack. "Do you think he'll call?"

"I really don't know," Joseph admitted. "I'm conflicted about it, to be honest. On one hand, I really, really want him to, and on the other..."

"On the other, you know what a relationship with him would mean for both of you," Rafaél pressed. He was trying to be consoling, but the facts of the matter were too obvious. "Do you need me to spell it out for you?"

"No, I get it."

"Do you, J?" Rafaél kept his voice kind and soft. "Best case scenario is a long life together, where you end up heartbroken for decades after his death. But before that, while you stay, well, *you*, he becomes increasingly frustrated at growing old and feeble."

"You don't know that," Joseph insisted.

"I do," Rafi said quietly. "I really do."

The moment hung in the air between them, so thick it could be cut with a blade. Joseph felt a well of sorrow in his heart for this man, who just a blink of an eye ago had been a boy, learning how to live without his parents in a new world with a completely new person. The years had flown by and now he was greying, slightly paunchy but in respectable shape for a man of... fuck, sixty-seven? Could that even be right?

"Rafi..." he started but didn't know what to say.

"No, listen, that wasn't fair of me. You gave me a life I could never dream of. If I *ever* make it seem like I'm not grateful beyond words, I apologize for it." The elder-looking of the two of them paused, then looked his adopted vampire father in the eye.

"That being said, no matter how much I know you love me, and I *do* know you love me, it is often frustrating being a regular old human living in the shadow of an immortal." Rafaél turned his hands in a shrugging gesture.

Joseph set the half-full bag on the counter behind him and moved to the opposite side of the island from where Rafaél was sitting. He pulled out a stool and sat down. "I wish I could give you that gift, Rafi. I really do. You are a much better man than I was when I was turned. If anyone deserved it..."

"I know why you can't. And hey, we're still working on the cure for death down at Tetractys, you never know." He smiled, half-joking, but turned somber again. "J, the advances *your* company has made in medicine and related fields have saved the lives of *millions* of people and improved billions more. Whatever kind of man you were, you *are* a great man now. And an amazing father." Rafaél reached out and grasped his former guardian's hand and squeezed it.

"But?" Joseph prompted, addressing the unfinished topic of David.

Now it was Rafi who put up his hands, signaling surrender on the topic. "No. Dammit, I'm sorry. David knows who you really are now, all of it. It's his decision to call or not, and if he does, I hope you both have all the happiness in the world for whatever time you have together. No one deserves it more. The end."

Joseph tried in vain to contain the grin of pride blossoming on his face. How he ever managed to raise such a smart, capable, and good man was quite beyond him. Especially considering his previous experience with Alexander.

"Rafi, you are an incredible son." Joseph and Rafi rarely got sentimental but realizing suddenly how old his boy had become made the vampire want to grab every single moment and never let go. "You are my heart. From the moment I saw you, that first instance in the alleyway when you looked at me with defiant determination in your eyes. I love you, kiddo."

"Oh, okay, *Dad*," Rafaél chided, before adding, "I love you, too."

The moment grew to bursting between them. Before it got too weird, Joseph threw up his hands. "That's it! I'm making you soup."

Rafaél laughed. "Okay, sure, that sounds great. What have you got?"

"Oh, several, but I know you want the split pea with ham," Joseph said, already getting a can out of the cupboard and a pot to warm it. "The question is, do you want a grilled cheese to go with it?"

Rafaél raised an eyebrow. "The question is, do you still remember how to make those? What has it been, forty years?"

Joseph scoffed. "Psh, it's like riding a bike!"

"Have you ever actually ridden a bike?"

Joseph pointed a slotted wooden spoon at him. "Not the point. I said it's *like* riding a bike. In that, you never forget."

Rafaél chuckled while he watched a vampire make him comfort food. Who he was trying to comfort wasn't a hundred percent clear, but it didn't matter.

After the soup was in the pot and the induction burner turned on, Joseph worked on the sandwich. Pre-shredded cheese packet in hand, a thought occurred to him. "Hey, Rafi, how come I've never had to counsel you in affairs of the heart?"

"Never needed it, I suppose."

Joseph turned to look at him. "I'm honestly embarrassed to have to ask this, but have you ever *been* in love? I mean, I know you've had girlfriends, much to my disappointment, but..."

Rafaél replied, "To be completely frank, I don't think so. I think I know what it is, from seeing you and Robert, and of course other friends and acquaintances, but it never was something I felt I needed."

Joseph pondered the answer for a moment, then with a "Hm," turned back to the slices of bread he'd set out.

Rafaél continued, "I've only recently begun to understand that side of myself, to tell you the truth. When I was young, I never really felt attracted to anyone of either gender. Dating women felt *more* right, but it didn't do for me what I knew it did for my friends and classmates. Just a few years ago I learned about asexuality and realized that's probably what I am."

Joseph put down the knife he was using to butter the outsides of the ungrilled sandwich and looked at his protege. "You are remarkable, you know that?"

Rafaél smiled. "I'm aware."

Joseph shook his head and turned back to the food. "Christ, what a pair we are."

"Right?" Rafaél agreed. "A gay vampire and a mixed-race asexual orphan. Someone should make a sitcom."

Joseph laughed. "You know, I very nearly started a movie studio back in the early nineteen hundreds. Deciding not to was the biggest mistake of my life. I thought moving pictures were a fad!"

CHAPTER 12

David sat in his car looking at his phone.

It was Monday night. He had spent the day driving. Dana had called immediately after getting his message on Saturday morning, before she even got out of bed. He had found that he didn't know what to say to her. He couldn't tell her the truth, but he had no idea how to pare the story down to details that he *could* tell her while getting across enough information for her to be able to help him.

He'd just sat quietly on the bed as she asked him what was going on, was he okay, did he need help, was he sick, was he injured, what? Finally, he'd said he was fine, and he'd call her later.

It wasn't fair to her, and for the rest of Saturday, he had *that* guilt to deal with in addition to the confusion and anguish caused by the previous twenty-four hours. At one point in the afternoon, his empty stomach had to not-so-gently remind him he hadn't eaten in at least a day, so he'd forced himself to get out of bed to make the bare minimum. A bowl of cereal and some coffee. Fortunately, he'd already gone through the effort of cold brewing a batch of Sumatran blend, so he just had to add water and heat a mug in the microwave.

David made it to the couch and turned on the TV but couldn't pay attention to anything. Dana called twice and left messages to check on him, but he didn't call back. Another bowl of cereal and a bag of popcorn later, he recognized the most dominant emotion he was feeling was loss. Thinking about Joseph, his heart ached. It was incredible to think all of this had happened in just this week. Every day had been an experience of working out a complex series of events in his head, and he was mentally exhausted.

As daylight gave way to dusk, David suddenly realized that the apartment was dark except for the light given off by the flat-screen TV. He panicked and dashed to each room, flipping on light switches. Only when the apartment was flooded with illumination and every closet was checked for potential intruders (*vampires!*) did he relax. His heart was pounding, so he closed his eyes and willed his breathing to slow.

Strangely, of all the people David wished were with him to hold and comfort him, the one he realized he was wishing for most was Joseph. Yet still he couldn't call him. It was all too fantastic, in the worst way.

Instead, he finally called Dana back, who threatened to call the police or his parents if he didn't prove he was okay. It was an empty threat. She didn't know his parents, and contacting the police was too extreme for her. He did invite his best friend over, though. David didn't want to be alone. He told Dana in advance that he might not feel like sharing, but at least they could watch a movie and order takeout, which is exactly what they did.

They ordered Thai food, both getting the orange chicken with fried rice, and watched action movies on Netflix until they fell asleep on the comfy couch, heads on each end and legs intertwined.

Sunday morning, Dana had refused the suggestion that she had better things to do than hang around with David all day but did insist they leave the apartment. They took turns showering, Dana borrowed a fresh T-shirt, and they went to get brunch at Grub. Grub was one of those little places on a side street in LA that used to be a house but was now a restaurant serving comfort food. Every table got a bowl of Trix cereal with their free tap water when they sat down, and menu items included croissant French toast, pumpkin pancakes, and their famous crack bacon (glazed with cayenne pepper and maple syrup). They had to wait a bit due to it being brunch time on a Sunday, but being outside in the daylight with a familiar face made David feel better than he had since Friday night. They had sat together on a bench along the sidewalk in the shade of a young tree.

During the breakfast, David didn't talk much. Dana towed the line of conversation, noting his discomfort, and kept topics superficial and lighthearted. Her natural humor raised his spirits, but it was obvious he was bothered by something important. When they got back into her car, she turned to him.

"Okay, spill it, D," she ordered.

He didn't bother asking what she was talking about. Not only did she know him about as well as anyone else in the world, but he *wanted* to tell her, and he had pretty much figured out what he was going to say.

"I was attacked Friday night in WeHo on my way to meet Joseph for dancing," he said.

"Holy shitballs, are you serious? Like *in* West Hollywood?" When David nodded, she asked, "Are you okay? Were you hurt?"

"Just a little, that's what the Band-Aid is for." He pointed at the large bandage on his neck, which he'd put on to replace the larger dressing Joseph had supplied. He took a deep breath, exhaled, and went on. "It would have been worse, but Joseph saved me."

Dana's eyes went wide. "Oh. My. God. Like, literally *fought them off* saved you?" She had begun gesticulating with her hands; the information was too much to contain.

"Yeah," David said simply, looking forward and staring at the back of the car in front of them. It was decorated with the COEXIST bumper sticker. Each letter was a different religious symbol.

"David, that is fucking incredible! Did the police do anything?"

"I didn't go to the police." This is where the fibbing began. "It was dark, and I didn't see much. There's not much I'd be able to tell them." He paused. The next part was the trickiest bit. "I was out of it, so Joseph took me to his place..."

"Did he do something to you? David, did he ... force himself on you?" She had been about to say *rape*, he realized. This was not a line of thought he'd predicted, and he wasn't quite prepared for it. He automatically jumped to Joseph's defense.

"No! No no no, he took care of me! He... he was a complete gentleman. Made me soup and ginger ale." David averted his gaze from the outside world and looked down at the interior of the car, lost in thought.

Dana took a second to process. "Oh. That's a lot of horrible and wonderful all in the same story." She reached out to run her fingers through the hair on the back of his head, something she had started doing in college when they watched *Simpsons* in the common room. She knew he loved it. "David, are you okay?"

"Not really," he admitted. He drew in a longer, slower breath and let it out. This was the person he told everything to. This was the moment to say what he needed to say and get the friendly counsel he required. "The thing is, Joseph and I said we love each other. Well, we texted it. I mean, we basically texted it. Never mind. We said it. I do. He does."

"Okay, I get it." Dana put a stop to the rambling. "That's great, right? It's really fast, but it's good?"

"Yeah," David said with some reticence. "I don't really get it, but I'd kind of resigned myself to experiencing it. The thing is... the *really* hard thing I don't know how I'm going to handle..." He turned to look at Dana and concentrated on picking his words. "Joseph showed a side of himself Friday night that really scared me. A violent side. A dangerous one."

"Ahh," Dana said and grabbed his hands comfortingly. "I think I get it. But, like, he was violent protecting you, right?"

"Yeah." He waited for her point.

Dana spoke carefully, thoughtfully, "In the short time you've known him, has he given any indication that he would act that way towards you? I mean, *really* think about it. Has he ever yelled at a waiter, said something mean about someone driving another car, raised his voice to you, anything like that?"

David thought the metaphor was wearing a bit thin. He wasn't talking about abusive spouse violence. He was talking about a goddamned vampire. But he realized that Joseph had never indicated any kind of behavior that could be construed as meaning him harm.

"No."

"Okay." Dana concluded her point, though she seemed cognizant of the possibility that she was giving an opinion contrary to what David was wrestling with. "So, it seems to me like he is kind of a catch. He defended you physically by putting himself in harm's way. He sounds romantic as fuck." David had to chuckle every time he heard this pixie of a girl drop the f-bomb, and it broke him out of his downward spiral. "And he said he loved you. Or whatever you two weirdos said or texted each other. Yeah?"

David absolutely saw her point. "Yeah, but there are some things about him I found out, stuff he can't really help, I guess, but they worry me."

"Like what?"

"I can't tell you," he told her. "I'm sorry."

"Well, I can't help you with any of that, then." She put a hand on his leg. "But I will stay with you all day and all night until I have to go to work, and then I'll cover for you for as long as you need. Okay?"

He smiled genuinely for the first time in what felt like weeks. "Thank you. How do I deserve you?"

"You don't. I'm insane for spending so much time with a man who will never please me physically." She leaned forward. "Come. Give us hugs."

The rest of Sunday was spent binge-watching TV shows and eating a shocking amount of junk food. Between each episode, she would ask him,

"Need to talk?" to which he would decline. By midnight, they were both passed out on the couch again. This time they'd had the foresight to grab a blue queen-size fleece blanket beforehand.

Monday morning Dana had checked in with him before leaving for work to see if he was going to be okay alone. He told her yes and was pretty sure it was the truth. He had made them both coffees, giving her his favorite Zojirushi insulated mug to take with her to work, and she promised to return it ASAP under penalty of death.

David sat on the couch sipping his coffee and had a sudden urge to go driving. He didn't have a destination, he just wanted to go. The only thing that dictated the direction was the traffic. Los Angeles traffic breathed like a living thing. In the morning, cars streamed towards the city center, and at the end of the workday, downtown exhaled, sending them back out to the suburbs from whence they came. Thus, in the morning, traffic was light heading north, so that's where David went.

He took the 101 freeway north, but as it veered west, he kept heading north on the 170, until it merged with the 5, which took him through the San Fernando Valley and past the LA Aqueduct Cascades, a man-made river of stairs that always caught David's eye. It was flowing heavily this close to the end of spring as winter runoff fed into the thirsty city.

From there, he passed by Valencia and Six Flags Magic Mountain. David loved theme parks, but only went to Magic Mountain on their yearly gay night in the fall. The tickets were cheaper, and the lines were nonexistent, so you could go on everything twice in just a few hours.

Some unknown guide told him to take the exit for Highway 126 a few minutes later. The smaller highway meandered into the southern foothills of the Santa Ana Mountains, until he reached a small town called Fillmore. The name rang a bell, but David had never been there, so he pulled off the highway to wander for a while.

Fillmore was a town out of place. It seemed like it came straight out of Iowa from the 1980s and transplanted itself to Southern California to chase its dreams. There was a railway station with brightly painted steam engines, and the quaint town square area was several decades behind the rest of the world. It even had a bandstand shaped like a large gazebo. David suspected the town was built or at least maintained by the movie studios; it was so perfectly out of time. Regardless, it was a cooling balm on his soul. He felt like if he walked into the drugstore, they might offer him a drink from the soda fountain, and would have no idea what a smartphone was.

He ate lunch at a local cafe, and the meal of homemade pot roast and broiled veggies was perfect midwestern: comforting, delicious, and reasonably priced. Afterwards, he wandered the rustic town for an hour before getting back into his car and continuing westward.

Soon, he reached the end of the smaller highway and rejoined the 101 freeway. He turned his little Honda onto the 101 south (which in reality headed almost due east), but when he saw the sign for the 1 freeway, the Pacific Coast Highway, he took it.

After a few minutes, the PCH passed the Point Magu Naval Air Station, and David saw the Pacific Ocean ahead and to the right. No matter how many times he saw it, the sight of the endless blue expanse always took his breath away. He frequently tried to imagine what it would have been like to be an explorer or native, hundreds of years ago, seeing the land fall away into the infinite field of water. The feeling must've been overwhelming, considering how powerful it was for him, when he'd seen it a hundred times before.

The PCH followed closely along the coastal cliff, sometimes so close the shoulder was nonexistent, just a ledge falling straight into the placid sea. When he approached beachy areas, David realized what he wanted. After the long weekend, after all the introspection and wandering and talking with Dana, the endless ocean somehow made everything clear.

At the turnoff for El Matador Beach, he pulled into the parking lot and found a spot pointed straight into the ocean. The parking lot was on a bluff above a long wooden staircase that led down to the beach, so from up here, in the car, it almost looked like he was flying over the water. He pulled his phone off the car mount and pulled up Joseph's number.

He sat there, looking at the small screen for five minutes.

Finally, he tapped the number. He expected to leave a message since the sun had not yet dipped into the waves, but the call connected, and he heard Joseph's voice.

"David? Are you okay?" For a moment David's breath caught in his throat, and his chest tightened.

"Hi, Joseph, yeah," he said finally. "I didn't expect you to be ... up. You know, since it's still daytime."

Joseph's voice softened. "I can be awake in the daytime. My house blocks all the sunlight." It was the first time he hadn't hesitated when discussing an aspect of his vampire nature.

"Oh." David wasn't sure exactly how he wanted to say what he wanted to say, but he knew he didn't want to do it over the phone. "I'd like to talk. Can I see you?"

"Of course," Joseph said, the surprise apparent in his voice. "Do you want to meet somewhere, or...?" He left the question open-ended so David wouldn't feel pressured in any way.

"I'll come to your place. I'm out on the PCH right now; I'm not sure how long it'll take. It's getting to be rush hour," David said. His voice didn't betray his intention.

"Okay," Joseph said cautiously. "I'll text you the address."

"Thanks. See you soon." David ended the call and waited for the text. Joseph's message with the address came through moments later, and David noted that he had followed the texting etiquette of not typing anything other than the address itself. He opened Waze and shared his trip with Joseph so he could see the estimated time of arrival.

David looked out at the ocean one more time as the sun ignited the horizon with oranges and reds, then pulled back out of the parking lot and onto the PCH.

The sun set before David arrived at Joseph's house. He pulled into the driveway and for the first time really saw the impressive edifice. The house wasn't lit up like its neighbors with intricately-designed landscape illumination, but there were simple security lights, the moon was half-full, and it never really got *all the way* dark at night in LA. Joseph's home looked like a modern castle. Built from large stone blocks, with slim slits for windows that weren't even wide enough to fit through. David thought it might be able to withstand a nuclear blast, it looked so much like an aboveground bomb shelter. Then he saw Joseph waiting in the entryway just outside the front door.

David parked, turned off the ignition, and took a measured breath. He unbuckled his seatbelt and got out of the car, using every moment to internally confirm his decision. Looking at Joseph, standing patiently on the front step. Making eye contact, seeing his soft smile. Knowing the pointed weapons that smile hid, the dangers they entailed.

"Hi," he said, taking a few steps from the safety of the car. For a moment, David felt physically vulnerable out in the open, but when Joseph closed the gap between them, stopping only an arm's length away, the fear subsided rather than grew worse. It was the last piece of confirmation David needed.

"I love you," David said simply. "I don't know how I know that so surely already, but I do."

Joseph waited in case there was a *but*, but there wasn't one. He reached out with both hands to David, who took them. "I love you, too, David. And I feel the same way." The pair stood in the driveway, touching but not embracing, yet. They each had things they needed to say before they could move forward.

Joseph started. "Uh, so I rehearsed what I was going to say while I waited for you to get here, but I forgot how it was going to go."

The admission elicited a smile from David. Some five centuries old and this guy standing in front of him was still just a guy who got flustered sometimes. It was good to know.

"I'll just say, I promise that you know the worst thing about me. I can't help what I am. I can't change it. But I think the more you know, the ... better you'll like me? That sounded stupid." Joseph shook his head at his lack of vocabulary, which made David laugh.

"I get what you're trying to say," David said. "I really want to get to know you better. I can't say it's not weird, knowing what you are—"

"You're going to have to say it at some point," Joseph needled amiably.

"*Vampire*." David stressed the word.

"There you go."

"I thought about it a *lot* this weekend, and I realized I don't care. I love you, for whatever reason. I think I did pretty much right away, and everything you've done and said has only made me love you more. What kind of asshole would I be to hold something against you that you can't control?" The irony of what David was saying wasn't lost on either of them. David had experienced prejudice for being gay and had felt the pain of it. The understanding had helped shape his thinking about Joseph.

Joseph inched slowly closer to David. "I am *really* glad to hear you say that. I have missed you these last few days. I wanted so badly to call you to see if you were okay. I want you to be comfortable with this. So, as slow as you need me to be, I'm fine with th—"

David abruptly leaned forward and kissed Joseph hard on the lips, eliciting a surprised "mmph." They wrapped their arms together and made out in the driveway for five long minutes that felt like forever. When they finally parted to catch their breath, Joseph said, "Do you want to come in?"

"Desperately," David said, a sense of relief washing over his body.

As they got to the door and Joseph entered the code, he heard David's stomach rumble. "Are you hungry? I still have soup. And I recently found out I'm still pretty good at grilled cheese."

They moved into the house, the heavy oaken door closing heavily behind them, and David pushed Joseph up against the wall next to it. "Maybe after."

Joseph took half a second to figure out what *after* meant. "Oh! Okay—" he barely got out before his lips were covered by David's again.

They tore at each other's clothing as they moved clumsily to the stairs and down to the bedroom. A trail of shoes, shirts, pants, underwear, and socks recorded their path as they collapsed on the bed, writhing and grinding against each other.

They made love for the second time since they'd met, but this time there were more words. Each of them felt as if they were the lucky one to be here with the perfect man, and they no longer had to be coy about it. *I love you's* were breathlessly uttered as they assumed a variety of positions for over an hour. Each topped and bottomed for the other, and each was mildly amazed they had no clear preference for who got penetrated.

Afterwards, as they laid together, bodies curled together in a perfect fit, David was the little spoon, looking past the bed at a piece of art that hung on the wall, barely visible in the gloom created by the light from the bathroom. He was content to be wrapped in Joseph's arms and feel his breath on the back of his neck. It was warmer than normal breath. Finally, he said softly, "I have questions."

"I assumed you might," Joseph said, his voice gentle in David's ear. "I promise I will be completely honest with you if you promise to tell me how you genuinely feel along the way."

"I can do that," David said thoughtfully. He asked questions about Joseph's nature, and Joseph was honest and forthright, as guaranteed.

Joseph talked about his life before being turned, living in Bavaria under the rule of the Holy Roman Empire and the experience of being turned and mentored by a vampire who was born a thousand years before that. He assured David again that he hadn't fed on a human since he accidentally turned Alexander in the mid–seventeen hundreds. Joseph briefly described his diet of animals for many centuries until the practice of blood transfusion, and by extension blood donations, was created. Joseph got in early in the blood business, and thus Tetractys was born, and the vampire with a distaste for killing humans had a steady human blood supply.

David turned so he was face to face with Joseph. "What about all the stuff in movies? Garlic, crosses, that kind of thing. Oh my God, can you turn into a b—"

"No, I can't turn into a bat. Or a wolf or mist or anything other than what you see right now," Joseph snickered.

"Oh," David feigned disappointment. "So just a sexy guy with a body like a Greek statue, then. Fiiiine."

Joseph couldn't resist the urge to lean forward and give David a smooch. "As for the rest, yeah, I have an intense aversion to garlic…"

"Aww."

"…and I never understood the deal with crosses. It's just a thing, and religion is made up, so how they could possibly be harmful has always baffled me."

David clutched imaginary pearls. "Do *not* let my mom hear you say that."

"Oh, am I meeting your mother, then?" Joseph asked, raising an eyebrow.

"Ah, that might take awhile. I've only introduced one boyfriend to my parents, and it did not go well."

"Hmm," Joseph interjected. "So we're boyfriends, then? Officially?"

"What are you, in middle school?" David joked, then became earnest. "Look, I am not currently madly in love with anyone else, so I can say with some confidence that I want to be with you and only you for the foreseeable future."

The newly anointed couple stared into each other's eyes for a moment before coming together for another kiss, though neither of them could had said who initiated it.

Joseph squealed when they parted, doing his best imitation of a teenage girl, "Oh my God, I have a boyfriend!"

This made David hoot with laughter, and he had to turn his head away. When the giggling subsided, he said, "Okay, what else? Can you fly?"

Joseph sighed. It was actually a bit of a release to talk about this side of himself in a positive way. "No, I'm basically human. Think of vampires as a close cousin of homo sapiens. Like Neanderthals, we've lived side by side on Earth for hundreds of thousands of years. We just happen to still be around."

"So literally you just subsist on blood and hate the sun and garlic? That's it?" David said, unable to hide his disillusionment.

"Well, no," Joseph admitted. "There's also immortality. And we are generally stronger than humans and get stronger the older we get."

"Huh." David absorbed this.

"We also have heightened senses. Like, all of them." Joseph felt like he was bragging if he said anything more.

"Like what?"

"Well, like I can hear your stomach growling like a lawnmower," the vampire replied, poking David in the abs.

"Come on, really?"

Joseph grinned. "I can hear the blood flowing through your veins if I try."

"Well. Okay, that's a little creepy."

"Oh! No, I didn't mean it like that. I was just trying to say that something really quiet is something I can hear."

David grinned. "You are *adorable* when you're flustered, you know that?" Joseph slapped him playfully on the chest. "But now that you mention it, it's been a while since I ate, and my *boyfriend* gave me kind of a workout, so…"

With another kiss, Joseph slipped out of the bed, pulled on a pair of lounge pants, and grabbed a robe for David. As they made their way to the kitchen, decisions were made about what soup to heat up (creamy tomato bisque) and whether to make grilled cheese (hell, yes). David slid onto a kitchen stool where he could watch Joseph cook and they could keep talking.

"It should be said, you look fucking hot, Mr. Shirtless Chef."

"Why thank you, my dear," Joseph replied, bowing slightly for his robed audience.

David folded his hands while he watched Joseph move smoothly from the stove to the cupboard and back. There was something nagging at him that felt more awkward than the other vampire topics they'd already broached.

"So…" he started tentatively, "I think I experienced another one of your skills Friday night." Joseph set the soup on low and turned to give David his attention. He didn't speak, just waited, one eyebrow raised slightly. "When… what's his name, Alexander?" Joseph nodded. "He did something to me where I couldn't move. Like, I forgot how. My body felt like it was encased in carbonite or something."

Joseph nodded knowingly. "Yeah. First, I love that you know that reference, and we're going to come back to that. But yes, we have an ability to hypnotize prey, in a way. To project our will on them, kind of?"

"It helps with the hunting?" David offered.

"Yeah."

"I have to ask. Have you ever—?"

"No," Joseph assured. "Never with you, I swear."

"Okay. I believe you," David smiled.

Joseph shrugged slightly. "That being said, there are uses for that particular skill that aren't related to hunting…"

"Oh?" David said, intrigued.

"Mmhmm." Joseph took a few steps and leaned over, his elbows on the counter opposite David. "Uses that greatly enhance lovemaking."

"I am officially intrigued, but let's take baby steps, okay?"

Joseph placed his hand on David's. "Absolutely. Never without your permission, my love."

David shook his shoulders. "Oooh, *my love*… I like that."

Joseph straightened and returned to the soup preparation. "Anything else?" he asked, inviting more questions about his vampire disposition.

David was aware of the challenge Joseph was dealing with, being so open about himself and wanted to help by asking questions. "Do you have a reflection?"

Joseph chuckled wryly. "The history of that particular vampire myth is interesting, but yes. We don't actually do anything that defies physics."

David nodded. Then something occurred to him. "Are you going to eat with me?"

Joseph paused stirring the creamy red soup but didn't turn around. He just looked at the pot, which was starting to steam. "You mean...?"

"You must be hungry, too."

"Are you sure?" He turned his head to the side and spoke over his shoulder. "I mean, that you want to see that?"

"I've thought it through, babe," David spoke assuredly. "I mean, we've exchanged bodily fluids. Aaaaand I've eaten a rare steak before. It's not that big of a leap when it really comes down to it."

Joseph shook his shoulders the way David had. "Oooh, *babe*... I like that." He smirked at the man he was finding it so easy to love. Their banter was so effortless and natural. Every moment he felt he was falling more and more for this gorgeous hunk sitting there in his robe. "Yeah, okay, I'll eat with you."

While Joseph finished making the grilled cheese and soup, he answered questions about his long past. More detail about his life before being turned and about his travels around the world after. He gave David the broad strokes about his long relationship with Connor, which took enough time for the food to be ready. He set down the crispy browned sandwich and the bowl of soup in front of David. He went to the fridge and removed one of Rafaél's ginger ales, which he gave to David, and a bag of blood, which he put in the microwave to warm.

David watched curiously and then asked, "Um, I don't know if this is impolite, but—" he gestured around, indicating the house, everything in it, and its location "—just how rich are you?"

Joseph leaned on the counter in front of the microwave. "Well, I don't *want* to be coy, but I'm going to be. For now. A little." He smiled and David smiled back, accepting this limit to the sharing. "Let me just say, we'll be able to go on some amazing dates, and you'll never have to pay for a thing. Okay?"

"I can live with that, I guess," David said, basking in what he felt was his good fortune.

"Good," Joseph nodded. "I've lived a fairly isolated life. I don't tend to open myself up all that often. But I do love to share what I have with those I love." He pointed a finger at David and waggled it around playfully.

The microwave beeped, and Joseph grabbed the approximately body temperature blood. He pulled a stool around to the opposite side of the counter so that he and David could look at each other. David had already eaten some of the tomato soup but had waited to start the sandwich. Now that they were both seated, David lifted half of the grilled cheese (*sliced diagonally, perfect*, he thought) and Joseph raised the plastic bag of red fluid. David went first, biting off a corner while maintaining eye contact with Joseph. Then Joseph, hesitantly, extended his fangs and bit into the bag, drinking his dinner.

Joseph was expecting David to be repulsed and disgusted, throw down his sandwich and dash to the bedroom, grab his clothes and race out into the night. Instead, he smiled around his mouthful of cheese and bread, and without swallowing, took another, bigger bite. Just to be equally as awkward.

Joseph pinched off the holes made by his fangs and looked adoringly at David. "I love you."

David chewed his extra-large mouthful of food. "I know." He winked.

"Oh, we are definitely going to get along," Joseph said, returning to his dinner.

Joseph finished his liquid dinner before David was done with his meal and took the opportunity to ask his own questions about his new beau. David told him of his parents, who were still married in Colorado, but as staunch Republicans, he had drifted apart from them in recent years. David had a brother who was two years younger. Kyle worked as an architect in Denver and tried to bridge the growing gap between David and his parents. They spoke politely on the phone to their eldest son but knew better than to ask him about the details of his life, which they generally disapproved of.

David was a dog person. Joseph was indifferent but generally enjoyed canine company.

They glossed over their pop culture likes and dislikes, though it was clear Joseph's tastes veered more to classical forms of entertainment—opera, concerts, live theater—while David was enamored with film and television and had little experience with classical music. Joseph casually mentioned that he'd met Johann Sebastian Bach, and David countered by saying he worked on a show with Lucy Hale. Joseph said he'd never heard of him and David sprayed chunks of grilled cheese over half the countertop.

Joseph was getting a supply of paper towels when David finally voiced a question he'd wanted to ask. "Okay... I have a serious one."

"Yeah?" Joseph wetted the paper towels and began wiping the counter.

"Let's say we still love each other next week..."

"Lofty goals, Romeo."

"Who's that?" David joked, unable to resist the callback.

Joseph picked up a tiny bit of half-chewed bread and threw it at David. "Ha ha."

"Okay, seriously. Let's say we still love each other next month, and next year..."

"Mmhmm?" Joseph had an idea where this was going but didn't want to lead him, just in case.

"...and ten years from now. *Just hypothetically,*" David stressed the purely theoretical nature of the question.

Joseph played. "Wow, planning our future already?"

"That's just it. You won't die, right? You don't get old?" David put his spoon down in the mostly eaten bowl of soup and pushed it away gently.

Joseph seemed intent on the counter, focused on cleaning. After a moment, he confirmed, "No."

"But I would just ... grow old and die."

"Like a normal human," Joseph pointed out.

"Would you ever consider turning me? I mean, assuming we loved each other enough? So we could be together forever?"

Joseph looked up at David, a mix of adoration and sorrow on his face. He set the soiled paper towel aside and sat back down across the counter. "I can't," he said.

"But you said you made a vampire before."

"Yeah." Joseph finally made eye contact again and took a slow breath. "Okay, first of all, it's not that I wouldn't want to. The fact is, we can't change people at will." David looked puzzled but curious and said nothing to interrupt. Joseph went on, "We call it Decimus. It's thought of as something of a curse among my kind. When we try to turn a human, it's only successful about one out of ten times. It works kind of like it does in the movies; a drained human must drink vampire blood. But ninety percent of the time ... they just die."

David saw something behind Joseph's eyes. "How many times have you been in love?" he asked.

Sadness swept across Joseph's features like a thin cloud. "Three. Which is how I know what I feel for you is real."

David smiled softy but got to the point of the topic. "Have you tried to turn someone you loved?"

Joseph regained his composure. This was something he had dealt with centuries ago. "Yes. My first. His name was Marcus. He was a soldier who fought in the Thirty Years' War. Do you know it?" David shook his head, and Joseph continued. "It was... well, it was pretty horrible. Over half of Germany died as a result of fighting or starvation. Wars were sort of a common occurrence in Europe in those days."

Joseph shook himself out of his slight reverie. "Anyway, Marcus and I met and fell in love, and I tried to live as normal a life as I could. It seems surprising how long I was able to hide it from him; eventually he found out, but wasn't frightened of me."

David was unconsciously touching his lips as he listened. "That's surprising because you're really quite terrifying," he commented dryly. Joseph stopped his story and looked at David, who had a deadpan expression on his face. Until it broke with a smirk as he waggled a finger at Joseph's head. "Like in the face area especially. Super scary."

Joseph smiled. "Quiet, you. Want another ginger ale?"

David shook his head slightly. "Keep going. I'm sorry I interrupted."

Joseph found he hadn't minded a bit. "Okay, so, after about six years together, enjoying the new European peace, he asked me to turn him."

"Did you know about the odds?" David asked.

"The vampire who made me told me, but I didn't believe him, I guess. I thought love was more powerful than nature. Marcus died in my arms."

"I'm so sorry," David sympathized, and reached out a hand, which Joseph took.

"It was centuries ago, but thank you." Joseph brought David's fingers to his lips and kissed them.

"That's why you were with Connor so long?"

"Good memory. Yeah." Joseph softly caressed David's hand with his thumb. He could see David was working it out in his head. Problem-solving.

"You said you were in love three times. There's Marcus, six years, and Connor, a lifetime..."

Joseph sighed. This was the last of it. Their secret spill completed after less than a week. "The third was Robert. We were together for seven years, and he died tragically in 1982."

"Wow," David said simply. It was a lot to process on top of everything else.

Joseph didn't elaborate on Robert's death. How he had been the victim of a hate crime and beaten to within an inch of his life in the middle of Pan Pacific Park. How, in the middle of a torrential rainstorm, Joseph had been desperate to try to save him and did the only thing he could think of; he tried to turn him. He drank the blood of the man he loved while Robert lay in agony in the cold rain, and then he bit his own wrist to feed him his lifeblood. It hadn't worked and Joseph had been lonely ever since.

Until a week ago when he walked into a club and ran smack into the man whose beautifully light brown eyes he was staring into right now.

Joseph squeezed David's hands, and they both said, "I love you," simultaneously, before cracking up.

The couple made love twice more before David finally fell asleep. He made no move to leave or indicate that he needed to go home, so Joseph lay with him until he was sound asleep, then got up, took a look at emails that had piled up over the weekend, and looked into a couple of potential surprises for David.

Before the sun came up, he crawled back into bed and snuggled up behind his man, who was on his side hugging a pillow. The house was designed to not let any direct sunlight in. All the windows were narrow, the walls were thick, and the glass was heavily UV fortified. But the bedroom was actually built *into* the hill. It had no windows at all, so there was no cue of daylight to wake David up. The weekend had been so taxing emotionally that he slept until noon.

When he roused, Joseph woke with him. On explaining again that he could indeed be awake in the daytime, as long as he was out of the sun, the new couple showered together, where they had sex again, and then set about planning for the day. Joseph had had groceries delivered in unnecessary quantities, wanting to make sure there was something David would like to eat. They shared a breakfast: blood for one and blueberry oatmeal with coffee for the other.

David checked in with Dana at work and told her everything was as good as it could be, recapped the highlights, and told her he was going to be out of work for a couple of days. She assured him she'd cover, and since production wasn't ramping up for another week, it was no problem.

The boys retired to the bedroom at 2:00 PM, naked and frisky. They tried a position they hadn't done yet, starting with a sixty-nine and transitioning to a mutual rimming, then back to simultaneous blowjobs. After they'd cum in each other's mouths, they snuggled on the bed, David cradling another cup of coffee and Joseph with herbal tea.

"Want to watch a movie?" Joseph asked.

"Sure," David replied contentedly. "Do we have to go upstairs, or do you have a screening room in this place somewhere?"

Joseph chuckled and grabbed his iPhone from the bedside charger. "Close your eyes."

David did as he was told, and Joseph opened the app on his phone to control the six-foot television that was embedded into the wall opposite the bed. It was so big that it looked by all appearances like a huge tapestry. The blacks were so black and the pixels so dense, unless David got up right next to it, he wouldn't be able to tell the surface wasn't real.

Joseph pulled up a comprehensive library of movies and started one. He skipped the iconic studio logo and said, "Okay. Open sesame."

David grinned as he opened his eyes, just as STAR WARS appeared on the screen. The accompanying John Williams fanfare filled the room in surround sound. He laughed and clapped his hands in appreciation of the choice. "Jesus, that's big!"

"That's what *he* said," Joseph quipped. "Want popcorn?"

"Nah, I'm good. This is perfect," David said, and snuggled up to watch the rebels take on the Empire.

After Luke blew up the Death Star, David rolled onto his stomach. "Can you scratch my back for me? Not like I have an itch, but like long and slow?"

Joseph knew exactly what he was asking for. He had trained with practitioners of Eastern medicine some time ago and was familiar with the relaxing pleasure that could be derived from therapeutic touch. He reached over with one hand and as Luke and Han got their medals (*not Chewie, though, those rebel racists*) lightly ran his fingers up and down David's back. Joseph knew the optimum speed for stroking human skin was three centimeters per second, and he was very good at it. Sometimes, he used all his fingers, or just a couple, sometimes with his nails, sometimes with the fingertips.

David moaned softly. "Mmm, that feels so good. I was worried you wouldn't know how to do this..."

"If there is anything I do that you don't like, or something you want me to do that I'm not, I want you to tell me, okay?" Joseph whispered.

David turned his head to look up at his new boyfriend. "Okay. You, too."

"I will." The movie ended, and they let the brilliant score play while Joseph found a handful of freckles scattered across David's back. He traced them like a connect-the-dots puzzle. They made no particular shape, but David noticed the change.

"Draw a message and see if I can guess it," he suggested.

"Mmkay." Joseph went with the first thing that popped into his head.

David said the letters as they were traced on his back. "I ... L ... O ... V ..." He laughed. "I know what this is." He rolled over and sat up to kiss Joseph. "I love you, too."

Joseph stroked David's arms as he settled in next to him. He let his fingers barely trace the hairs on David's arms, tickling him from his knuckles up to his shoulders.

"Here's a question," Joseph began casually. "If you could, would you rather go on a road trip to Santa Fe in an RV or visit Paris?"

"Ooh, boy, those both sound fun for different reasons. I'm an adventurer, so road trips are always fun. But I have always wanted to see Paris. Have you ever been?"

Joseph chuckled lightly. "I used to live there. I've been most places in the world. I also love exploring," he shared.

"We should go someday," David said dreamily, snuggling up against Joseph's toned, warm body.

"I was hoping you'd say that. We have reservations for dinner tomorrow night at the Eiffel Tower."

David blinked a couple of times, then sat up. "What?"

"Dinner. Tomorrow." Joseph said it as if it were the most regular thing in the world.

David was confused. "At a French restaurant?"

"Oh, yes. Very French." Joseph enjoyed watching David take this mental journey.

"... Called the Eiffel Tower?"

"Actually, the restaurant is called the Jules Verne," he corrected. "It's just *in* the Eiffel Tower."

David looked away from Joseph as he reviewed the last several sentences of the conversation, then made quizzical eye contact again. "I'm sorry, what?"

Joseph didn't want to torture the boy. He gently placed his hands on both sides of David's face and spoke slowly. "We are flying to Paris tomorrow for dinner. I made us reservations at *Le Jules Verne*, which is a restaurant in the Eiffel Tower." He couldn't help but smirk. This was romantic as hell.

"There's a restaurant in the Eiffel Tower?"

"Two of them," said Joseph. "Plus a champagne bar on the third floor."

David squinted his eyes, scrutinizing the other man. "Are you showing off to me?"

Joseph's smirk turned into a full grin. "A little. You like it?"

David returned the grin. "A little." Then the realization of the news hit him and he squealed. "Oh my God, we're going to *Paris*!" He bounced a little on the bed and straddled Joseph's legs, kissing him passionately.

"I'm glad you're excited," Joseph smiled when they parted. "Do you have a passport?"

After ordering delivery for dinner and then fucking, showering, and fucking again, they arrived at the Burbank airport after midnight. Their Lyft swung by David's apartment so he could pick up essentials, including his passport and some nice clothes. Joseph had offered to take him shopping on the *Champs-Elysées*, but David demurred while promising that they could do that on the next trip when Joseph asked.

The plane was a private Gulfstream G450, and as they boarded, David could barely contain his amazement. The main cabin split into three separate living areas with a dozen seats, including a full-size couch. There was a credenza, two bathrooms, and a shower. Several of the chairs reclined flat, and the couch pulled out into a bed. Panoramic windows featured UV-blocking materials and blackout shades.

Joseph explained that the plane technically belonged to the company. He wrestled with the ostentatiousness of it over the years, but it had been Rafaél who insisted on purchasing it about fifteen years ago since Joseph couldn't very well fly commercial with his special environmental and dietary needs.

David had barely flown anywhere in his life, and when he had, it had been the cheapest ticket possible. He had never traveled pre-9/11, so the idea of just driving up to the plane right on the tarmac and getting in without having to go through the indignity of a TSA screening, or throw away his coffee or a shampoo bottle that was bigger than three ounces...

"This is incredible. Thank you," he said as they cuddled on two plush seats, and the jet took off into the dark sky.

"This is just the plane ride," Joseph said, gazing lovingly into David's eyes. "You're going to love Paris."

"You know, I already said I love you. You don't need to impress me," David teased.

"Eh, we'll see," Joseph replied. The jet leveled off after a steep initial climb. It was still rising at a shallow angle and would until they reached their cruising altitude of forty-one thousand feet.

The couple were lost in each other's eyes when Joseph absently said, "You know, in Hebrew, David means beloved."

David got a bemused look on his face. "I did ... not know that."

"Mmhmm. It's a good name," Joseph continued. "David was the second and greatest of the kings of Israel, ruling in the tenth century BCE."

"You're going to tell me you met him, right?" David teased.

"I'm not that old!" Joseph said, giving David a playful poke. "Several stories about him are told in the Old Testament, including his defeat of Goliath. According to the New Testament, Jesus was descended from King David."

"I did know about Goliath, actually," David said, laying his head on Joseph's shoulder. "I went to Sunday school for a hot second before I rebelled."

"A wise man I once knew once said, 'Give your children religion because it will give them something to rebel against other than their parents.' What's funny is that he was a minister." Joseph chuckled at the memory.

"Well, joke's on my parents, I rebelled against them, too."

Joseph turned his head towards David's. "You know, I really respect that about you. It's hard for children to grow past their parents' beliefs sometimes."

"Eh," David muttered as his only explanation. After a moment, he asked, "What does Joseph mean?"

"Oh, it's dumb," he replied. "Another bible name, but this was just a guy with a colorful jacket."

David poked him in the ribs. "But he got a musical written about his life."

"Actually, so did King David, written by Alan Menkin and Tim Rice of all people," Joseph pointed out.

"*The Lion King* guys?" David said, surprised he'd never heard of it.

"Well, Rice was *Lion King*, Menken was *Little Mermaid*." Joseph tilted his head up, thinking. "I think they might have worked together on *Aladdin*?"

"Crazy," David said. "I have to see it now."

Joseph laughed. "No, you really don't. *King David, the musical* lasted something like nine performances."

"Oh."

"The cast album isn't bad, if I remember. They cut a lot of the boring stuff."

David didn't bother to reply. He felt no need to fill quiet moments with chatter, and was perfectly content to just be here, flying across the country, and soon the Atlantic Ocean with this man, this vampire, with whom he'd impossibly fallen in love. One thing did cross his mind, however. "Are there flight attendants on the plane?"

Joseph shook his head. "No, you can grab anything you want, the galley is pretty well stocked." He lowered his voice conspiratorially. "Besides, there's things I want to do to you on this aircraft that I don't want anyone to see..."

They made love and slept on the flight, alternatingly. Upon their arrival at Charles De Gaul airport in Paris, the pair was reasonably well-rested and had made use of the shower and bathroom facilities to freshen up for dinner. The jet taxied for several minutes into a hanger since it was still daylight. They transferred into a private SUV fitted with darkly tinted windows which appeared almost black looking in, but David found he was able to see out through them. He observed a bit of the French countryside which gave way to the populated outskirts of Paris.

David was struck by something almost immediately. "Hey, we're driving on the right side."

"Yeah?" Joseph replied. The *So?* was implied.

"I thought they all drove on the other side of the road in Europe," David said quizzically.

"Oh, that's just England, and the countries they colonized. India, Australia, parts of Africa..." He furrowed his brow. "And Japan, oddly enough, but I can't explain that one."

"Huh. Well, that's cool," David enthused. "Points for France!"

By the time they arrived at the Eiffel Tower, the sun had set, and the edifice was lit up like a glittering Christmas tree, twinkling in the middle of the city. David opted for the romance of climbing the wrought iron stairs to the second floor and the fancier of the two restaurants. Joseph warned David that it meant a six-hundred-step climb, but he insisted, saying no one told stories of taking an elevator to the top of anything. Unlike American buildings where the first floor was at ground level, the first floor of the Eiffel Tower was itself a climb of three hundred stairs and one hundred eighty-seven feet, with the second floor being twice as high.

When they reached the second level, they were shown to their table overlooking *Le Champ du Mars*, a huge green park space spreading out before them, the whole of Paris laid out beyond. David downed his complimentary water immediately, having exerted himself more than his extra-human companion.

Dinner was exquisite. The lovers were served a seven-course meal with different wine pairings for each menu item. Joseph sipped on the wines and poked around his plate so it would at least appear that he ate. He would smell a forkful of lamb or of lobster to experience each ingredient as much as he could, but then set it back down. After the dessert of warm chocolate soufflé and espresso, the men decided to go to the top of the tower, as long as they were there. They laughed together when they were told that they had to take the elevator, much to the confusion of the maître d'.

After a spectacular ride in the glass-walled elevator, they emerged on the third level to see Paris laid out below them. The noise of the city barely reached up here, and Joseph could hear David's heart racing.

"Are you scared of heights?" he asked, wrapping David in his arms as they looked across the Seine River at the *Arc de Triomphe* a mile away.

"I have a healthy fear of falling to my death from a great height," David replied jovially, though he could not tear his eyes from the view.

Joseph noticed and felt a welling of affection for this man. Fear didn't dissuade him from experiencing something new. "When it was built, the tower was the highest thing in the world," he said absently. He wasn't showing off his knowledge or anything, just sharing a thing. If he'd been showing off, he would have said he helped finance the building that would replace it, the Chrysler Building in New York.

"We are two hundred and seventy-six meters up in the sky." David turned his head and gave Joseph a kiss. "That kiss was two hundred and seventy-eight meters high," he grinned.

"You're a nerd, and I love you for it," Joseph sighed. He initiated his own kiss, which lasted longer than the first, and they turned and wrapped their arms around each other.

The kiss lasted several moments, until they heard an old woman say, "Ah, le jeune amour!" *Young love!*

If she only knew how not young one of us is, thought Joseph, but replied in French, "J'espère seulement que nous sommes si amoureux quand nous avons votre âge, ma chérie." *I only hope we are so in love when we are your age, my darling.*

The old woman giggled, waved a gloved hand at them, and walked away blushing. David pulled Joseph's chin toward him. Looking into his eyes with a charmed smile, he only shook his head with amazement.

"Well, I told you I lived in France," Joseph said. "Say, there's a champagne bar up here. We could share a toast as we look over the city, if you think you have room for a glass."

"I will make room, yes, please," David replied enthusiastically. He'd already had more food and alcohol this evening than any time since college, but the wine was giving him the perfect buzz and made him especially susceptible to romantic suggestions.

They made their way to the opposite side of the platform where large red letters announced the champagne bar. "Would you like white or rosé, boyfriend?" Joseph inquired with a wink.

"Uh, pink champagne on top of the Eiffel Tower? Yeah, I think I am exactly that much gay," David laughed, and Joseph went to retrieve a glass for each of them. When he returned, David was looking out over downtown Paris, lost in the wonder that they were even here and together. The champagne flutes were illuminated so that the bubbles glowed and danced in the liquid. They clinked glasses and looked into each other's eyes as they sipped. The effervescence tickled David's nose and made him giggle. They turned back to the city view and stood arm in arm as the rest of the world momentarily fell away. The cool night breeze ruffled their hair and made David pull Joseph closer into a sideways embrace. They leaned their heads together. "This is amazing," David said quietly. "Thank you."

"Thank *you* for sharing it with me," Joseph replied. "It's been a long time since I've been this happy. I hope it's the first of many amazing dates."

David replied simply by giving his new love a squeeze. Joseph gave two squeezes in response.

The flight home was similar to the flight to France, though it involved more sleeping. Both men were exhausted from the trip, the food, the stair climbing. Before they retired, David had insisted on seeing if all those stairs had made Joseph's ass look any different. Once pants and underwear had been removed, he had determined a closer inspection was warranted: first by tongue, then by finger, and finally by his hard tool.

After, Joseph ate dinner from a supply of blood he'd brought aboard while David looked on. David wanted to show that he was comfortable with it, even if he wasn't *totally and completely* comfortable with it. Joseph could tell he was making an effort and was grateful for it.

They flew with the direction of the sun on the way home, so it was dark the entire way. The flight to France had taken nearly twenty-one hours including the time zone change, but they arrived in LA only three hours after they left Paris. They were back in their plush chairs as they touched down. They each took their phones off airplane mode and waited for them to connect to the cell networks.

"I'm not at all ashamed to say I don't even know what day it is," David said, laughing. "Time zones mess me *up*." His phone buzzed with a text from Dana, checking in. He tapped into the messaging app to reply.

Joseph's phone began a steady series of buzzes as dozens of missed texts, calls, and emails came flooding in.

"Babe, do you get messed up by time zones?" David asked, still typing his reply to Dana. "Like, do you have some sort of innate sense of where the sun is, or do you just travel enough to—"

"Oh, fuck," Joseph said.

David looked over. Joseph was poring through messages on his phone. On any other person, David might have described his expression as vexed, but he knew Joseph well enough to know it was downright panic.

Joseph unbuckled his seatbelt and rose as the jet taxied to a stop near a waiting SUV. David followed suit, unsure if physical closeness was appropriate for the moment. "Joseph? What's wrong?"

Joseph was pacing like a trapped tiger, waiting for the plane to stop. He paused suddenly and looked at David. It was as if he'd completely forgotten he was on the airplane. He went to him and took his face gently in his hands to reassure him. "David, I'm so sorry. I have to go. It's an emergency. I'll have the pilot call you another ride to take you to the house so you can get your car."

David grew instantly concerned. "You're not going home? It'll be morning in a couple of hours." He held up his phone, showing the current time.

"I'll be okay," Joseph assured him as the jet slowed to a stop. Joseph stooped to look out the window and make sure they were near the car. Then, without even a kiss goodbye, he went to the door and opened it himself, leaping down the steps to the runway and sprinting to the SUV, circling his finger in the air to signify that they needed to leave immediately.

He didn't see David looking after him as the vehicle sped away. Joseph's attention was on his phone as he took in the information that was sent to him from a dozen different sources.

Those sources were telling him that approximately eight hours ago, just after sunset, the Tetractys Medical Research building had been destroyed.

Initial reports suggested a bomb. A handful of people were inside the building after hours.

One of them was Rafaél.

CHAPTER 13

Joseph tried calling Rafi's phone. It went straight to voicemail. *Don't be stupid, of course it did, the phone was destroyed along with him*, his mind shot back.

The messages on Joseph's phone were mostly automated alerts about the Tetractys tragedy. It was all over the news and coming in from dozens of different outlets. Rafi had done a very good job of insulating Joseph from the day-to-day operations of the business. Very few people had his private number. There were a dozen or so texts and calls from his personal assistant, Brandy, who Rafi had hired just in case Joseph ever needed anything (she had set up the Paris trip and made all the necessary reservations. She'd also had to reserve and cancel the RV and hotels in Santa Fe in case David had chosen the road trip). Brandy didn't usually contact Joseph directly, but she was being inundated with calls from the press and the police and the FBI and didn't know what to do. She had initially tried and failed to contact Mr. Loya (*It failed because he's dead*, Joseph's mind shouted) because she knew Joseph was in Paris, but then the police had informed her that Rafaél Loya was one of the victims of the explosion and she really didn't know what to do or who she should talk to and could he please, please call her back?

Joseph gave the driver a new address and moments later the car pulled a U-turn on Burbank Boulevard to head east for the 5 freeway. He thought for a moment. He didn't want to engage with police, that was a bad idea. And certainly not the FBI, that was an extraordinarily bad idea. He made a call to the Tetractys' chief of corporate security. He instructed him to get Brandy into protective custody and give her a lawyer, and told him to oversee interaction with the authorities, while coordinating with the company's legal team. That should keep everyone busy for at least a few days.

Joseph had business to attend to.

The apartment door of former Uber driver Bahir Ismat burst inward, tearing off the top hinge. Inside, the air was musty and dark.

"*Alexander!*" Joseph roared as he strode inside, moving assuredly and with the confidence of rage. He had tracked Alexander and Roxana after their attack on David, but at the time decided not to confront them here in case he needed to find them again. He didn't want to frighten them from their roost. He assumed he currently had the element of surprise. He was wrong.

Roxana struck the back of Joseph's knee with a fluid kick and followed through with a gripping strike to the back of the neck. She would have had him face down on the floor if his own martial arts training didn't have him instantly move with the momentum of the blow, tucking into a forward roll faster than she could follow. He dove forward, pushing off his good leg, and crashed through an old wooden coffee table. Despite the obstruction, he carried the roll to his feet and spun back around to face his attacker.

Foolish, he chided himself. Now he was in an enclosed space with two opponents, and he only knew where one of them was.

Except he didn't even know that. He should have been able to see Roxana in the light spilling in from the hallway and knew it was her that struck him. The strength of her blow, the sound of her exhale, and, of course, her smell. When her attack failed to incapacitate him, she'd moved quickly and disappeared.

Joseph fixated on his senses. His irises opened to allow more light than a normal human eye and had greater dynamic range, capable of seeing into the infrared and ultraviolet spectrums. His hearing focused on the room, creating an auditory 3-D map of anything that made the slightest bit of sound. His nose was his best tool. He could *see* odors. Recent smells looked like trails of color to his olfactory cortex, while older scents dissipated and mingled together to create a general smell for any given place.

The man whose apartment they stole was of similar Middle Eastern descent, but he saw Roxana's trail and within half a second located her in the room. She blended in, olfactorily speaking. Alexander, on the other hand, stood out like a sore thumb. Whatever things this woman had taught him over the centuries, an abundance of stealth was not one of them.

"Why?" Joseph demanded when it was clear they weren't immediately going to attack him.

"We considered your proposal, *Father*, and we're afraid we will have to decline the offer," Alexander replied.

The use of the word *father* made Joseph's blood boil. Images of Rafaél flashed through his mind. Rafaél as a boy, alone and scared, living in a cardboard box. Rafaél graduating high school as valedictorian. Rafaél making Thanksgiving dinner that only he and Robert would eat. Rafaél at his kitchen counter only days ago.

"Don't you dare call me that," Joseph spat. "I had a son. You are not him."

Alexander feigned surprise with a melodramatic hand to his heart. "Oh my, are you telling me there were *people* in that building?"

"So you admit it? You blew up my lab?" Joseph said, somewhat shocked. In the world he had occupied for the last hundred years, one did not simply admit to casual terrorism.

"Why not?" Roxana commented. "What will you do, Bavarian? Will you tell the human authorities that your vampire progeny destroyed the blood bank you used to feed yourself?"

"Why, then?" Joseph demanded. "Why did you do it?"

"*Why?*" Alexander hurled back. "You attacked us, threatened us, *demeaned us for a human!*"

Joseph's eyes glowed with pain and rage as he stepped towards the younger vampire. "My son was in that building. You *killed* him."

"*I am your son!*" Alexander screamed with the fury of two hundred years of pent-up resentment. "You made me! You brought me into this new life and then you abandoned me. I might have died if not for Roxana."

"You were an abomination, and if death is what you seek, I shall give it to you," Joseph growled.

"No, Bavarian, you will not," Roxana interjected. "You had the upper hand one time, but we are at full strength now. You could not possibly win against us."

Joseph's eyes narrowed threateningly as he shifted his attention to the older and more powerful female vampire. Roxana was one of the most ruthless vampires on the planet. Joseph knew it was part of what drew Alexander to her. Their wanton passion for killing and mutual certainty of human inferiority made them a perfect couple. In a way, Joseph was jealous of their love. It was, if nothing else, true. "I offered you wealth. I offered to take care of you."

"You offered us *half*," she responded coolly. "We want all of it."

"And you'll destroy me to get it, I suppose?" Joseph sneered.

"No, no, no, you child. You are important to what you have built. We know that." Roxana took one slow step forward to demonstrate her lack of fear. "But we will destroy everyone and everything you love."

Alexander glided forward to join Roxana. "The truth is, we didn't know your human pet was in the building." Joseph bristled at the insult to Rafi but made no move. Alexander continued, "We only meant to cut off your food supply to encourage you to embrace your true nature. But ... your love for these frail beings is a weakness that has only been illuminated by this." He gestured at Joseph, simmering in his fury.

Joseph was unable to hide his shock at hearing that Roxana and Alexander had not only learned that he was getting his human blood from donations but somehow tracked the source. He deflected by grasping at the more important tragedy. "Love is not a weakness," he retorted, though in truth he felt weaker than he had in recent memory, and he knew his odds of winning either a fight or an argument had evaporated.

"No, of course not. After all, it is my queen's love for me and mine for her that makes us so powerful. But you—" Alexander waved a hand derisively at Joseph "—what you do is a derangement. Should a wolf love a rabbit? It's unnatural."

Joseph tensed at the implied threat to David, but then forced himself to relax his posture. If there was a fight here, he would not win it. Talk was needed. Strategy. "If you aren't trying to kill me, tell me what you want."

Alexander looked to Roxana, offering the moment to her. She pulled herself to her full height. The pair grinned deviously. "We propose a bargain."

CHAPTER 14

David drove home in a daze after picking up his car at Joseph's house. He'd had one of the most incredible experiences of his life, and it ended so suddenly he didn't know how to feel. It was as if he'd been scuba diving, seeing another world of gloriously colorful coral formations and sea creatures, and then instantly ascended back to the surface world. He had the emotional equivalent of the bends.

In his apartment, he wandered aimlessly from the kitchen to the bedroom to the living room and back. He wasn't hungry or tired. He didn't want to watch TV. He wanted to know what was happening to Joseph. What had frightened him so badly that he had to run off without any warning?

David considered calling Dana, but what could he say? He had no idea how to frame the problem, let alone discuss it without spilling Joseph's secrets. He was in a moral cage.

Finally, he opted to take a shower. The long flight home had been sweaty with sex, and they hadn't showered on the eleven-hour flight back from Paris. He used the tub in the guest bath because the small standing shower off the main bedroom reminded him of Joseph. As he stood under the hot water, letting it scald his back slightly, David tried to think through the events of the last seventy-two hours, but his mind kept yanking him back to the last moment he saw Joseph's face, and the panic he had seen on it. After ten or fifteen minutes in the shower he realized that he was crying, and his legs turned to jelly. He sank to the bottom of the tub, and the best idea he could come up with was to put the stopper in, so his shower turned into a bath. A bath was the best cure for most problems, his mother had said.

Thinking felt like walking through a swamp in the fog. It was slow and lugubrious. An image of a movie from his childhood drifted to the forefront, of a character trying to pull his horse through the swamp but eventually the swamp swallowed the horse. David spent a few minutes trying to come up with the name of the movie. *Ah, right, The NeverEnding Story.* Just remembering that felt like some kind of achievement.

David then tried to work out what day it was. For some reason it seemed important to know. He could have looked on his phone, but the device was way over in his pants pocket on the bedroom floor, and he didn't particularly feel like moving. Even lifting his wrist to look at his Timex felt like too much effort.

He was pretty sure it was early Thursday. Very early, as the sun was only starting to lighten the alleyway outside the bathroom window. This revelation led to another. He was severely jet-lagged. Or was he? Was jet lag a thing that happened whenever you flew, or was it just in certain directions? And if so, did flying one direction and then turning around and flying the other counteract the effect like spinning in a circle and then spinning the other way?

David woke up in the bathtub after the water cooled enough it was uncomfortable. His first thought was to add more hot water, but almost immediately, he realized he really ought to get out of the tub. He dried himself, and wearing only a towel, plodded to the kitchen and prepared a mug of cold brew coffee to put in the microwave. While it heated, he thought again of Joseph.

He rushed to the bedroom to check his phone. No messages from Joseph. He realized that his reply to Dana's check-in had never been sent. It was just before 6:00 AM, too early to call back, so he just texted.

<I'm back, can't work today but I need to talk when you're up>

David hung the towel in the bathroom and wandered aimlessly into the bedroom, realizing that his body was unconsciously encouraging him to get more sleep. He slid naked under the covers and pulled one of the pillows down from the top of the bed, hugging it as he curled over on his side. It felt like no time had passed when his phone began buzzing and woke him up, but looking at it, he saw that it was almost an hour later. He answered and heard Dana's voice on the line.

"You're back, like you went somewhere? Or you're back, like you're back in civilization after disconnecting for a while?"

David realized he hadn't told her he was leaving for France with Joseph; it had all happened so fast. "Actually, Joseph did take me somewhere. But that's not what I needed to talk to you about."

Dana interrupted him, "Did you hear about the explosion?"

"What explosion?" David asked.

"Jesus, turn on a TV," Dana scolded. "It's all over the news! Some laboratory by the beach exploded last night. The police think it was a terrorist attack."

"Holy fuck," David said. His sleep-addled mind was having a hard time parsing this new information along with everything else it was dealing with. "Slow down, I just woke up and I'm a little bit jet-lagged."

"Jet-lagged?" Dana asked. "Where did you go?"

"We kind of went to France," David replied sleepily.

"Holy fuck," Dana echoed. "Now I need the whole story. Are you sure you can't come in today?"

David turned onto his back and looked at the cottage cheese–style stucco ceiling of his apartment. "Okay, I'll do a half day. I still need a little bit more sleep to get my brain working."

"Okay, let me know when you're on your way in. I'll wait to take lunch until you get here. We can chat before we go to the office and then chat some more."

"Copy that, see you in a few hours." David ended the call and clumsily placed the phone back on the bedside table. Pulling the hugging pillow to his other side, he curled up again and instantly fell asleep.

"So, did you hear the news?" Dana was eating her panini and sipping an iced tea in the studio commissary.

"Oh, no, I forgot you told me about that. I needed some music on the drive here, so I was listening to that," David replied as he sipped a coffee and nibbled unenthusiastically on a blueberry scone.

"Dude, the city is under attack! But in like the dumbest, least important way possible," Dana said behind mouthfuls of panini.

"What do you mean?" David asked

"Apparently the building that was destroyed was some sort of blood bank. Like a Red Cross center but a private company. Hang on." Dana pulled out her phone and started googling information. "It was called Tetractys. But, like, if you're going to attack the city, why attack something that has so much redundancy and seems so unimportant? There's plenty of blood banks, authorities say it doesn't affect our supply all that much—" Dana stopped talking when she saw David's mouth was agape. "What?"

"Give me your phone," David demanded.

Dana handed him her iPhone, and he looked at the website she had pulled up detailing the explosion.

"Oh, shit," he breathed. It was Joseph's company. That's why he had been so panicked on the plane. "I'm sorry, I have to call someone." David stood up without taking his tray and walked to the outside door, pulling out his own phone.

He called Joseph's number three times, each time going to voicemail, before he finally left a message. "Please call me. I just saw the news and I know why you were freaked out last night. Please let me know if there's anything I can do to help." He paused before adding, "I love you."

David stood out in the sun, feeling impotent for a moment, before remembering that Dana was still inside. He reentered the commissary and rejoined her at the table. She looked at him with eyebrows raised. "You're being weird," she said simply. "Do you wanna talk about it?"

David sat and looked at his partially eaten scone. "I do. I really do," he told his friend, "but there are things I can't tell you. I don't know if it's safe for you, or…" He trailed off, not knowing how to finish the sentence. "Or other people."

Dana reached out and grabbed one of his hands with hers. "Sweetie, as far as I know, I am your best friend. I am here for you no matter what is going on, okay? You can tell me anything, and it wouldn't change things between us."

I'm dating a vampire, David wanted to say. *Vampires are real, and my new boyfriend is one of them.* But of course, he couldn't. "I know, I really do," he said instead.

Back in the office, David tried calling Joseph on the phone nearly every hour, but only got his voicemail. He tried to give Joseph the benefit of the doubt, saying to himself that it was daytime, and he must be sleeping. But he also knew that Joseph didn't need to sleep in the daytime, and with such an emergency going on, probably wasn't. In one of his messages, he said exactly that.

Finally, around 5:00 PM, David's phone rang, and Joseph's name showed up on the caller ID. "Are you okay?" David answered instead of a greeting.

Joseph's voice came from the other end of the line, sounding ragged and tired. "David, I need to take some time away for a bit. I…" He trailed off. It was a long pause, David dreading the rest of the sentence, and Joseph apparently dreading having to say it. "I think it's best if we don't see each other," he finished finally.

David's stomach felt as if he was on a roller coaster, and his throat tightened. "No..." It was all he could get out. The room started spinning, so he closed his eyes and focused on trying to breathe.

Dana heard him and looked at David's desk. She recognized right away that something was very wrong. "Guys, go get some coffee and give us the room, okay?" she said authoritatively to the room.

"You're not our boss, Dana. *You* go get some coffee and give *us* the room," one of the writer assistants said, laughing.

"Yeah, that makes more sense," Dana admitted as she hurried over to David. "Carry on." She got to his side in time to hear the rest of the phone call.

"Joseph, please don't do this. You don't have to. Whatever it is, I can help!" David was grasping at straws. When Dana put her hand on his shoulder, he looked at her desperately. But there was nothing she could do, she didn't even know what was going on.

Joseph was very quiet on the other end of the line. "David... You can't help me," he said.

"Please!" David felt the pressure behind his sinuses building. His nose got that feeling before a sneeze, and his eyes welled up with tears. He was suddenly being loud enough to draw the attention of the whole room. Dana pulled him up and out into the hallway as the rest of the writing room staff looked on.

"Do you love me?" David asked forlornly.

There was another pause. "I do, but—"

"Well, I love you! That should be the most important thing. Love is more powerful than anything!" Tears were streaming down David's overheated cheeks. Dana recognized this side of this kind of conversation and grabbed David's non-phone hand, which was busily yanking at his shirt hem, and held it tight.

"David, you know I know things most people don't," Joseph explained, his voice laden with remorse. "You have to trust me that this is for the best."

"It's not, though! It can't be. Please..." David slid down the wall in the hallway to the floor. Dana knelt beside him.

"I need to deal with this, David, and I can't put you in danger. For now, at least, just stay away."

David latched onto the potential of the way Joseph phrased the words. "For now?"

"I don't know what's going to happen. I'm really sorry I can't say more," Joseph replied carefully. "I do love you."

"I love you, t—" but the call had ended. David stared at the phone, willing the timer on the call to keep going, but it was done. His arm fell to his side and he slumped down, his chest against his knees. Dana wrapped her arms around him.

"I'm so sorry, D," she whispered. After a moment, as David was able to catch his breath and compose himself from the worst parts of his emotional outburst, she asked, "What happened?"

David just looked at his knees. "Joseph owned the building that was blown up."

"Oh, fuck," Dana said.

"Yeah."

After a moment of thought, she apparently tried to see the situation analytically. "Well, shit, David, that's a huge thing he's got to deal with. But, like, he said he loves you, right?"

"Yeah."

She hugged him tight. "Okay, so that's not your problem to worry about. But Jesus Christ, dude. You own a building that gets firebombed, you have to deal with the FBI and the police... fire department, the city, insurance, lawyers... Fuck, there were *people* inside, I heard. No offense, babe, but you're not the biggest thing on his plate right now."

David turned his head to look at his friend. He took a deep breath and wiped his face with his hands. "Yeah, I guess. I'm just really worried about him. I want to help."

"Nothing you can do, sweetie," Dana said gently. "It's just sucky timing, but you gotta give him some space."

David groaned as he thumped his head against the wall. "It all just happened so fast. I didn't even tell you about the last few days."

"You told me you went to Paris, you lucky sonofabitch," she said, still hugging him but smiling, trying to lighten the mood.

"Yeah, that's just it. It was like something out of a fantasy, but it actually happened. But now this is exactly that feeling when you wake up from something you wish was real but isn't." He rubbed his face with his hands. "*Gaaagh*, I don't know how to describe it."

"I get it, D, I really do," Dana commiserated. "Hey, we're out of here in a bit, let's get takeout and go back to my place. You can catch me up, we can watch junky TV, and I can support you and be jealous at you for going to fucking Paris."

David couldn't help but laugh. Dana always was able to reach inside him and touch the thing in his brain that helped. "Okay, sounds good."

They helped each other up, and he took a quick detour to the restroom to freshen up before going back to work. But he couldn't stop thinking about Joseph. About what he could do to help, if anything.

CHAPTER 15

Joseph hung up the phone from his call to David. His heart felt like a ball of lead in his chest.

He had spent all day dealing with the emergency surrounding the destroyed Tetractys lab, taking calls from the company's security chief and head lawyer. They assured him they could handle almost all of the necessary red tape and paperwork caused by the attack. He was sufficiently insulated from the police and other law enforcement scrutiny. The only thing was, as Rafaél's only official living relative, he would have to authorize certain elements pertaining to the care and handling of his remains. Identification wasn't necessary, or even possible, visually. They had used dental records and would confirm with DNA analysis. Rafaél had believed that the American funerary industry was a giant scam, so there was no need to debate the potential of an open casket. He had already arranged to be turned into a tree or some such environmentally sustainable thing.

Joseph liked the idea of Rafi being a tree. It was a living thing that would grow and *be* there. A live thing Joseph could go to and see and touch, unlike the cold solidity of a granite headstone. He wished there were trees he could visit for the handful of other people he'd lost over the centuries. The only other loss in recent memory had been Rob, and his family had taken their son's body and not allowed his "roommate", as they called Joseph, to take part in the funeral. Joseph had only visited his grave, tucked away in the corner of a medium-sized cemetery in Augusta, Georgia, once.

Joseph had not slept all day. He knew he should rest but was not tired. As the sun set, he walked from his house to Mulholland Drive, which snaked along the top of the Hollywood Hills from just west of the Hollywood Sign all the way west to Calabasas about twenty miles away. Joseph decided to head west, because it was longer, and walked.

Over the course of his life, Joseph found that walking outside was the best way to clear his head. He had walked through the forests and fields of Europe, through jungles in India and South America, though deserts and savannas of Africa, and more. Most humans had no idea what the world was like at night. It was not, until very, very recently, the domain of man. And the night, as they say, was still very dark and full of terrors.

The thing Joseph missed most in this modern world was the stars. Los Angeles had a lot going for it, but in the last century, light pollution had obliviously erased billions of stars from the night sky. Joseph could still see more than most, especially when he focused on wider wavelengths of light, but they still counted only in the hundreds. They were his friends, though. Permanent fixtures in the sky, looking down on the Earth and marveling at the folly of mankind and its treatment of the planet. Joseph felt a kinship with the stars. His extended life was to a human what a human's was to a mouse. Very few life-forms on Earth knew what it was to live so long as vampire kind. But the stars... they looked on life itself and saw it as a blink of a cosmic eye. Humans thought of stars as forever things, but even stars were finite in their existence. They were born, they lived and grew and had families in their planetary bodies, and they died. And just like living things, they died in different ways. Sometimes slowly and quietly, shrinking into dense balls of matter. Others died violently, explosively, spreading their elements across the cosmos. *We are all made of star stuff*, Joseph thought, looking upwards. Sometimes he wished brilliant humans were made vampires. Carl Sagan would have made wonderful use of immortality.

Joseph rambled along the backbone of Los Angeles, occasionally passing a jogger or a dog walker, until the hour approached midnight. He had passed Coldwater Canyon hours ago. Had looked over the sprawling estates of Bel Air and Benedict Canyon. Passed Beverly Glen, and the ostentatious strip mall that catered to the super wealthy yet still had a Starbucks. He walked until he crossed the fourteen lanes of the 405 freeway, which was currently unclogged and running smoothly, and into the Santa Monica Mountains. He saw and smelled the scorched trees of fire seasons past, which had pushed right up into civilization. Wealth could not protect from nature's fury, or the wrath of a changing climate that humans blindly instigated.

As he walked, Joseph thought of David. Their time together was unquestioningly wonderful. He felt connected with him in a way that surpassed any emotional attachment Joseph could remember. But surely all this was too much to make the average human deal with, wasn't it? Just look what happened to Rafi...

Lost in thought and keeping a brisk pace in an attempt to tire himself, Joseph was soon surprised to reach another highway. Road signs indicated it was the 101 freeway. Joseph had thought that Mulholland continued along the spine of the mountain range, but realized he hadn't driven it this far in some time. He turned around, noting that he'd have just enough time to get back to the house before sunrise.

The return journey was occupied predominantly by thoughts of Alexander and Roxana. Joseph had offered them half his company during their confrontation in the park, thinking he could give them enough to sate their desire for wealth, but when his anger foolishly sent him into a trap, they increased their demand to all his wealth. "A bargain," they'd said, throwing his own words in his face. The problem was Joseph didn't know how much they knew. Rafi was the one who could have moved things around to make it look like the vampire couple were getting a lot when they would only be touching a small bit of Joseph's actual fortune. But now, they'd proven a willingness to destroy huge amounts of Tetractys to get what they wanted, which indicated they were aware of its reach. Worse, they were perfectly happy to kill anyone Joseph cared about until he capitulated. They had turned the tables on him and given him a week to accept their demand.

There were potential solutions to his vampire problem. One was, of course, to attempt battle with Alexander and Roxana. Joseph knew he could dispatch Alexander without difficulty. Joseph was older and stronger, and the younger vampire had no discipline. He had never taken to the combat training Joseph had offered after his turning. Roxana, on the other hand, was a different matter entirely. She was far older than either of the males, and besides being stronger, she was vicious. An outcome where Joseph emerged victorious from combat with the bloodsucking couple seemed extremely unlikely.

The other problem with this action would be repercussions among the vampire community at large. Vampires simply did not kill other vampires without consequences. There were too few of them, and the odds of successfully turning a human made it difficult to make more. Accidents happened, and the rare vampire hunter still roamed the world, so vampire-on-vampire violence was forbidden in a strict if unspoken code.

Joseph considered wiping the slate clear. Leaving his life in Los Angeles and going into hiding. He had been alive over five hundred years. It seemed like a waste to cast all that progress away, but without the fear of mortality pushing him, throwing everything away was a real possibility. He could rebuild his life. What would the next hundred years look like on this planet? Humanity was on the precipice of either taking major leaps in technology or near-absolute destruction. In five hundred years, they could be traveling the stars, which would certainly make keeping to himself easier. On the other hand, a lot of Joseph's work was meant to help keep a darker future at bay. Joseph's business and technology empire combatted climate change, cured disease, researched sustainable energy and food production, and funded anti-corruption campaigns in governments around the world. What would happen to the planet without that positive influence?

Joseph thought about the impossibility of turning David as he'd suggested. It was a nonstarter, of course, but Joseph's mind wandered nonetheless. He imagined what it would be like to have a partner, as so many others of his kind had, who he could travel through history with, passionately and unconcerned with the trivial matter of aging and death. There were thousands of vampires in the world. But just as in the rest of nature, only a fraction were homosexual. Then half of them were female. Pickings were slim. This is why Joseph so acutely felt the truth of Decimus being a curse. Without it, it would be so easy to find a human to love who would embrace immortality, turn them, and be happy. Of course, then the world would be absolutely overrun with nightwalkers.

These fantasies of an immortal life together with David took him all the way back to his house, and despite the tragedy of the last day, Joseph couldn't help but smile as he stepped up the two stairs of the front stoop and raised his hand to unlock the oak front door.

That big, heavy, oak front door with no doorknob, the fancy new electronic keypad security system, and cold-rolled steel deadbolt lock.

It was wide open.

CHAPTER 16

Joseph's whole body shifted immediately into a defensive predator mode. His muscles tensed and his senses reached out to provide hyper-detailed information about the environment. First, he noticed the door. Most of the damage was in the jamb itself, as the wood had been battered in by something heavy. The deadbolt had bent slightly but the jamb had given way, splintering into the house. The smell of stained lumber was tart in his nostrils.

Inside, the darkness was heavy, but Joseph's night vision cut through the gloom better than military goggles. He could see splinters of wood strewn on the floor from the impact on the door and something else. Scrapes of skin on the stone that were barely perceptible. He crouched down closer to the floor, keeping half of his attention directed into the house in case the intruders were still present. Joseph guessed that the dermal residue was from the bare feet of someone walking—or being dragged—into the house.

The cool, environmentally controlled air tingled his skin as he adjusted from the outdoor warmth of May. He inhaled deeply. His sharp sense of smell, evolved to stalk prey, turned to the task of identifying the interlopers. Joseph detected three distinct pheromone signatures. He almost saw the smells like one might see colors in the air, drifting and mingling. Two of them were familiar. One of those was *very* familiar. And there was something more. Something which excited and concerned him deeply. Blood. Joseph rose to standing. He turned and pushed the oak door closed as far as it would go with the mangled deadbolt sticking out of the side.

He called out into the cool darkness. "Alexander!"

A form stepped from around the corner, shrouded in darkness. Joseph could smell the other vampire's essence, but also dirt, grass, leaves... *disinfectant fluid?* ... and blood.

"Hello, Father," he said coldly.

"You said a week," Joseph replied.

"Oh, I just had to see you again. Family is *so* important," Alexander needled.

Joseph felt the verbal jab but forced himself to be calm. His anger had already exposed him once to these two. "You broke my door. I just got the new lock installed," Joseph replied, still tensed in case of trouble.

"And it was very strong. It took me two whole tries to bust it in. But then, you didn't leave a window open for me, so what other option did I have?" Alexander was playing with him, adopting a petulant tone that hinted to something devious up his sleeve. It had been a hundred years since they'd spent real time together, but Joseph still knew the other man that well.

"Where is she?" Joseph could smell Alexander's companion.

"In the kitchen. We wouldn't dream of visiting without bringing a gift." Alexander's eyes flashed dangerously. "She's keeping *it* company, Father."

"*Don't* call me that. I'm not your father." Joseph advanced slowly toward the younger vampire, his body shifting from a defensive stance to an attack posture: tall, imposing.

"Nonsense, you're more of a father than the human who shot his seed into my whore of a mother. I never knew the bastard until I tracked him down and tore his throat out."

Joseph remembered it. Alexander's obsession after his turning was finding his biological parentage and wiping them off the face of the Earth. He fed on his mother and then hunted and slaughtered his father. Joseph had tried to stop him, but his efforts had been futile. It was then, when Joseph witnessed the savagery of the being he had given this power to, that Joseph truly understood the ramifications of turning a new vampire, and vowed never to do it again.

"If you were concerned with manners, you should have let me know you were coming," Joseph growled.

"Ah, but that would have ruined the surprise."

"A week, you said." Joseph took another step toward the younger vampire.

Alexander turned his head and smelled the air deeply. "Even now, I smell them on you and in this house. One of them pervades this space, and the other—" he brought his nose up against Joseph's face "—is newer. You bedded your human recently."

"You've fucked humans."

"Not in decades," Alexander scoffed. "Not since New Orleans eradicated Yellow Fever."

Joseph controlled his emotions so that they wouldn't betray him. "You should. They're much cleaner these days."

"They're as repulsive as you are."

As the two men stood nose to nose, tension building to a crescendo, Roxana called from the kitchen. "Come, my *batal*, dinner is getting cold!"

Joseph suspected the answer, but he asked anyway, "What did you bring into my house?"

Alexander grinned wickedly. "Your surprise..." he whispered and turned away into the kitchen.

Joseph followed his younger progeny into the next room and was taken aback. He knew whatever Alexander and Roxana had planned would be bad, but this was some kind of awful torture theater.

Tied and gagged to a chair in the middle of the dining area was a young woman, perhaps twenty years old, wearing no more than a grimy summer dress which hung torn off one shoulder, revealing her breast. She was scratched and dirty, and Joseph could see and smell that she had been living on the street for some time. But the worst thing was that she was drenched in blood. Joseph knew it wasn't hers; two empty blood bags lay flaccid next to the woman's chair. She looked at him with terror in her eyes, and he looked back with pity in his. He knew she would not survive the night.

Joseph glanced at the refrigerator and saw the blood leaking out. They had found his supply and destroyed it. The very thought of food made him realize he hadn't eaten in over twenty-four hours and was thus in a weakened state.

Roxana bowed her head theatrically to Joseph. "For you, *Herr Knoblauch*. We have already eaten this evening, so you may have your fill."

It was a game for them.

"No," he said firmly.

"How very rude." Roxana went to Alexander and stood by his side, draping a sinewy hand up over his shoulder.

Alexander kissed it before moving behind the tied-up woman. "We found your *bagged* blood and figured for some unfathomable reason you prefer it, so we warmed it for you." He traced a finger through the thickening blood on the homeless woman's arm and across her clavicle and her neck, then brought it to his mouth to taste, an expression of revulsion coming over his face. "It's still disgusting."

"Get out of my house. Now." Joseph's mind raced, trying to figure out what he could do for the terrified young woman. Every scenario ended badly. If he somehow managed to get her out of the house alive, she would still have been abducted by two vampires and taken to the home of a third vampire, and they could all be identified.

"Tsk, tsk, father. We didn't come here to make you kill a homeless wench. There's business to attend to." Alexander turned and took his opposite hand to the woman's throat. With a small puncture device affixed like a claw to his thumb, he pierced her neck at the jugular vein. It was so fast and the claw so sharp the woman didn't even scream. There was only a look of surprise in her wide, horrified eyes. Alexander held his hand in front of the blood as it came in spurts from the wound.

"Don't want to make more of a mess than we already have, now do we?" He grinned happily. As the initial spurts gave way to a steady stream of blood from the wound, he licked the fresh gore from his hand. "Mmm, much better. You really should try it." He held out his hand to Joseph invitingly. "Please, you didn't do the killing, your precious conscience can rest easy. It's just so much better than the reheated garbage you subject yourself to."

The woman moaned as she felt her lifeblood oozing from her body. This was going to take a while. Joseph made visual contact with her and flashed his eyes, trying to will her to be less aware of her own impending death. But Roxana stepped between them. "Ah-ah, Bavarian. The fear makes it taste better."

"You're sure you don't want any, father?" Alexander chided him.

Joseph knew he was being baited but refused to engage. As it was, as soon as these two had snatched the woman from the street, her death had been inevitable. "You're an animal."

"We are animals all, father," Alexander retorted. "Nature has an order, and it is you who refuses to acknowledge it. You are a predator. You should act like one." He sighed. "Well, there's no point in it going to waste. My darling, help yourself."

Roxana gave a small purring squeal that sent a shiver down Joseph's spine as she moved to the homeless woman and pushed her head to expose the puncture wound. As she drank, Alexander approached Joseph until he was within arm's reach. "Now to business. We want all of it."

Joseph blinked. The change in subject was so abrupt he didn't realize what Alexander was referring to. "All? Of what?"

"Your empire. The family business. I'll give you credit, father, you saw what the world was becoming and built something powerful. And we want it."

Joseph looked at Alexander, whose demeanor had turned almost contrite, and then back to Roxana, feasting on a woman tied to a chair in his kitchen, and then back to Alexander, who looked expectant, like he wanted an answer to the absurd demand.

"I see you're at a loss for words. I'll make it simple to understand. You have power in this world. Real power, with influence over millions. It's more than I have, and I want it. I'd have settled for half, but then you had to go and act all holier-than-thou, and made me look weak in front of my darling wife. I really don't want to kill you, Joseph. If only because I don't know what that would do to the thing I aim to take from you. I want to keep it as valuable as possible. But we will kill you. If you make us. You can't possibly stand against both of us in a fair fight. Look at you."

Alexander stepped back, and took his own advice, looking Joseph up and down, and continued. "For as powerful as the thing you have built is, you yourself are, in reality, soft and weak."

Roxanna finished drinking from the woman, who was still semiconscious, and stood tall next to Alexander. When she spoke, her silky voice betrayed her physical power. At nearly fifteen hundred years old, she was easily the strongest of the three of them. "Your progeny has come home to you, Bavarian, and we have proven our capacity to harm that which you love. Do not presume you are in a position to negotiate. You are not."

She used Joseph's own words from their encounter in the park against him before she turned and walked from the kitchen. Alexander cocked an eyebrow at Joseph and shrugged his shoulders as if to say *"Women. What can you do?"* and followed her.

He stopped at the doorway to the kitchen and looked at the woman in the chair, and then at Joseph. "Be a predator, *Father*. We'll be in touch to arrange details. In the meantime, I have yet to experience *all* the flavors of the City of Angels."

He left. Joseph heard the door creak open and their footsteps out the front stoop. He turned to the woman in the chair, who was looking at him, her eyes begging. He held her with his gaze and willed her pain away. Her eyes went glassy like a patient on morphine, and her head lolled. Joseph licked his lips, unaware that he was slowly moving towards the woman. His stomach rumbled, and his heartbeat quickened as a need overtook his senses.

CHAPTER 17

Joseph awoke with a start and took a few moments to realize where he was. The scent of his bedding and the coolness of the windowless stone helped identify his own bedroom. How did he get here? He sat up in bed and took a few deep, calming breaths. Memories of the previous evening slowly came back to him. Alexander and Roxana in his house torturing the homeless woman. His own exhaustion after his urban walkabout. What happened after the murderous pair finally left...

It had been so long since he had fresh human blood. For two hundred and fifty years, he had been able to resist the temptation. But a large part of his decision had been the act of the hunt itself. He abhorred the thought of hunting and killing a human being, something he himself could remember being. He had been so turned off to the idea that for many decades he had subsisted on animal blood. It was not as good as human, but it was okay. Then, as the years progressed, he was able to find a steady supply of donated human blood, and satisfied his thirst without the moral quandary of having to take it from the source.

But last night, weak from days of emotional turmoil, fighting with his wicked progeny and his vixen of a wife, a sleepless day and his night out walking the breadth of Los Angeles, Joseph had found himself in his kitchen with a bleeding corpse that wasn't quite dead yet. He hadn't done the killing, and in that moment, his hunger had done the thinking and rationalizing for him.

He had fed on the poor woman.

A wave of guilt swept through him like a cold front, making him shiver even though he wasn't physically cold. He fell back on the bed, covering his face with his hands.

I have to deal with the body.

The awful thing was that it was so *good*. The ecstasy of having a full meal of hot, fresh, human blood (a young woman at that, full of spicy fear), along with his exhaustion, had made him drunk, and he'd barely been able to stumble down the stairs to his bedroom. He'd slept more soundly than he had in—

Joseph opened his eyes and took his hands away from his face. A sound came from upstairs.

Someone is in my house.

Joseph bolted up and over to the staircase leading up to the main level. Barefoot, he soundlessly took the stairs two at a time. He reached the main floor and the metallic smell of congealed blood filled the air. To his nostrils, it was a fog of overpowering odor. It should have been dark in the living room. The sun had set at least half an hour ago. But there, in the doorway to the kitchen, a figure. Backlit against the light from above the cooking area, the features were indiscernible, but Joseph recognized the silhouette immediately, and his heart sank in his chest.

"David?!" he said more loudly than he had meant.

David, who had been staring wide-eyed at the gory scene before him, screamed at the sudden interruption of the silence.

"No! David, it's just me, it's okay!" Joseph moved forward, hands outstretched.

David turned to see him. The light from the kitchen made it easy to see the blood on Joseph's shirt, hands, and mouth.

"Stop! Don't come any closer!" He had no weapon to back up the command if Joseph had been unwilling to obey, but Joseph did stop. David took in everything he was seeing and could barely speak from the awful picture it formed in his mind. All he could say was, "Did you...?"

"No," Joseph quickly defended himself from the unspoken accusation. "No, I didn't kill her. It was Alexander and Roxana." He gestured frantically to the front of the house. "You saw the front door? They broke in this morning and tormented that poor woman in front of me. They killed Rafaél, David. He was my son, and they killed him. They blew up one of my buildings, and he was inside."

Joseph realized he was beginning to ramble and forced himself to stop talking. He needed to get the lay of the land as far as David was concerned.

David, for his part, was barely handling the situation. This was the first dead body he'd ever seen, and it wasn't *just* a dead body. There was blood *everywhere*. It looked like a horror movie. If he hadn't already known for a fact he was in the home of a vampire, he might have assumed it was an excessively decorated set piece in a film. There was just too *much* blood.

"Wh-who..." David stammered. "Who is...?" He didn't need to get more specific.

"Homeless. I don't know. They pulled her off the street. They were toying with me, torturing *me* because I tracked them down after they attacked you and told them to leave town. They wanted me to drink from her because they were disgusted that I wouldn't feed on humans, so they pulled a random woman—"

"Did you?" David interrupted.

"What?" Joseph realized he had said too much.

David paused. It was a tough question to get out the first time. It was even harder to repeat into the silence between them.

"Did you ... *feed* ... on her?"

Joseph couldn't answer. To give voice to his sin would be ten times worse. The sanctity of human life was the closest thing he had to a belief system. He had betrayed himself in a colossal moment of profound weakness.

The silence was answer enough for David. He turned his back on Joseph, unable to make eye contact. That only brought him to face the corpse sitting tied to the chair in the kitchen. It was less shocking now, and he was able to take in other details. He saw the blood bags on the floor and the thick red liquid dripping out of the refrigerator.

Joseph took a solitary step closer before stopping himself. "Please believe me, David, I didn't kill her. I couldn't bear it if you thought I..."

David averted his eyes from the scene and brought a hand to his mouth to hold back the vomit rising in his throat. He retreated into the living room and sat on the sofa. "I believe you," he said as he tried to take deep breaths.

Joseph, meanwhile, moved to the entryway to the kitchen and took in the scene with fresh eyes. He wept with pity for himself and for the innocent person that sat within.

He felt David's eyes on him and turned to meet his gaze.

"What are you going to do?" David asked.

Joseph shook his head. There were so many things he could be referring to. Joseph's whole world seemed to be crumbling around him. Rafaél's death, Tetractys, Alexander and Roxana, the body in his kitchen, his relationship with

David... He didn't know which one David was asking about. But it didn't really matter because he didn't have the answers. One thing was certain, however.

"You have to leave, David. We can never see each other again."

"What?" David started. "But I came to check—"

"No, stop," Joseph interrupted. "It's not safe. I already lost the most important person in my life. They will hurt you if they know how much you mean to me." Joseph turned his head to indicate the contents of the kitchen. "Or worse."

David was terrified by the obvious truth of what Joseph was saying, but he was unable to break himself of his love for this man who was in such trouble. He was a problem solver by nature. It's what made David a good director. His first instinct with this situation had been to start thinking of a solution. "Joseph. Maybe if..." He had hoped to have an end to the sentence by the time he got there but nothing came.

"David." Joseph took a step forward and tried to make himself authoritative. "You have to leave. Don't call, don't check on me. Leave. *Now*."

David stood up so fast he stumbled a bit. *Fuck you* is what he wanted to say, but he knew he didn't mean that. He had already gone through all the reasons why Joseph was having an impossible time right now. His whole body was tingling and he felt disconnected.

"I love you," he said quietly.

Joseph held his tongue. He wanted desperately to say it back, to run over and hug David and tell him not to go, they'd figure something out... but he knew it was wrong. He had to let David go for his own safety.

David waited a moment for an answer, then steadied himself and turned to the broken door. He had not tried to close it when he came in, so it stood wide open, moonlight spilling into the foyer. He stopped at the threshold and looked back at his immortal lover with tears falling in streams down his warm and very mortal cheeks. "Please. Be careful."

Joseph nodded. "You, too," he replied, willing himself not to show the same remorse.

He watched David walk out the door and did not follow. The door of the little Accord opened and closed a moment later. He heard the engine rev to life and the wheels crunch the asphalt as it reversed out of the driveway. Then David drove away forever.

CHAPTER 18

Joseph waited motionless until the sound of David's car had faded completely into the background noise of the city before he moved a muscle. He went to the door and cleared away as much of the debris as he could and pushed it closed. The bent deadbolt prevented it from shutting completely and it remained slightly ajar. Better than nothing. Joseph moved a three-legged hallway table, which had previously been home to a rather expensive vase, in front of the door so it would make noise if someone tried to push it open. The vase it had held, a blue-and-white Chinese piece from the Ming Dynasty, lay in a hundred shards on the floor. Dealing with that would have to wait, however.

The homeless woman sat cold in her death chair, covered in her own blood and that of anonymous donors. Joseph gazed over the scene, contemplating various options. The body must be disposed of. The room needed cleaning. This whole floor of the house needed to be scrubbed top to bottom. A plan was coalescing in his head, and his first instinct was to call Rafi, but Rafi was gone, his death caused by the same people who created this horror show. Joseph felt anger rising up his spine but pushed it down. Now was not the time for impotent rage.

He needed a vehicle. For the first time in years, a Lyft or Uber would not do. Privacy and discretion were the words of the day. Joseph surmised that renting a car in his name in order to move a corpse was also probably not the best idea. Then a possibility came to mind. He took out a phone and rang the head of corporate security, Hayes Burton. Rafaél was the only person Joseph trusted with sensitive personal matters, but whenever Rafi had needed assistance, he had turned to Burton. A former Marine officer in the Special Operations Command with several classified jobs on his resume, he was a get-things-done-and-don't-ask-questions type of guy. Which was exactly what Joseph needed right now.

"Yes, sir, Mr. Walter, what can I do for you?" Burton answered the phone.

Joseph could swear he heard him standing up stiffly at attention, even over the phone. He had learned that Hayes Burton preferred a no-nonsense approach. No chitchat, no personal talk. "What's the status?" He didn't particularly feel the need to know about what was happening surrounding the explosion. In fact, he felt it was probably best if he didn't. But it might seem odd if he called and *didn't* ask, especially when he was about to make another odd request.

Burton gave a recap of the body count (four dead and six wounded, a surprisingly low number considering over two hundred people had worked in the building), estimated damages ($1.3 billion including the high-tech lab equipment and computers, not including the incalculable loss of experimental data and intellectual property), and cause of the explosion (homemade bomb using ammonium nitrate).

Joseph was about to ask for a company car when he suddenly remembered that Rafaél had brought him his blood shipments in a delivery van. "Burton, do you know where Rafaél's truck is that he used to transport sensitive cargo?"

"Yessir, I believe it was in the lot and is intact," the former military man said in his no-nonsense gruff.

"I need it, please. Be sure the LoJack and GPS tracking is deactivated. I'll order a car to pick me up and be down in..." Joseph looked at his watch and made a quick calculation that every LA native became adept at: estimating traffic. "Ninety minutes."

"Copy that, sir. I'll make sure it's ready." Joseph wondered if the combat vet had saluted. "I won't be able to meet you, but I'll have Elmer waiting with the keys." Elmer Fox was one of his lieutenants within the company.

"Thank you. Good night, Burton, and good work."

"Sir?" his voice cut in before Joseph ended the call.

"Yeah?"

Burton's voice assumed an uncharacteristic degree of empathy. "Sir... I'm sorry, sir." Joseph pondered the words for a moment. No one knew Rafaél's true relation to him, but perhaps knowing they were close was enough. Or maybe the old Marine was referring to the building and the damage done to the thing that Joseph had built. He couldn't possibly know the true value of the food supply the building contained...

"Thank you, Burton." Joseph ended the call.

Usually, he got a bit of enjoyment out of calling the man by his last name. It had been a request Burton made the first time they'd met when Joseph had congenially called him Hayes. The last name thing was a military holdover, and it took Joseph back to his own days of having comrades-in-arms. Tonight, it felt grim and joyless.

Eighty-six minutes later, the Lyft dropped him off at what was left of the Tetractys offices and lab building. It was in a newly developed area of town called Playa Vista, and the building itself was a converted airplane hangar which had been used to manufacture aircraft during World War II. Joseph had bought a lot of property in the area and leased some to tech companies like Google and Adobe. He had gutted the massive structure and installed state-of-the-art facilities for biomedical research and blood processing and storage. It was almost totally destroyed. Half the building was rubble, and the rest was heavily damaged. Joseph had been informed that it was a complete loss.

The parking lot across the street was untouched, except for some detritus from the explosion. It was now home to a small village of emergency vehicles and a portable terrorist response lab. On the far side of the lot, Joseph spotted Rafi's delivery truck, and he pointed the Lyft driver there.

Elmer was waiting next to the van as promised, and he made sure Joseph was situated, treating him with a respectful deference of a boss who rarely interacted with his employees and thus held a sort of mythical eminence. Joseph tried to be kind and put the young man at ease. He offered to give him a ride home with the Lyft, but Elmer declined, pointing out his car a few spots away.

Joseph drove the truck to a nearby home supply store and grabbed large plastic bags, several containers of heavy-duty cleaning solution, and other cleaning supplies, and was about to drive home when Burton called.

"Sir, I'm sorry to disturb you," the former Marine said gruffly, his voice indicating he wasn't so much sorry as being polite, "but I just received a call from the FBI lead investigator. They requested to be able to ask you some questions about the explosion."

"Requested?" Joseph repeated wryly.

"Insisted, sir." Burton read his meaning without it needing to be spelled out. It was one of the things Joseph really liked about the man. "But it does seem more of a formality and shouldn't be too much of a concern. Are you still close?"

Joseph tapped a finger absently on the steering wheel. Talking to the FBI about one crime while driving a truck filled with materials he intended to use to cover up another crime didn't exactly seem like the best idea, but Joseph suspected he knew the types of questions they wanted to ask him. They would ask him the same questions they would have to ask most of the people who worked at Tetractys, but speaking with the owner of the privately held company was surely essential to any investigation. He wouldn't be able to avoid speaking with them. It might as well be now, after sunset, than try to arrange a time tomorrow or the next day.

"Yeah, I'm still in the area. I'll swing back. Who am I looking for?" Joseph replied.

"Agent Kane from the Joint Terrorism Task Force," Burton replied curtly. "I'll meet you. I can be there in ten."

"Perfect." Joseph ended the call and took an extra-deep breath. It wouldn't do any good to get frustrated. *Just go and answer their questions and be done with it*, he thought.

Joseph stopped at a Starbucks drive-thru to equip himself with the prop of a green tea, which served two purposes: to eat up some time to allow his security chief to arrive first, and to make Joseph appear so at ease that he was just sipping his green tea, no big deal, I don't know nuthin' about no terrorist attack, Officer.

He arrived back at the small tent city a few minutes later and recognized Burton's giant Range Rover immediately. It was just the sort of car an ex-Marine would have. Bulky, overpowered, and much too large for a city. Parked next to it was a Tesla Model X with a vanity license place reading LAWGRRL, which Joseph recognized as belonging to the Tetractys general counsel. Sure enough, when he got out of the van he was met by Burton and Pamela Alwin, a woman of about sixty years of age who could best be described as fierce. But as Ru Paul would say it. With a few finger snaps.

Joseph had fallen professionally head over heels for Pamela when Rafaél had brought her on. She was like a lawyer version of Sigourney Weaver in *Aliens*. Supremely competent, confident, and could surely strap a couple of M41A Pulse Rifles together when she had to venture into a courtroom setting. She also had a sense of humor, as evidenced by her vanity plate, but woe to the man who got on her bad side.

"Pamela," Joseph greeted her (*Pamela, never Pam*, he reminded himself, as he did every time he met her), extending his hand.

"Hello, sir, it's been too long. You look good, all things considered," she said, grasping his hand firmly, her perfectly manicured nails pushing lightly into the skin on the back of Joseph's hand.

"You, too," he returned the compliment. It was true. Pamela didn't look a day over forty-five and was dressed smartly yet alluringly in a charcoal grey Armani pantsuit with a light purple shirt that showed just the slightest hint of cleavage. Rafaél had told Joseph that she had worked as a Playboy Bunny to put herself through law school, a fact which Joseph absolutely loved. "Thank you for coming."

"It seemed prudent, given the circumstances," the lawyer said, adopting a caring, almost motherly demeanor. She added her other hand and held Joseph's, looking into his eyes sympathetically. "I'm so, so sorry for Rafaél. He was a good man."

Joseph felt a lump appear suddenly in his throat, and he swallowed it down. "He was, thank you." Then he looked to Burton to include him in the conversation. "Shall we get this over with?"

They traversed the sixty or so feet to a large trailer serving as a command center for the FBI task force. Pamela and Burton briefly prepped Joseph on the way. Agent Kane, a tall, slightly overweight man of Midwest origins and closely cropped hair, breezed through introductions before moving on to the questions at hand. Joseph took a strategically timed sip of his green tea while Agent Kane spoke.

"Sorry to have to bother you with this, but of course we have to try and figure out what motives the terrorists might have had to attack your company specifically," Agent Kane explained.

"Of course, whatever I can do to help. My counsel and chief of corporate security have filled me in so far." Joseph held his cup with both hands and leaned in slightly, taking on a concerned look.

Agent Kane held up an audio recorder. "Do you mind if I record this for reference?"

Joseph didn't care a bit, but dutifully looked to Pamela, who nodded. "No, it's fine," he told the agent.

Kane pushed the record button. "I only have a couple questions. You are the current owner of Tetractys, correct?"

"Yes," Joseph confirmed, though didn't elaborate on the company's history of being passed down from grandfather to father to son, all of whom were the same person.

"Do you have any enemies that you can think of who might want to attack your company?" Agent Kane asked bluntly. Without needing to take notes, his attention was focused on Joseph.

Joseph returned his gaze and allowed his will to spill into the agent, just a bit. "No, as far as I know I don't have any enemies," he lied. "I try to be a positive influence in the community, and the work we do helps people."

"I see," the agent said, his speech slowing somewhat, like he was thinking through a fog. "What about corporate enemies? Competition from overseas that might go so far as industrial espionage?"

"Not that I'm aware of, but surely Mr. Burton would be a better person to ask about such things. My involvement in day-to-day operations is ... minimal," Joseph replied assuredly, maintaining eye contact with the agent. His goal was to instill a sense of trust, so that the questions would be kept to a minimum, without need for follow-ups.

"Sure, sure," Kane replied, pursing his lips. The next question was a tad delicate. "Rafaél Loya was the Managing Director of Tetractys, and also—" he checked his notes on a smartphone app "—your brother, by adoption, correct?"

Next to him, Joseph felt Pamela stiffen somewhat at the mention of Rafi's name, and he heard her heartbeat quicken noticeably. *Interesting*, he thought. Was this a professional reaction to the inclusion of her only other boss into the conversation, or was there something more? As far as Joseph knew, the stately head counsel was not married herself. Rafi had always seemed too busy with work for personal connections, but perhaps he had managed to combine the two. Joseph's mind flitted briefly to their recent conversation where Rafaél confidently revealed his asexuality, and he wondered briefly whether his son had any physical interactions at all.

He returned his attention to the FBI agent. "That's correct, yes." Joseph had adopted Rafi when he was living under his previous name. Legally speaking, when he was his own father, making Rafaél his brother.

"I'm sorry for your loss," Kane said with a hint of genuine sympathy. "Did *he* have any enemies that you were aware of?"

Burton let out a subtle *humph*, which Joseph also found interesting. It seemed to indicate that the very idea of Rafaél having anyone in his life that could come close to being called an enemy was preposterous.

"I would be shocked if he did," Joseph said. Out of the corner of his eye, he saw Burton nod almost imperceptibly.

"I see," the agent said. "That's all I need for now, but if you think of anything that might help, let me know."

"I've got your number, Agent Kane," Burton said, being very clear that the conversation had ended. Kane nodded and turned on his heel, returning to the command trailer. *Another military man*, Joseph observed. *Intelligence, though, not special forces.* Joseph had known countless military types in his life. They generally fit neatly into a certain personality type, and when they entered the service, they usually wound up sliding into a slot that fit them.

Joseph apologized to Burton and Pamela for needing to leave, and they apologized for making him come in the first place. He put them at ease, blaming the FBI for needing his answers personally. He drove the delivery truck laden with cleaning supplies back to the house via Venice and La Cienega Boulevards rather than getting on the 405 freeway. The highways weren't always faster in LA, and Joseph wanted to stay on surface streets to give himself time to think. It had been a long time since he'd had to dispose of a body, and he only just realized that he didn't know exactly how he was going to do it.

He had fleetingly considered hiring a service to take care of the homeless woman's corpse and the mess. There were such resources available to the super wealthy, but he had never availed himself of them. The fact was, Joseph considered the cleanup to be penance for falling off the wagon of abstaining from feeding on humans. It would be gruesome and messy work, the smell of old blood and death already permeated the kitchen, but Joseph ultimately decided to handle it by himself. If Rafi were still alive, he'd have said the old vampire was wallowing. Forcing himself to live in anguish and self-pity. That was never quite right.

Joseph felt a small but constant and gnawing guilt in the depths of his soul. He felt, whatever vampires were and however they came to exist on the Earth, they could be better than the myths and legends they failed to live up to. They were superior to humans in many ways. Stronger, faster, heightened senses, impossibly long life. Nature had balanced these strengths with some limitations like extreme sensitivity to sunlight, allergies to garlic, and the difficulty in propagating that they named *Decimus*, but for all the gifts evolution had given them, what did they do with them? Less than nothing.

On top of it all, vampires were in a sense the worst predators on the planet. In nature, predators weeded out the sick and the old from the prey populations, but vampires, oh no, they fed on the young, the strong, and the most virile of humans. Joseph knew they could be better. Could give something back to the planet which had brought about their existence. The early centuries of killing and living by his basest desires had happened, and they will always have happened. So, Joseph atoned.

Tonight, that meant sawing through the flesh, muscle, and bone of an innocent woman, praying forgiveness from her and any other spirits that may be watching as he did so.

In the moment when he asked Burton for the truck, Joseph had assumed that he'd have to drive the body somewhere remote and bury pieces all over the Southern California desert. It wasn't until he held a grimy severed foot in his hand that he realized he might have the solution right in his very house.

The house was equipped with a Volkan medical grade butane incinerator system, installed precisely for disposing of blood bags and any other materials related to Joseph's nocturnal proclivities. There were chutes that led from the kitchen and the garage, though they weren't big enough to accommodate a whole body. Even a foot or a hand might get stuck, Joseph suspected (perhaps the best thing about being old was that he was able to foresee accidents before they happened, unlike his younger human self, who constantly had to clean up messes as a result of foolish pride).

The incinerator was located in the subbasement of the house, and it had a direct access panel measuring twelve by twenty-four inches. With a bit of sickening disassembly, Joseph was able to fit all of the body parts into the burn receptacle and reduced the woman who died in his kitchen to soft grey ash.

The cleaning of the kitchen took longer. Even with his enhanced strength, Joseph's arms ached from scrubbing sticky, drying blood from the marble floor tiles. They were stain-treated, and the blood left no trace after a little elbow grease was employed. He also had to scrub the refrigerator inside and out, removing all the shelving to be sure he left no trace. Seeing the empty spot where his bags of donated blood usually sat reminded him that he hadn't eaten in almost twenty-four hours. He checked his watch to make sure, but sunrise was coming, which meant it had been a whole day since he succumbed to the urge to feed on a human being.

He wasn't hungry. Joseph knew he should be, given how long ago his last meal was and how taxing the last day had been, both physically and emotionally. He suspected he was in a bit of shock and running on adrenaline as he cleaned. Perhaps he was depressed. He certainly felt hollowed out, and that small, gnawing feeling of guilt he usually had was now large and festering right in the middle of his chest.

He finished the cleaning process by burning the chair to which the homeless woman had been tied. Joseph was reasonably certain no one would come to his house in search of her, but he did another pass on every surface in the kitchen just to be safe, then the floor from the kitchen to the entryway. There, he swept up the debris from the broken front door, and, seeing that the sun was up, called the company that had installed the door and agreed to pay the expediting fee for them to come to fix it that day. He told them it had been broken in by firefighters responding to a faulty alarm. The receptionist on the other end of the call said he hoped they were paying for the replacement, and Joseph faked a laugh and said he hoped so, too.

All that taken care of, Joseph was faced with an age-old dilemma. Too tired to eat, too hungry to sleep. The problem was solved for him when he realized there was no way for him to get food. Rafi was dead and was the only one he could have called. Anyway, Tetractys' blood lab was destroyed, and that was where Rafi would have gotten his supply. So Joseph put the table in front of the front door again as a makeshift alarm and descended to the bedroom. He didn't think he'd be able to sleep; his mind was swimming with guilt and sadness and worry and what felt like a thousand decisions that needed to be made, but he put his phone ringer on as loud as it could go just in case and set it in the charger on the bedside table. He laid down on the bed and passed out from exhaustion as soon as his head hit the soft pillow.

CHAPTER 19

David felt empty, hollowed out. There was a dull ache in his chest, and if he weren't a young man in good health he might have worried he was having a heart attack. He had been in love and experienced heartbreak before. This was different, for a myriad of reasons. The speed of his romance with Joseph, the *completeness* of their love for each other, and the suddenness of the breakup. But mostly, it was the fact that he knew they both loved each other. They were being torn apart by circumstances beyond their control.

The night after he drove away from Joseph's house for the last time, David didn't sleep well. He tossed and turned, and when he did drift off, he had fitful dreams of being strapped in a chair while vampires drained him from all parts of his body, but he never seemed to die from blood loss.

David woke up a final time well before sunrise, sweating, his breath coming in ragged gasps. He could still feel the bites on his skin from the dream and was compelled to check himself for wounds. Content that he was uninjured, he got out of bed and washed his face with cool water. He pulled on a pair of gym shorts and slipped out the front door to the outdoor walkway connecting the apartments to the elevator and stairwell. His apartment was on the third floor of a building that was three sides of a square. His view was of a courtyard area that featured a swimming pool and served as a mingling point for the gays in the building. Next to the courtyard, a recessed driveway gave access to parking under the building, and across from that an identical building to his, but in a mirrored design, complete with its own pool, made up the complex .

The air was almost cold, and the sheen of sweat on David's body chilled him. He looked down at the calm water of the heated pool and thought for perhaps the fiftieth time since he moved into the building about what it'd be like to jump into the pool from the third floor. He'd never tried it and never would. It was actually in his lease that it was not allowed, which made him wonder, also not for the first time, how badly the person who tried it had gotten hurt.

David suddenly had the feeling he was being watched. He scrutinized the other apartment doors on his floor and in the building opposite the courtyards but saw no one else out at this hour. His rational mind knew he was imagining it, but his primal lizard brain was screaming at him nonetheless. It was like when he was younger and would swim in a dark pool and suddenly get the feeling he was going to get eaten by a shark. It was a fear he had learned to dismiss, because obviously sharks weren't abundant in swimming pools. This time, though, it was harder to ignore. He now knew for a fact that vampires were real and fed on human beings.

At this clear thought, David's logical brain began problem-solving and he stood straight and returned to the apartment, taking special care to lock the deadbolt and the doorknob behind him. He turned to the small dining area and regarded the table and chairs. They were a mismatched set. The table had been a gift from a friend when he had moved into the apartment with his ex-boyfriend. They had found a complete set of kitchen chairs in decent shape with soft padded seats that showed no stains or tears while walking around the neighborhood a few blocks east. They hadn't thought anything about it at the time. The neighborhood was heavily populated by Russians who had fled during the fall of the USSR, and it was customary in that culture to put something out on the curb when you didn't want it, free for anyone to take.

David tipped one of the chairs on its back and placed a foot on the leg that lay along the floor. Crouching down, he grasped the opposite leg firmly with both hands and pulled. He didn't know how well the chair was assembled. It wasn't as cheap as a piece of IKEA furniture, and it had never wobbled, but in his current state he didn't want to take time to carefully disassemble the chair with tools. He pulled up, straining with his legs, back, and shoulders, until the chair split apart at the joints. David stood, holding one of the legs, the end split and jagged. He tested out his new weapon with a thrust into the air. Yeah, this would do.

He spent the hours until sunrise whittling the legs of the chair into stakes. They turned out to be single pieces of a sturdy wood, not the particle board/fiberboard combination found in certain Swedish furniture pieces, and with a little sanding work became perfect instruments of bloodsucker destruction, at least by David's estimation. Stake through the heart wasn't one of the myths he and Joseph had discussed, but he suspected that pretty much everything died if you put a stake through its heart. They also hadn't discussed the element of mythology that said vampires needed express permission to enter a home, but David's furtive glances at the front door drove home the fact that he didn't believe there was any reason that myth should be true. His time with Joseph had made vampires a very real thing, which meant they were less likely to be restricted by arbitrary rules that had no basis in biology and science.

David managed to fashion six good stakes and a handful of smaller ones from the one chair, and for the first time since the attack on Friday so long ago, felt his anxiety and fear subside somewhat. He was taking control of his safety, and that helped. He didn't bother tearing apart any of the other three chairs, knowing that if he couldn't defend himself against two vampires with six full-size stakes, the problem was definitely not a shortage of stakes.

Sitting on the living room couch with the sharpened stakes arrayed before him on the coffee table, David glanced again at the front door and saw that the sky outside had gone from dark obscurity to the clear blue of a Southern California morning. His stomach rumbled, and he realized it had been almost a full day since he had eaten. He slipped one of the stakes into the waistband of his pants and wandered into the kitchen, texting Dana on the way to say he was so sorry, but he was going to be staying home again today. There was just no way he was going to be able to work with his mind trying to fly in a dozen different directions at once while also suffering from lack of sleep. He couldn't seem to focus on one particular thing, until he had poured a bowl of cereal and stood frozen, staring down into it. One urgent problem that needed solving.

Joseph needed food.

Several pieces of a puzzle came together in David's mind. The plastic bags on the floor of Joseph's kitchen and the blood oozing out of the refrigerator (*don't think about what else was in the kitchen*) which he'd seen Joseph take his meals out of and stick them in the microwave for warming. Alexander and the woman had destroyed his supply, David realized. Which sparked another realization. The building that blew up had been a blood bank and research center. And it was Joseph's company. The vampire couple destroyed that, too, to take away the source of his food supply!

How long could Joseph go without eating? Not long, David guessed. He'd seen him consume at least one bag of blood per day when they were together at his house and on the trip to Paris.

What was the reason for destroying his supply of donated blood? To weaken him in preparation for a confrontation? To force him to feed on humans? Joseph would never—

The thought stopped in the middle of making its way across David's mind. Of course, Joseph would feed on a human. He already had. And the look on his face had said that it was tearing him apart.

So a fight, then. They wanted to make him weak. Surely Joseph would eat animals before hunting humans, wouldn't he? Yet hunting in the concrete jungle of Los Angeles would be much more difficult than the last time Joseph had tried it, what, a hundred years ago?

And they'd killed Rafaél, Joseph's son and closest confidant. If there was anyone Joseph would have gone to for help in this situation, it would have been him. Joseph had no one left, as far as David knew.

Okay, then. This was a problem David could help solve. It was one thing to walk away from known danger, but it was quite another to let the man you loved face it alone when you could do something to help. He finished pouring milk over his crunch flakes with almonds and heated up a cup of cold brewed coffee. Usually, he cut it half-and-half with water, but today he drank it full-strength. He'd need the caffeine.

He took his breakfast to the computer and started brainstorming. After some overly complicated fits and starts, David stumbled upon an obvious solution, and opened up the maps app to search for grocery stores. Then after a moment looking at the list, searched for butchers instead. He reviewed the list, noting that most of the shops didn't open for another few hours, exceptions being the several that overlapped with his grocery store results. When he'd drained the last of his milk from his bowl, David started to make calls.

First, he researched foods that used blood, so he could have a story to tell when he made his unusual requests. The second web search led to an article titled "Dine Like a Vampire With These Blood-Based Culinary Delights," so he decided to mix a bit of truth into his lie. He prepared himself with a simple request to get blood for a specialty food event and, if pressed, would say it was for a gathering of people who pretended to be vampires. It didn't get that far, though. It only took three calls to learn that butchers weren't a source for animal blood. The third provided him with the source for their raw meat, a halal slaughterhouse within driving distance of LA.

David had to wait until 9:00 AM to call them, so he set his phone timer for an hour and leaned back on the couch, hugging one of his newly carved weapons to his chest. He didn't expect to be able to nap, but as soon as his head relaxed against the couch cushion, the alarm went off. He jerked up, forgetting that he was holding the stake, and sent it clattering to the floor, startling himself even more.

David polished off the last of his extra-strong coffee, which had grown cold, and called the abattoir. His heart was beating hard in his chest, a combination of having just woken up from a deep nap, plus the pressure of this mission and the nervous energy of preparing to tell his lie to complete it. As it turned out, the receptionist who answered the phone didn't need to know why he needed the blood, just how much he needed. David hadn't actually thought about that. A part of him had assumed he would have to work so hard to obtain each cup and pint that he'd eventually reach a point where he had to stop. He asked if a couple of gallons was okay, and the receptionist told him the minimum size was five-gallon buckets. David asked to buy one and was told it would be ready to pick up that afternoon.

He hung up the phone and barked out a laugh. When the idea came to him, David initially thought he'd have to find some friend of a friend who worked at the Red Cross and bribe him somehow to steal donated blood. He had even began formulating a plan to do that, by offering Joseph's wealth by way of a huge donation to the Red Cross, plus maybe a little extra on the side for the person stealing the blood. He had images of an *Ocean's Eleven*–style heist in his head, and in the end, he was able to get five *gallons* of blood and all he had to do was drive to San Bernardino in the inland empire, just an hour and a half away with traffic.

The drive would get him there several hours early, but David started feeling antsy sitting on the couch trying to watch YouTube videos on the living room television, so he stuffed the stakes into an empty backpack, prepared an insulated mug with more coffee, and left the safety of the apartment, taking the stairs down to the underground garage.

Waze took David on his normal commuting route over the Barham pass to the 134 freeway. He drove east past Glendale and Pasadena, where the 134 transitioned into the 210 freeway, and David felt his anxiety ease somewhat. He felt safer in his car, driving away from the scene in Joseph's kitchen, the location of his recent attack, and of the perpetrators of that assault. He felt certain that vampires couldn't move as fast as a car and, however strong their hunting senses were, couldn't follow him when he was surrounded by his steel and glass tanklet.

He planned on getting to San Bernardino and puttering around until his order was ready for pickup, but about halfway there, his vision started to blur and he struggled to stay awake. He pulled off at the exit for Duarte, a place he'd been several times as a younger man, attending swanky summer holiday parties at a home on the side of the Angeles Mountains, and found a parking spot in the shade of a Costco. He cracked his car windows and set his phone alarm for two hours before reclining his seat. A leather jacket lay in a pile in the passenger seat, left when the weather became too warm for it. David used the light-proof material to cover his face, creating a cocoon of darkness in which he quickly descended into a deep sleep.

His dreams were vivid. He was laying in Joseph's arms, being cradled and loved. His whole body was hot and cold at the same time, tingling with what his dream-brain assumed was a post-sex glow, though the dream didn't include any actual sex, unfortunately. David saw through the eyes of his dream-self, Joseph's face looking down at him with so much love in his eyes it was overwhelming him with emotion. David felt at ease, as he had since the first time they slept together. He had always felt comfortable with Joseph, even after learning of his true nature. Even when he was looking on the gore and blood in Joseph's kitchen, he hadn't been afraid for his safety, at least as far as his immortal lover was concerned. Here in the dream, he felt that same security, even more than the sexual desire.

David's dream awareness moved outside of his body then, in that way dreams have of disassociating one's self, and he saw his own body. He was covered in blood, and Joseph was baring his fangs...

The small Honda rocked as David awoke with a start. His head had slipped into the sleeve of the leather jacket, and the darkness was complete. At first, he forgot where he was and panicked when he couldn't see. He clawed at the material covering his head and face, pulling the coat off. Even parked in the shade, the California sun was shockingly bright, and David had to press his palms against his eyes while his brain caught up. Keeping his eyelids pressed closed, he reached down next to the driver's seat and lifted the lever that brought the seat back into an upright position. Then he was able to relax and breathe deeply a few times, focusing on slowing his exhalations.

He opened his eyes and looked around, getting his bearings. The Costco loomed large in front of his car, and there were cars parked on both sides of him, but the larger parking spots meant they weren't too close for comfort. On the passenger seat sat the open backpack with the rudimentary impaling implements poking out. The stake he'd been holding had fallen next to the seat. He fished it out and decided it was probably a good idea to run in and pee before driving the second half of the trip.

An hour later he was back on the road, bladder empty, with a venti Americano from Starbucks and munching on a Crunchwrap Supreme from Taco Bell. David felt more normal than he had in what seemed like a very long time. As long as he didn't think about the fact that he was driving to a slaughterhouse to get blood for his vampire boyfriend. *Ex-boyfriend?* his brain asked, but he pushed the thought away. It didn't matter. They loved each other, whether they could be together or not, and David would be there for Joseph in any way he could be.

He was still early when he arrived at the small, family-run operation, but the receptionist told him to wait while she went through a swinging door to the main abattoir and returned minutes later with a sealed five-gallon pail on a cart. David paid for the blood on his credit card and was allowed to use the cart to get the pail to his car. It must've weighed fifty pounds as he hoisted it up into his trunk, pushing aside several pieces of accumulated junk to make it fit.

The drive home took nearly twice as long, nap not included, as rush-hour traffic reached its peak. The sun was just beginning to dip towards the horizon when David turned onto the last winding road that led to Joseph's castle-like home. He got stuck behind an old pickup truck that was laden with lumber and tools, with rigging built into the sides to hold it all. There wasn't room to pass on the narrow, winding roads of the Hollywood Hills, but David took a breath and took himself into a Zen place, rather than get frustrated that he couldn't get to his destination a few minutes sooner.

He ended up following the truck all the way to Joseph's house, where it turned off the road into Joseph's driveway. As it did, David saw the name of the company on the side, Door and Peace, and he realized why they were there. He didn't want anyone else around when he spoke to Joseph (if he spoke to Joseph), so he kept driving. He had Siri find him the closest Starbucks locations and had the AI voice give him directions to the one on Beverly Glen and Mulholland. It wasn't the closest one, but he didn't feel like driving down the hill and back up again. Plus, the views of the LA basin and the Valley would be worth the extra time. The sunset spread glorious oranges and reds across the Valley as it sunk into the horizon, and the endless blanket of lights twinkled on across the caldera of what had once been an ancient volcano.

David sat for a couple of hours on the sidewalk in front of the coffee shop, nursing a grande almond milk latte and picking at a blueberry scone. He absently watched the rich people walk to and from the restaurants he'd never been able to afford to go to and the boutiques at which he wouldn't even bother to window shop. He made sure to text Dana to let her know he was okay and he'd tell her everything that was happening soon, but otherwise, David's mind drifted while he intermittently browsed Facebook on his phone.

When he estimated enough time had passed for the big old door at Joseph's to be fixed or replaced, David walked across the small lot back to his car, now laughably parked next to a Lamborghini. He drove back to Joseph's, and the driveway was empty. Getting out of the car, he tucked a stake into the back of his belt and covered the end with his shirt. He walked up to the door, which was locked, but visibly not completely repaired, and knocked.

David took two steps away from the door. He didn't know why, exactly. Maybe it was just polite to not be right *there* when the owner answered. Or maybe he wanted to let Joseph know he wasn't here to pressure him for anything. Just drop off the blood and go. But he still inhaled sharply when Joseph answered.

The pallor had left the vampire's face. He wasn't gaunt, but there were dark shadows under his eyes. Upon seeing David standing there, Joseph exhaled, like he had been holding a breath, as someone does who is pretending not to be sick when they are.

"David..." Joseph said, like he was disappointed to see him.

"I know, I know, but..." David started to defend his presence, but Joseph's exhausted face stopped his excuses. "Have you eaten?" he said instead.

Joseph looked confused at the question. Then he lowered his eyes as he did some mental calculations. "It's been a couple days," he said, shaking his head.

"Okay, well, I got some for you," David said, gesturing towards the car.

"Some...?" Joseph asked, not completely sure what David was talking about.

David lowered his voice as if there were people around and he didn't want to be overheard. "*Blood*. I drove out to a place in San Bernardino and got some. I figured... I didn't say it before, but I'm so, so sorry about Rafaél. And about your building. I really am." David desperately wanted to step forward and hug Joseph, to help him, but stood still.

Joseph was still confused. He had been very clear that David was to leave and never come back. "Why are you here, David?"

David shook his head a little to focus himself and communicate that Joseph needn't worry. "I just realized that you didn't have any food, and that—" he slowed down and chose his words carefully, not wanting to hurt Joseph with a sensitive topic "—Rafaél would have probably been the one you went to for this particular problem." Joseph still looked confused, so David decided to be simple and blunt. "I have five gallons of fresh cow blood in a bucket in the car."

Joseph's eyebrows shot up. "Oh! Okay, thank you." But he didn't move.

David got a bit annoyed. "It's in the trunk. Should I get it?"

Joseph looked past David to the car, and then around the front of the house, like he was searching for trespassers. Which, David realized, he might have been. "Yes, please," Joseph said.

David went back to the car and heaved the pail out of the hatchback. He struggled to walk in anything resembling a dignified manner while he brought it back to the house, and was getting a little miffed that Joseph with all his super strength didn't bother to help. No, he just stood there in the doorway, watching David while also scanning the nighttime surroundings. If he saw the stake poking out of David's belt, he didn't say anything about it.

David began to move it inside, but Joseph stopped him. "It's okay, I've got it. Thank you."

David set the bucket down at Joseph's feet. "Yeah, no problem," he said automatically, shaking out the cramp that had formed in his hand, biting into his palm. They stood for a moment while David waited for Joseph to say something more, and Joseph waited for David to leave.

Joseph bent down to pick up the bucket, and despite his fatigue and relative weakness, it appeared to weigh no more than a gallon of ice cream. He pulled it inside, and David felt his throat tighten like a small ball of iron was forming just behind his chin. But it didn't fall to his chest with the rest of his despair as Joseph retreated into his house wearing an expression of broken guilt. Instead, the iron ball turned momentarily white-hot and shot straight up into David's head.

"Is that it? Thank you?" he lashed out at Joseph, who stopped moving, but did not make eye contact. "I come in here yesterday and see ... what I saw. And still I worry for you and put in, I mean, a *lot* of effort to track down something for you to eat so you don't starve, or *worse*—" David leaned to emphasize his unspoken words "—and all you can say is 'Thank you'?" He tossed his arms up in the air, at a loss for words.

Joseph still refused to look at him.

David took a couple of breaths, then stepped closer to the door. "I... I know you've lost a lot, and that you're still in the middle of it all. But you don't need to push me away, Joseph. You can depend on me. I can help." He gestured at the bucket swaying from Joseph's hand. "I can *help.*"

Joseph shifted the bucket from one hand to the other, and the thick liquid sloshed inside. His shoulders hung low, and his head wouldn't rise to meet his former lover's eyes. "Please go, David," he said simply.

Joseph turned into the house, and David thought he saw tears fall from his eyes before the heavy door closed behind him.

David stood impotently for a few moments, wrestling with the urge to pound dramatically on the door until Joseph relented, opening it and wrapping him in his arms, after which they would retreat into the house and make love and, and, and...

But David knew it wouldn't do any good. He turned his back on Joseph's fancy door and walked back to his car. His legs and arms operated as if by remote, like he was a marionette and someone else was pulling his strings. He was so angry and sad and pissed and dejected but still knew Joseph was doing what he thought was best for David.

Sitting in his car, looking out past the house and out over the Los Angeles basin, David cried softly. He was so powerless to change what was going on. He had had something so amazing, and even worked through seemingly giant problems, like, say, his boyfriend being a vampire, and now it was torn away from him and there was nothing he could do about it. He felt completely and utterly exhausted, mentally and physically, from head to toe. He barely felt the warm tears trickling down his cheeks.

Finally, he closed his eyes and focused on his breath. David wasn't a habitual practitioner of meditation, but he believed in the power of mindfulness and would sometimes take a moment in a stressful time at work to pause and breathe. After a couple of minutes, he felt a bit more clearheaded. He didn't know what he was going to do, exactly, but was ready to take one step at a time. The first was to go home and get some sleep. Tomorrow, go to work. Get back into a routine. After the last week of complete disarray, routine sounded absolutely divine.

David started the car and pulled out of the driveway, forcing himself to not look back at the house. He wound down the narrow mountain road and turned east on Mulholland Drive. The night was still and rush hour had passed, so there weren't many other cars on the high road. David felt relief seeping into his body the more distance he put between him and Joseph, though he felt the logical and emotional halves of his brain wrestling for control.

His logical brain tried to be optimistic, and he thought, *I will love again, I don't believe there's only one person in the world for everyone*, but then the emotional part of his brain focused on how much he loved Joseph and how he wouldn't have *that* love again, and he began to cry, much harder this time.

In moments, the tears were coming hard and hot from his eyes, and his nose was running from the effort to hold back the waterworks. David leaned over to open the glove box for some napkins he kept there for emergencies, taking his foot off the gas pedal but keeping one eye on the road as he rounded a curve. Still, he didn't see the figure standing directly in his path until it was too late to slow down.

David shot back up in his seat and yanked the wheel, attempting to swerve out of the way. The car's path managed to shift to the right, missing the person standing in the middle of the road. *Is it two people?* his brain screamed as time seemed to slow to a crawl. *Why would you go for a walk in the middle of the road?* The swerve brought him dangerously close to the edge of the embankment, where there was not even a guard rail between him and the steep drop down the side of the mountain.

As his car lost traction, David registered two things. The first, he'd seen the same terrifying face from the alleyway, glaring at him from outside the window, mouth twisted in a snarl of hate and malevolence, fangs bared. The second, he'd narrowly missed hitting Alexander with the car, but the vampire had parried in order to push David's little Honda further into its skid.

Then David was flying over the edge.

Gravity took a vacation inside the car. David's backpack, spare pens, and his supply of laundry quarters lifted from their places and seemed to float around the cabin. David's seatbelt kept him strapped to the driver's seat, but he saw the world outside the windshield turning over and over while the car tumbled down the steep embankment. It rolled four times, each impact dangerously crushing in the roof. David heard screaming but wasn't aware that he was making any sound himself.

The world just kept spinning and spinning and spinning.

CHAPTER 20

T he world stopped rotating as the hill flattened out into a dog park, and the car hit a chain link fence, flattening it but coming to a stop right side up. The tires had been torn off and the roof was a mangled sheet of metal. Broken glass twinkled in the moonlight from the top of the fifty-foot descent and down the steep hill scraped bare of vegetation along the Honda's path.

David sat in the driver's seat, stunned but alive. The rending of metal had ceased and there was silence, save for a ringing in his ears. Acrid smells assaulted David's nose from smoke and leaking fluids. An image flashed in his brain of the gas tank bursting into flames, the car exploding like in the movies. A surge of adrenaline cleared the fog of the accident, and he was suddenly panicked to get out of the imminent deathtrap. The driver's side door was crunched and semi-open. With a firm push, he was able to make the gap big enough to get out, but when he tried to scramble free, he found he couldn't move.

David panicked briefly, suspecting he might have broken something in the fall and was now paralyzed, but then he realized his seatbelt was still fastened and was squeezing his body. He reached down and unbuckled it and felt the release of pressure he hadn't been cognizant of, and involuntarily drew in a full breath. Nothing seemed to be broken, but a throbbing, stinging sensation on the crown of his head drew his hand up to investigate. It came away bloody. A warmness ran down the back of his neck.

Okay, he thought, *I'm injured, but I need to get out of the car before it blows up.*

With the seatbelt undone, David leaned out of the car, gingerly pulling his legs out of the compacted area under the steering wheel. Standing next his faithful ride, he marveled. The roof had caved in further than where his head should have been. He was lucky to be alive. He knew he should have been woozy or lightheaded, but the adrenaline was running and he barely felt his body.

Just then, there were sounds of something coming down the hill. David turned and saw two figures descending rapidly, jumping and running down the near-vertical grade. A fight-or-flight instinct kicked in, and David dove back into the car to grab his backpack. At first, he couldn't find it. Not only was the vehicle a disaster, but nothing was where it was supposed to be. After a few interminable seconds, he found the pack wedged in between the passenger floor and the center console. He yanked it and thankfully it came free without a fight.

David retreated from the approaching vampires who were already down the hill. He tripped awkwardly over the chain link fence the car had landed on and headed into the dog park.

"Help!" he screamed into the night. "Somebody help me!" The park was closed after sunset. There were no owners with their dogs, and being situated at the top of the Hollywood Hills, the Laurel Canyon Dog Park was not a place homeless people bothered to hike to for a night's sleep. David was alone.

The park was a large dusty bowl of land, and the nearest houses were fifty yards away, back up the ridge along Mulholland Drive. They were too far away. David's only chance was down, but that meant running half a football field away from two beings who were faster and stronger and hadn't just been in a car wreck. He fumbled with the backpack as he loped as fast as he could. He barely registered that he was limping from a leg injury that was just starting to throb. He hadn't closed the pack's zipper on the pack and feared that the chair legs he'd whittled had all fallen out when the bag was flying around the car, but he got a hand in and felt several of the wooden weapons inside. David prayed a silent thanks to a God he hadn't believed in for fifteen years and wrapped a hand around one of the stakes.

A hand with nail-like claws raked across David's back, knocking him off-balance. He tumbled into the gravelly dirt, losing the backpack as he rolled, and skidded to a stop on his shoulder. He felt the sting of deep lacerations on his back where the thin fabric of his t-shirt had done nothing to protect him and scrapes on his chin and arm from sliding over the rough ground.

Retreat was no longer an option. He screamed once again for help and scrambled to his feet to face the vampires. In his hand, he still gripped one of the stakes. He held it out like a foot-long blade.

"Oh, look, my love, the whelp has claws," Alexander said derisively. "Are you a vampire hunter now, boy?"

"Get away from me!" David shouted, waving the stake wildly. He kept his eyes on the pair but cast quick glances around, looking for help or a way to escape. There was nothing and no one. No place to hide, not even a tree to put between them, assuming he could even make it to one.

"If we leave, how would we kill you?" Alexander replied amiably, while Roxana purred a small chuckle. "That doesn't make any sense at all, does it?"

David saw the futility of the situation and panicked. Tears once again flowed, making streaks through the dirt and grime on his face. "Why are you doing this to me?"

Roxana advanced menacingly, watching the weapon David waved at her with a keen eye. "Don't be stupid, little boy. You know what we are. We prey on humans."

"Of course, normally we'd be much quicker about it," Alexander said, his voice lowering to a dangerous growl. "But *your* fear in particular is something I very much want to taste." Alexander hissed and bared his fangs, projecting all of his hatred for Joseph at the one living human he loved. Feeding on this mortal, and making it painful, would bring his progenitor to the brink, after which he and Roxana would destroy him completely.

Roxana leapt forward, parrying a thrust David made with the stake, and swiped across his chest with her sharpened, knifelike nails. They left four long gouges along his torso. Thick blood immediately welled from the wounds. David's scream pierced the dry night air and echoed briefly around the bowl of the canyon before falling silent.

David knew he was about to die but couldn't reconcile the realization. He couldn't just give up, but fighting was impossible, and running equally as futile. Every emotion seemed to be crowding in to have its last shot at his consciousness.

Despair for all the things he would never do and for the people he would never see again. Outrage that he was being singled out just because he had dared fall in love with someone. Terror beyond anything he had experienced in his life. Above it all, David felt physical pain so intensely it was making it hard to think. Fire burned through the nerve endings in his chest and back, and his head throbbed worse the more blood he lost from Roxana's slashes.

Then, all the fury he had ever felt about the injustice and tragedy in the world focused to a pinpoint of white-hot rage at this monstrous woman who was trying to kill him. David's thoughts coalesced into one simple directive: *Live.* Kill this thing in order to live. Plunge the stake he still held into her heart. If he was to die, he would take this personification of evil along with him.

David squared his body sideways, his childhood martial arts training taking over with the memory of how to move and ready yourself for attack. He naturally took on a variation of a tiger stance, left heel raised off the ground as his weight settled on his back leg. This made his front foot available for defense or attack. He raised his left hand to guard his face and pulled his right back like a bow string, holding the dagger-like stake at his shoulder.

Roxana sneered. "So the puppy is a tiger..."

Alexander stood several steps behind her and cocked his head. "Take care you don't get scratched, my queen."

Roxana's sneer pulled into a humorless smile, and she kissed the air over her shoulder. *This will not be difficult*, said the wordless message to her lover. She turned her head to lock eyes with her soon-to-be victim, but David's eyes were focused on her torso. Smart, for a human. Roxana feinted forward, causing David to reflexively step back. The move put him off his optimal defensive posture, and Roxana took the opportunity and struck.

David saw the move coming. Instead of dropping back, he shifted his weight onto his front foot. What would it feel like to plunge the stake into her? Would it be hard or soft? Would it get stuck? How fast would she die? Would he have time to get another stake before the other one attacked? The questions flashed in a fraction through his brain but were pushed aside by the needs of the moment. Putting momentum into his weapon hand, he sent it forward into that point of rage in the middle of the bitch's chest, aiming directly for her heart.

Thrust. Push. Kill.

Roxana was far too fast, with hundreds of years of fighting experience compared to David's eight. She swept up and to the side with one hand, deflecting David's thrusting attack and grabbing his wrist at the same time. Dodging to the side, she let his momentum carry him forward, while using the thumb blade on the other hand to slice the tendons in David's wrist. His hand went instantly limp, and the stake clattered to the ground.

David had planned on an impact to stop him, with the female's body between him and the male bloodsucker, but now his momentum put him between them. Roxana had a grip on his wrist and he was turning, the park spinning wildly one hundred eighty degrees before stopping suddenly. He was now facing the opposite direction, and Alexander had him by his other arm.

A hand grabbed him by the hair, fingernails raking David's scalp as his head was yanked backwards. He tried to flail, to wrest free, but Alexander's fingers dug into the inside of the elbow of his left arm, his superior strength making it impossible to move. David saw only the grey night sky of Southern California. A smattering of stars—maybe a planet or an airplane—

and that was the last thing he would ever see. He made a choking cry as Roxana clamped her mouth over his gushing left wrist.

David felt the bite on his neck from Alexander. Compared to the rest of the pain searing his body, it was barely a bug bite. However, the pressure on his neck cut off any sound that he could make. Quickly though, the feeling in his extremities began to fade. The pain in his chest and back dulled. It didn't go away, really, but David's nerves weren't screaming quite as loudly. The sky darkened. The unceasing glow of the city around his peripheral vision dimmed. A blackness crept in from the edges. He was glad to be rid of the pain. If this was what death was, it wasn't so bad, once you couldn't feel anything.

As his pulse slowed more and more, the absence of the constant background noise of a heartbeat made the audioscape of the city come through in sharp relief. David heard cars honking and sirens wailing. He heard dogs barking and the flying fauna making their mating and hunting calls. He heard a mountain lion roar. It was really close. Was it in the dog park? Was it going to eat his body when the vampires were done with him? It sounded almost like it was roaring right *next* to him...

David's head jerked as Alexander's mouth was torn away from his neck. The grip that the vampire had had on him vanished, and though Roxana was still holding him by one arm, David sank to the ground as darkness closed in and his consciousness left him.

Joseph had just begun to drink his second glass of cow's blood, heated to a pleasant level in the microwave, when he heard a crash echoing faintly over the hills. He felt something deep inside of himself, too. A reverberation, like standing too close to the giant subwoofer at a concert. Whether it was a vibration in the ground or something unexplainable within him, it was jarring enough to force him to set the glass down and grab the counter with both hands.

He focused his senses. He could hear the sounds of a car rolling. It wasn't the first time he'd heard something like this. Drunks sent their vehicles off the side of winding Mulholland Drive with some frequency. But this was different.

Joseph knew it was David.

Adrenaline surged through his body as he pushed himself from the counter and out of the kitchen, racing to the front door. He nearly tore it off its already-weakened hinges as he yanked the thick oak open like it was balsa wood. Once in the driveway, Joseph paused, forcing himself to focus all his attention into his ears, to pinpoint the direction of the crash. East. He took one breath, using it to center his mind, and ran.

He ran half a mile in just under a minute when he heard David's scream for help ringing through the hills. Fresh from his meal, Joseph's energy levels were at their peak, and he practically flew. His feet were a blur, his strides the length of a cheetah's, and in another thirty seconds, Joseph made it to the fresh skid marks leading off the edge of the road. He scanned the hillside, noting the damage done to the slope by the rolling car, the tracks following it down, and then the car itself. It wasn't on fire, but smoke was coming from the crushed engine compartment.

"No... nononono." From the top of the hill, Joseph could see that the door of the demolished car was open and no one was inside. He said a silent thanks for that much.

The park below was several acres, and Joseph was searching for any sign of David when he heard his choked cry and located him just in time to see Alexander sink his fangs into his neck. Joseph didn't waste a fraction of a moment. He sprinted two steps to the edge of the road and launched himself into the cool night air, traversing the fifty feet to the bottom in a controlled fall. He hit the ground hard enough to send up a billowing dust cloud and tucked into a roll to absorb the shock. He managed to get his feet under him and his momentum took him upright directly into a sprint.

A hundred feet from the trio, he hit full speed, roaring in anguish and ferocious wrath. Roxana and Alexander were so engrossed in their feeding they didn't have time to react before Joseph reached them. With a palm strike to the head, he pulled his younger offspring away from David. Blood flew in an arc from Alexander's mouth. He uttered a surprised *hurrggghh* as Joseph came to a stop and brought his other hand up to grip his progeny's head on both sides.

Joseph saw David's body fall limply to the ground as Roxana gaped with a rare look of surprise, blood dripping from her fangs.

With a roar of despair and savagery, Joseph tore Alexander's head from his neck.

Roxana's expression turned to one of shock, and she screamed in impotent hatred at Joseph, who looked down at the only vampire he had ever created. The expression on Alexander's face was frozen in surprise, his lips still wet with David's blood and his ragged neck spilling his own crimson gore.

"You will die for that, Bavarian!" Roxana spat, David's blood forming a pink mist as she uttered her invective.

"You've taken everything from me, witch," Joseph replied in a low growl, tossing the head to the side. "I don't care if neither of us leaves here alive, but I swear to God you will not."

Roxana spat out what remained of David's blood from her mouth and wiped her lips with her sleeve as she circled, readying to fight. "I made the vampire who sired the one who sired you, Bavarian," she sneered. "You have no hope against me."

They circled each other. When Roxana reached Alexander's body and head, she crouched slightly to touch his hair.

While she was distracted, Joseph cast a glance at David and tried to ascertain if he was still alive. It looked like he might be breathing, but he couldn't hear a heartbeat from here, and didn't dare take focus away from Roxana. He looked back at her as she rose to standing and saw David's backpack on the ground a dozen yards behind her, the stakes strewn across the dirt.

Joseph already knew Roxana was quicker and more powerful than he was, but when he made the mistake of blinking, she moved so fast that she closed several feet in the time it took for his eyes to open. His reaction time was reduced to nearly nothing, and he was barely able to get an arm up to defend himself before her talons swiped across his forearm. A tenth of a second later, she would have sliced his face open.

He pushed away with his damaged arm and dropped, countering the movement with an uppercut using the other arm. He almost missed Roxana completely, only catching her under the arm she had used to attack. The impact sent her into a tight spin, and Joseph allowed his momentum to carry him forward into a diving roll. He got to his feet as fast as he could, using his senses to hear where she was before he turned to see her. She was cradling her forearm. Joseph didn't dare hope he'd broken anything, but even if he had, she was dangerous enough to emerge victorious from this battle. Joseph didn't dare risk a glance to see if David was moving or even alive, but the smell of his blood filled Joseph with passionate wrath.

"My night father is dead, Roxana, as is the one who sired him," Joseph snarled. "You will join them shortly."

Roxana moved her arms in a showy demonstration of form, sinking to the ground in a variation of a Shaolin stance, and Joseph thought she appeared very much like a scorpion. He adopted a defensive stance of his own. His left arm was oozing blood where she had gotten him, red fluid dripping steadily into the dry ground. He didn't want to move towards her so he egged her on, tilting his good hand up and giving her the "come on" gesture he'd seen in so many movies since the kung fu revolution began. He suspected Roxana wasn't the movie type.

She took the bait, rising up slightly from her stance. She spun in a circle on her approach, trying to confuse him with the extra movement. Joseph had a moment to wonder how foolish she must think him before Roxana released a cloud of dust from her hands. It hit him directly in his face. She *had* fooled him, somehow loading up on sand and dirt without him noticing. Granules of grit dug into Joseph's eyes. He staggered backwards away from the attack, but it was too late. She was already on him.

Her first impact was a kick directly to his knee, and Joseph felt the kneecap pop as the two large bones separated. He howled in pain as Roxana followed through with a clawing swipe at his jugular, but his reflexive motion to pull in his arms and protect his face succeeded in blocking her. Joseph pushed out with both hands and made contact with the mass of her torso, sending them tumbling away from each other.

He rolled back, the pain in his leg sending lightning bolts of agony through his body. He tried to disconnect the pain with a trick he had learned from one of his many teachers over the last centuries. *Imagine a light switch attached to whatever body part has been injured,* the old man had said, *and simply turn it off.* This worked very well for small injuries, but in this case it only muffled the trauma.

Joseph dared not expend too much time. Roxana was undoubtedly readying another attack. Blurred with dust and watering uncontrollably, his eyes were useless, so he ignored them. Instead, he reached out with his other senses and found her immediately. Mostly he heard her, but he also smelled her spicy scent, and even felt her movement in the ground, as her feet crunched the dirt and gravel.

She really was more powerful than he. Faster. Deadlier. Joseph only had one hope that he could think of. He crawled away, pulling with his arms and pushing with his one good leg, his injured leg trailing limply behind, screaming at him with each inch he dragged it along the dry ground.

As Joseph crawled, he felt Roxana launch herself into the air, meaning to pounce on him like a puma. To anyone else, she would have appeared silent, moving into the air along an arc, her claws outstretched to tear at his flesh and rip out his heart, but Joseph could hear her. Her dress rustled in the wind, her long black hair fluttering behind her. He heard her breath as she exhaled at the effort of launching herself from so far away. This was her killing blow, and she was putting every ounce of her power behind it.

Joseph reached his goal, however, and while he tracked Roxana's path through the air behind him, he grasped in each hand a sharpened stake from their resting places in the dirt. Squeezing tight, he rolled over to face the sky, contracted his core, and propelled his torso upward, thrusting his weapons up with as much force as he could create. Roxana saw too late what was happening and tried to shift her body, but she was too committed to the attack. The stakes speared through both sides of her ribcage and into her heart.

She writhed over Joseph, meaning to inflict as much damage as she could in her final moments. She made several deep cuts in his arms and chest before he lurched upwards again, throwing her much lighter body to the side and scrambling like a three-legged crab in the other direction to put distance between them.

Roxana landed gracelessly in the dirt, but refused to die. She got her arms under herself and pushed up onto her knees. She hissed and spat, a cross between a rabid cat and a viper, screaming words in Arabic that Joseph didn't understand. Once on her knees, she grasped the stakes protruding from her chest as if she meant to pull them out and use them as her own weapons, but they were embedded too deeply, and her life was fading too quickly.

The two-millennia-old vampire stopped suddenly. A look of confused sadness replaced the twisted rage on her face. She looked around the park that had served as their battlefield and found Alexander's body and head, laying a few feet from each other. Using a colossal amount of effort, Roxana crawled over to his corpse, picked up his head, and cradled it as she collapsed into a sitting position next to him.

Joseph's watering eyes began to clear his vision, and he could make her out as she stroked Alexander's hair into place.

"Goodnight, my beautiful *batal*," she whispered so quietly Joseph could barely hear. "I will see you soon..." Moments later, she slumped forward as much as the stakes would allow, and with a final wheezing breath, died.

Joseph focused on her for a moment to be sure she was gone, and then turned his attention to David. He pushed himself onto one leg and limp-hopped over to where his beloved lay in the dirt.

David was surrounded by blood. A growing pool of it had formed under him, and his clothes were drenched with it. His chest was moving imperceptibly, and his breath was so shallow it was almost undetectable. His heartbeat was similarly weak, the muscle fluttering desperately in his chest to pump what little blood was left in his system.

Joseph knew there was no hope to get him to a hospital in time. He felt the déjà vu of a moment he had already experienced, and he knew the outcome. There was only one slim chance, but Joseph refused to allow himself to hope.

He placed one hand gently under David's head and lifted him slowly, pulling himself underneath his once-beautiful man. With David's body leaning against him, Joseph bent his head down and said, "I'm sorry, David."

He was sorry for the pain David had endured this evening. He was sorry for what he was about to do to him. He was sorry if it didn't work, and, perhaps most of all, he was sorry if it did.

Joseph leaned further down and wrapped his lips around the jagged wound Alexander had left, and he drank. David was already unconscious, thank goodness. He wasn't aware of what Joseph was doing. What Joseph had sworn he would never do. Joseph listened to David's breath and his heartbeat. He let the awareness of David's life consume him until he was conscious of nothing else in the world. The city fell away, and it was just the two of them, alone in the universe.

Just as David's heart was about to stop from lack of blood to pump, Joseph ceased drinking and placed his arm, where Roxana had gouged several deep cuts, over David's lips. His blood flowed into David's mouth, over his tongue, and down his throat. He was too weak to swallow, but if it worked, that shouldn't matter. Whatever happened in the one-in-ten moment to turn a human into a vampire happened with only a few drops of ingested blood, once the human was drained of their own.

Joseph heard David's heart stop.

The last shallow breath leaked slowly from his lips.

Joseph waited. The tears in his eyes from the dust and sand became tears of anguish, which were thicker, and hotter. They fell onto David's skin, mixing with the grime and blood as Joseph gently rocked them both, praying to a God he believed had forsaken him five centuries ago.

He thought of Robert, the last man he'd fallen in love with, whose death mirrored this moment so eerily. Rob had been beaten to death because he dared to be gay, and as he lay battered and dying in a different park in this same city, Joseph had found him, and tried for the first time in centuries to turn a human being, to save him. He had failed, and that failure had ushered in decades of solitude.

The sounds of the modern city reasserted themselves in Joseph's awareness. Wild animals that had been frightened away by the commotion following the car crash slowly crept back, some returning to nests and burrows, others enticed by the rich scent of blood.

And Joseph waited.

The minutes crept by agonizingly, but after what seemed like an eternity, David's heart began to beat. Once, then another, then slowly but steadily. His eyes crept open, their hazel irises now speckled with amber and dark purple. They looked searchingly at the sky, confused, until finally, they found Joseph.

Sneak Peek of Book Two

DECIMUS

ANGUISH OF BLOOD

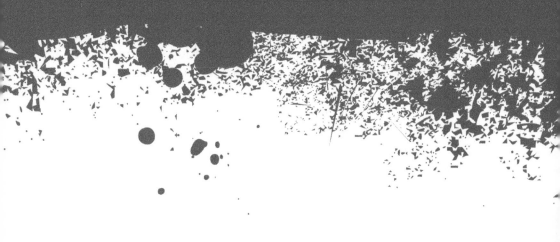

PROLOGUE

Xinjiang - Autonomous region of the People's Republic of China
Present day

Aynur lay on her straw mat, feeling the coolness of the stone slowly leeching the heat from her body, and thought how remarkable it was that the human mind could get so used to a thing if it went on long enough. So used to the hard floor of a cave, for example. So used to the light that was so dim she could barely see the chain attached to her ankle. So used to a sound that repeated so often and for so long that one was barely aware of it anymore.

She hardly heard the screams anymore.

As a child, Aynur's parents had praised her imagination. She had invented stories even at the age of ten that had enthralled her family and neighbors. Now she used that talent to take her from this dank cave back to a life that felt so long ago it could only *be* imaginary. Playing with other kids in the streets of her town. The licking kiss from the dog they had had. This thought threatened to bring thoughts of her mother and the soft kisses she used to give Aynur every night when she went to bed. One on the forehead and then gently on each eye—

No. Do not think of that. Aynur pushed the thoughts of the family she had not seen in months from her mind. Instead, she allowed herself to listen.

The screams were closer now. They were always closer. They mingled with the sounds of the other captives. Moans and cries for mercy from what must have been hundreds of voices mixed with their echoes and melded into a low cacophony of torment. But the screams were acute and represented something worse than simply being held prisoner in a dark cave somewhere. Being a prisoner was bearable, especially when there was no other option but to bear it. Once a day, they were provided with a large bowl of mush to eat. There may have been bugs in it for all Aynur knew, but she had stopped looking. She just imagined she was eating a rich porridge with fresh cream and monk fruit, and thus, it got more delicious every day for her. The darkness helped with that. Another captor would come once a day to collect the contents of the toilet buckets which were placed next to each sleeping mat.

Once an hour or so, through the din of agony that filled the cave (so amazingly easy to ignore after only a couple of days), a scream would echo against the limestone walls. There was usually a small chorus of accompanying wails from the same direction, but the main scream was one of deathly fear and pain. It was followed by a gurgling, choking sound before it went mercifully silent, leaving a slight rise of the persistent wailing, which would itself then reduce like a wave receding into the ocean.

There were two things that Aynur was aware of as she lay there in the darkness. Despite the scream-causing event being a fairly regular occurrence, the little side-chorus of wailing never went away. If her captors were doing something terrible to the prisoners, one might think the prisoners would become numb to it, perhaps even accepting or desiring the release of death, if indeed it was murder of some sort (which Aynur assumed, even at her young age). So whatever they were doing to the prisoners, it was so terrible as to be beyond imagining. And then there was the second thing.

The screams were getting closer. Day by day, they crept nearer and ever-so-slightly louder. Aynur had never been so terrified as when she thought about what might be causing those howls of excruciating pain and fear.

There was another thing. Twice a day or so—Aynur could tell time by the cheap Timex watch her grandmother had gotten her when she turned eleven—after the source scream and accompanying wailing and wordless chorus ebbed, a small wave of new shouting would begin perhaps ten minutes later. These would sound as if they were fueled more by shock and surprised fear than by terror. Within them, as they echoed through the cave to her ears, she could hear prayers to Muhammad and exclamations of disbelief. As their echoes died down, Aynur could hear anxious whispers spread through her fellow captors. This is how she had an idea that there must be hundreds of souls with her in the gloom. She had no idea what could be causing this commotion every ten episodes or so.

Closer. Day by day. Hour by hour. Aynur figured she had another month or so until she found out for herself what was making the prisoners wail so.

A month. Maybe only a few weeks.

Then she would know.

ACKNOWLEDGEMENTS

This book is dedicated to my mom, as probably everything in my life should be. She's the only person who has *always* believed in me, and from whom nearly everything I value most about myself derives. My creativity and love of the spoken and written word, certainly (her writing talent eclipses my own by many levels), but also my sense of optimism and adventure and delight in the beauty that surrounds us, even in the darkest times. She's an incredible human, and you should find and read her stuff.

That being said, *this* book would not be possible without a whole bunch of other people, and I feel honored and obliged to highlight them here.

First, my ex-boyfriend Rob Wood, who most likely will never read this, but with whom I learned the difference between loving someone and being *in love* with someone, and when the time came for us to not be *us*, taught me also about unbearable heartbreak. More concretely, though, our many hikes and walks in 2009, where I first remember formulating this story. Originally intended to be a movie I wrote and acted in. I'd still like to see this story on the big screen, though I'm afraid I've aged out of playing either of the leads.

Next is Melinda Snodgrass, a TV writer and novelist whom I've been a fan of since I was a youngster recording every episode of "Star Trek: The Next Generation" on my 13" combo TV/VCR. I'd pause during the commercials and could fit seven or eight episodes on a tape in EP mode. Melinda's incredible episodes and supremely memorable name made her an immediate conversation target when we happened to be at the CONvergence Sci-Fi convention in Minneapolis while I was in the height of the Inspector Spacetime craze. We sat and had dinner and chatted, and I'm pretty sure she only pretended to know who I was at first, but still took a liking to me. We became friends and she introduced me to a wonderful circle of creative people who also became friends (including at least two other Star Trek writers *and* one of my comic book heroes).

Then, in 2014, as I experienced the loss of my dog and another boyfriend and was truly alone for the first time, I decided to just write this story I'd had cooking in my brain as a novel instead of a screenplay. National Novel Writing Month was coming up and I had a friend or two who had had some luck in the self-publishing world. Plus, *Twilight* had been made into a movie, so even if what I wrote sucked, maybe someone would adapt *my* vampire story? Melinda told me to come by her house and she'd help me break the story. "Sure!" I said, having no idea what breaking the story meant.

It means come up with an outline. A framework of plot and theme and character arcs that you can take into the rest of the writing process. This moment is what made it possible for this novel to be as good as it is. That's not me tooting my own horn; just saying that without Melinda's guidance in this early moment, it should surely have been much worse. And when it was done and she deemed my work up to par, she referred me to her publisher.

The actual writing of the book was made possible by Barry Goold, one of the most generous people I've had the pleasure to know. I rented a room from Barry for three years in Los Angeles between my first and second boyfriends, and we got along fine, but didn't interact a *whole* lot. After I moved out we remained friends though; going to an occasional dinner or party, and trading dog-sitting favors.

In 2020 I landed an acting gig in Japan for which I felt very grateful. Mostly about not having to be in the US during the presidential election, but *then* the pandemic hit and I was able to say I was a working actor, which was suddenly very, very rare. And then I wasn't, when due to low attendance my employer was forced to cut back on the cast and I was sent packing back to America. I had very little time to figure out where I was going, and when Barry replied to a frantic Facebook post asking if anyone had a spare room. I gratefully went to stay with him in Nashville, Tennessee.

I was there when NaNoWriMo 2020 came around, and I was determined not to feel like I was wasting my pandemic. I wrote almost all of this book in about six weeks in November and December, and I was only able to do it because Barry made it possible for me to not worry about life for those months I was there.

Honorable mention goes to Barry's neighbors, who were a fantastic emotional support group while I was there.

(BTW, if you have a dog and are visiting Nashville, do yourself a favor and look up his AirBnB. It's a doggie paradise.)

Once the novel was done and I had done one pass of my own, several people volunteered to read this book and give me feedback.

The first one done with notes back to me was Noah Kopp, who I've known since I cast him as Puck, the role I'd *intended* to play myself, in a High School production of "Midsummer Night's Dream" my senior year. I was shocked and pleased that a straight male liked this book as much as Noah did. I didn't think that was a demographic I'd get much traffic with.

Lisa Klink was next in with very helpful feedback (unsurprising since she's one of those Star Trek writers I mentioned earlier).

Keith Hampton was next, with a critical eye. Keith is my best and oldest friend, with whom I created some of my first fantasy worlds as children together. These worlds were often mashups of various books we read in those young years.

Chris Neely and Naomi Ben-Yehuda each managed to catch many mistakes I and others had missed.

I have had the pleasure of working with so many talented people over the years. Thank you to everyone who has inspired me. And thank you, Dear Reader, for slipping into my world of love and vampires.

BOOK CLUB QUESTIONS

1) The main character, Joseph, says that he's been in love three times in his long life, and none of them were the same. Have you ever been in love? How was it unique?

2) If you were a vampire of the type in this world, what would you like most about it? Would you feed on regular humans?

3) What would you do if you could live forever?

4) The number 10 has special significance in this novel? Can you think of how many ways it shows up?

5) Being openly queer in the ways depicted in the book is based on real experiences by the author. How has that changed in recent history? Why?

6) Is the way David reacts to learning of Joseph's true nature the same as how you would react in that situation? How or how not?

7) How does the change to typical vampire mythology presented in Decimus effect the relationship potential between vampires and humans?

8) Discuss the allegory between fear of vampires in this world and that of homophobia and racism in our own.

9) Decimus changes the mythology of vampires from what we might be familiar with. In what ways are vampires in this world different from past iterations, and how does that effect the story?

ABOUT THE AUTHOR

Travis Richey is an actor/writer living in Hollywood, CA. He has had recurring roles on ABC Family's Pretty Little Liars as Harold Crane and NBC's Community as Inspector Spacetime, a role that launched him into the spotlight of Doctor Who fans. He also appeared on FOX's Sons of Tucson, NBC's The Event, and Sugar on AppleTV+, opposite Colin Farrell.

Travis has achieved international acclaim as the creator of several web series, including Robot, Ninja & Gay Guy, 2 Hot Guys In The Shower, Smiley Town, and the award-winning series The Inspector Chronicles: Untitled Web Series About A Space Traveler Who Can Also Travel Through Time.

His videos have been seen on CNN, Comedy Central, the Huffington Post, the UK Telegraph, PerezHilton.com, dozens of other notable blogs and websites across the internet, and have garnered over 4 million views.

MORE BOOKS FROM
4 HORSEMEN PUBLICATIONS

HORROR, THRILLER, & SUSPENSE

ALAN BERKSHIRE
Jungle
Hell's Road

ERIKA LANCE
Jimmy
Illusions of Happiness
No Place for Happiness
I Hunt You

MARIA DEVIVO
Witch of the Black Circle
Witch of the Red Thorn
Witch of the Silver Locust

MARK TARRANT
The Mighty Hook

STEVE ALTIER
The Ghost Hunter

PARANORMAL & URBAN FANTASY

AMANDA FASCIANO
Waking Up Dead
Dead Vessel

BEAU LAKE
The Beast Beside Me
The Beast Within Me
Taming the Beast: Novella
The Beast After Me
Charming the Beast
The Beast Like Me
An Eye for Emeralds
Swimming in Sapphires
Pining for Pearls

CHELSEA BURTON DUNN
By Moonlight
Moon Bound

J.M. PAQUETTE
Call Me Forth
Invite Me In
Keep Me Close

KAIT DISNEY-LEUGERS
Antique Magic
Blood Magic

Milton Keynes UK
Ingram Content Group UK Ltd.
UKHW042039081123
432235UK00018B/223/J